Death by
Mournful Numbers

John Vance

This is a work of fiction. Names, characters, businesses, places, events and incidents are either the products of the author's imagination or used in a fictitious manner. Any resemblance to actual persons, living or dead, or actual events is purely coincidental.

ISBN: 978-1-61296-595-6

PUBLISHED BY BLACK ROSE WRITING

www.blackrosewriting.com

Printed in the United States of America

Suggested retail price $17.95

Death by Mournful Numbers is printed in Palatino Linotype

Acknowledgements

Work on this novel was aided by the efforts of Matthew Carnicelli; by the suggestions of Adrienne Lombardo; by the encouragement of my daughter Hope and son Jimmy; and by the keen eye and unflagging support of my wife Susan.

Death by

Mournful Numbers

Chapter 1

The face was frozen in a sadistic yet ecstatic grin, suggesting immense satisfaction at the completion of some horrific act. Marshall Grayson knew he had seen it before.

He stood on the sidewalk ignoring the snowfall on this early January evening in Washington, D.C. He felt neither the cold nor the intensifying wind as he continued to examine the hideous gargoyle perched above the courtyard entrance. Beyond the neo-gothic quadrangle stood one of Washington's newest upscale apartment complexes. He wondered how many of the tenants found it chic to reside in a structure lorded over by a ghastly gargoyle. Without question, one of those particularly delighted by the gothic charm of the building was the woman with whom Grayson was about to have sex.

He checked the numbers on the small folded sheet of white paper he had just taken from his coat pocket: 6231 and 412. The street address and apartment number of Maureen Blakely, the young woman he had met two months before. They made fervent and unrestrained love the night they were introduced, and she had been his exclusive sex partner ever since. Whether he was hers, he couldn't be sure. Regardless, it was through his influence that she had secured an apartment in this "Gothic Paradise." Tonight would be the first time they'd make love at her new place, and he was particularly anxious because she promised to indulge him in one of his most active fantasies as a reward for all he had done for her.

Grayson glanced at his watch. He'd have to wait another two minutes before entering the building, for on this night perfect timing was everything. And why should that be at all unusual? Such exquisite timing had brought him to work here in the nation's capital—and to this very place he was about to enter.

Marshall Grayson had been twenty-eight when he first met the current Vice President of the United States, when Edward Malloch was running for his second term as governor of Missouri. Immediately impressed by Grayson's acumen and charm, Governor Malloch offered Grayson the job of chief political advisor. The sudden rise in Grayson's fortunes, however, caused friction among several senior staff members, and he soon discovered what it meant to have political enemies disguised as political allies.

Grayson heard rapid footsteps approaching behind him in the settling snow. He turned quickly and instinctively put up both palms of his hands to ward off an attack from the tall man standing less than a foot away. The man's own hands were gloved, and he wore a heavy dark green sweatshirt with a hood.

He locked his eyes on Grayson's. "Sorry to startle you, but you're one of the top aides to the vice president, aren't you?"

"No, I just get mistaken for him a lot." Grayson kept his hands up and repositioned his body to better defend himself in case the man pulled a weapon. Lately, Grayson had been preparing himself for such actions, prompted by his increasing suspicions that he was being followed.

The hooded man looked down at Grayson from a six-inch

height advantage. "If you don't mind me saying so, I think we elected the wrong guy as president. Your man and that asshole Evan Bedingfield ought to change jobs. Tell Malloch I said that, okay?" The man brushed some of the snow from his hood and walked briskly away into the darkness.

"Jesus Christ." Dropping his hands, Grayson checked his watch again. Two attractive women strolled past Grayson and toward the front door of the apartment building. Before they entered, the shorter of the two whispered to her companion, and Grayson could see the companion's mouth drop open. They seemed vaguely familiar to him. Yes, they were part of that group of five women always at the ball field from August through early October, when Grayson, his good friend on Capitol Hill, Senator Tom Roper, and others played softball. The other men were amused by the women's cheerleading and liked their gorgeous looks. But even then, Grayson found himself scanning the make-shift bleachers for other faces watching him when he played shortstop or stood at the plate. The two women outside the apartment complex nodded to him before opening the door and entering.

It was time to go up to Maureen Blakely's apartment. Grayson shot another glance at the gargoyle. He laughed, realizing where he'd seen that face before. It belonged to the current chairman of the Senate Judiciary Committee. It was the look old Chuck Hefferen gave Grayson last summer in the rotunda of the Capitol after discovering that the V.P.'s thirty-seven-year-old political director had been romancing Hefferen's twenty-four-year-old granddaughter.

Heading into the apartment complex at a brisk pace, Grayson gave further thought to those faces, both familiar and strange, which seemed to scrutinize him. He knew it wasn't simply because he had been the subject of a lot of media interest after a PBS documentary in the winter and early spring of 2012, when Ed Malloch was running a strong second to the eventual nominee, Evan Bedingfield. Determined to avoid any chance meetings, Grayson by-passed the elevator and opened the door to the stairwell.

As for his reputation as D.C.'s most intriguing Lothario, reports of his romances were eighty percent fiction, twenty percent fact. Still, Grayson was keenly aware that his major political enemy on Malloch's team, chief of staff Max Nettleton, would relish any opportunity to show the V.P. that his chief political adviser was acting irresponsibly in his sex life and placing himself and Malloch's office in jeopardy. Heading up the four flights couldn't shake his concern over Nettleton's or the Veep's having learned that he'd recently talked to a *Post* reporter writing a book on the first year of the new administration. And then there was Grayson's recent testimony to a grand jury-- which was likely to damage the Justice Department.

Grayson jogged up the four flights. He and Maureen had agreed that he would open her door at exactly 7:45 p.m. And he wouldn't knock because it would be impossible for her to answer.

She fascinated him not simply because of her intriguing face and stunning body but because she was dangerous—especially to him. He knew damn well he was risking everything by his intense affair with her. He didn't have a wife and family to gamble away, but still the stakes were high. There was his career and potential harm to the Vice President of the United States. But he had no intention to give up Maureen Blakely. He relished the daring imagination Maureen brought to their sex life and how she stimulated his own hunger for unconventional sex and erotic role-playing.

Grayson quickly reached the door of apartment 412. It was

exactly 7:45 p.m. He turned the door knob and entered.

He heard snow spatter against the windows. The room was almost completely dark and silent, except for the sound of the shower in the bathroom to his left. It was exactly what he expected to hear. He paused for a moment, giving Maureen time to arrange herself exactly as they'd discussed.

Grayson removed his clothing. He knew Maureen was aware of the exact time—7:46 now—because the digital clock in her bathroom was synchronized to the watch he had just tossed on her bed. The illuminated numbers of the clock and the flickering glow of several candles on her bathroom vanity counter provided the only light. But it was more than enough for him to find his way.

Completely nude and beginning to get aroused, Grayson stepped into the bathroom and spied the outline of his beautiful lover silhouetted on the other side of the sheer shower curtain. As he'd imagined over the past several hours, she was bent forward at the waist, hands thrust upward and coming together at the top of the elevated shower head. He had instructed her to place the sides of her feet against the edge of the tub and to wrap the rope around her wrists. That she could easily free her hands wasn't the point. She only had to imagine and make him imagine that she was helplessly bound.

Grayson pulled the shower curtain back, entered the tub and stood behind her. In a short quick breath, he took in her rounded buttocks and felt the warm water flowing over them and down her firm, smooth legs. He savored the water pooling down the curve of her back. But he hadn't uttered one word. Maureen knew he would remain mute until he was finished.

He gently touched her lower back—his cue to begin the role-playing in earnest—but she remained perfectly still. He moved his hands up her sides until they touched the outward edges of both breasts. Again no reaction. Now fully erect, Grayson was about to say the hell with it and begin his lovemaking without continuing the scenario they'd agreed upon, but then he caught sight of a white cord curled over the drain of the tub directly below Maureen's drooped head.

"No, no!" He pulled Maureen's water-soaked hair off the back of her neck. "Oh, no. Please God, no."

The ugly red and deep gouges on both sides of her throat told him she had been strangled.

"Oh, Maureen. Baby, please don't be..."

The searing pain came two or three seconds after he felt the intense pressure of a knife entering his upper back. The last thing he sensed was the removal of the blade. He never felt the quick reentry of the knife, nor the subsequent removal, followed by yet another careful thrust.

•   •   •   •   •

The man's gloved hand turned the shower off. He watched the flow of blood disappear down the drain with water from the shower. Without getting into the tub, he repositioned Grayson's body until it half drooped out of the tub—aware that it resembled the figure in Jacques-Louis David's *Death of Marat*. The man placed a folded piece of paper in Grayson's hand. He took the white rope curled around the drain and dried it with a bath towel. He also blotted dry Maureen Blakely's buttocks. Dipping the edge of the cord into the blood pooled around Grayson's wounds, the man wrote an "M" on her left buttock. On the right side, he made a "T." Finally, he double-checked the note in Grayson's hand. He was satisfied. On the paper were printed the numbers "20-18-11-19-07," the "20" crossed out with an "X"—all made with Grayson's blood.

Chapter 2

"Oh, dear heaven above us all, don't stop. That feels so incredibly nice."

"I was just moving up to your shoulders."

"I never thought a simple hand massage could make me wilt like forty-day-old lettuce."

"Lettuce?"

"Oh, my. Oh, my...God. I think my hand has melted off."

"That's fine, but I'm more concerned about melting your resistance."

"Like I had any to begin with." Robyn Meadows repositioned herself on the sofa so she could kiss him fully. "I mean really, Tom, how does one resist a young, handsome, witty, articulate, and brilliant United States senator with such sensual technique as you possess, my darling?"

Senator Thomas Roper couldn't resist laughing. "Jesus, Robyn, you certainly know how to shatter a mood. And I tried so hard to make the seduction as classy and memorable as I could."

"Tom, you've had me—what?—four dozen times already? This mission of seduction is already accomplished." She kissed him passionately. When she broke the kiss, she once again formed the puckish expression he had come to adore. "I don't understand why everyone on the Hill thinks you've lost your way, Tom Roper. As far as I'm concerned, your compass is in good working order."

"Tell that to the president and members of my party."

"Right. So perhaps we shouldn't get too cozy and familiar. You have to save all your strength for tomorrow's one-on-one with my bitter rival, Madam Majority Leader."

"Yeah." Roper sighed heavily and reached for his half-drunk bottle of Newcastle Brown.

Robyn immediately regretted teasing him about Monday's meeting, because she could see he was frustrated by the prospects of one more finger-wagging lecture by Carol McCrimmon. The politically hard-nosed and efficient McCrimmon was the party's brand new leader, having been voted to the post after the untimely death of Vincent Galino right before the holiday recess.

"Robyn, I really miss Vince." Roper lifted his bottle of ale and saluted the deceased majority leader. "He seemed to love the fact that I wasn't playing by the rules. He told me just a few weeks before his heart attack that he and I would be leaving the Senate at the same time. After my 'first and only' six-year term and his 'fourth and last' six-year term were over in January 2019. Old Vince knew I didn't have the temperament to thrive on Capitol Hill."

"Tom, are you really sure you won't be running again in 2018? Unlike almost all of your colleagues in Congress, you at least have the saving grace of your irresistible personality. The media gobbles up every word you say."

"If you say so." Roper grinned as he finished his beer. Robyn headed to the kitchen to get him another one.

"You're also a big hit with almost all the wives of your adversaries—of the opposing party and of your own. I remember sitting in the bleachers at your softball games watching them ogle and drool."

He called to her as she opened the refrigerator. "That explains my difficulty with the new majority leader. She doesn't have a wife."

Robyn returned with another Newcastle. "She's just trying to suppress her sexual attraction to you, that's all." Robyn put her arms around him and kissed him playfully. Before she completely broke the final kiss, she whispered, "Did I tell you I think you'd make a great president?"

"Uh-huh. "

"You'd be one of the, if not *the* smartest one ever to serve. You'd go down in history as the greatest newspaper and board game puzzle-solver ever to occupy the Oval Office."

"I should give all that up now. I'm in the Senate now, remember?"

She laughed and punched him playfully on the arm. "Like hell you should. How many times have you helped me with my little forensic problems since we became an item?"

"Just keeping my hand in, chief investigator Meadows." Roper simply loved the fact that Robyn worked for the D.C. crime lab.

"I wouldn't have received that nice promotion and raise had you not come up with the hidden code in the note left at the Cherie Markbreit murder scene. The terminal letter at the end of each sentence providing the county, city, and street where the murderer lived. Just brilliant. Sherlock Holmes's got nothin' on you, babe."

"Remember—you had to read all the letters from bottom to top to get it right."

"How does the famous saying go, Tom? 'You can take the boy out of intelligence but you can't take the intelligence out of the boy'?"

"My political opponents would beg to differ. I'm sure they're currently arguing that the intelligence was taken out of me the moment I arrived on Capitol Hill."

"Tom, seriously, why didn't you pursue a career in the CIA or the FBI?"

"Again, temperamentally unfit. But don't forget that I spent my three years in the Army working in intelligence. It was the only way I would enlist."

"I thought you enlisted to honor your father."

"I did."

"And you timed it right. What was it again—'Operation Desert Wolf'?"

"Close. 'Desert Fox.' A little four-day bombing party in late '98 supposedly to 'degrade' Saddam's ability to store and produce something they called, what was it again, 'Weapons of Mass Destruction.' Of course, many wise heads thought the real goal was to destabilize the Iraqi government. But we couldn't admit to that, could we? Sorry, I'm mounting my high horse again."

Robyn kissed him again. "I want you to tell me everything about your life, Tom. I mean that."

But Roper had not yet shared with Robyn his experience with the other side of that little bombing party. Owing to confusion, stubbornness, and some gross incompetence, U.S. missiles struck too close to the civilian population to let Roper's conscience rest easy with the familiar palliative that there was always unfortunate yet inevitable collateral damage in warfare. On one occasion he put the blame squarely on his own shoulders when he learned of the obliteration of a busload of

Iraqi civilians parked on the other side of a targeted structure. He chastised himself for not making his case forcefully enough when the location was chosen in spite of his contrary advice. He wouldn't forget that on this occasion he was the one who had initially gotten the intelligence wrong, leading to the death of thirty-one innocent women and children.

Robyn stroked his brow. "You couldn't help that your father was career military and that you wished to make him proud." At the time, General Nathan Roper ignored his gold stars and listened to his son as a parent, ultimately conceding that the three-year hitch would be Tom's first and last. And here the younger Roper was again facing another "one and done" with his Senate career. Still, he couldn't shake the fact that his father had always admired his son's active curiosity and ability to probe, sift, and resolve.

Perhaps it was a boyhood fascination with all that was labyrinthine, whether it was a difficult word puzzle or a complex tale of mystery, but Tom Roper couldn't let it go when it came to an intellectual challenge. Since they'd become seriously involved, he and Robyn had collaborated on a number of cases she was working on, although he insisted that his contributions remain unpublicized.

The phone interrupted their musings about Roper's intelligence and lack of political ambition.

"Robyn, wait. Before you take that call, I want to say in return that I think you'd make a great first lady. The first professional crime-solver ever to redecorate the White House."

"It needs it too. Hello?"

Roper could tell by Robyn's extended silence that it was serious—something likely to occupy her professionally for the next several days, if not weeks.

"I see. Victims identified? Wait. Would you say that name

again?" She shot a pained look at Roper. "Oh, dear God. Then when are you going to release the names? Oh, yes, of course. We must always be extra cautious when politics is involved."

Roper couldn't miss the sarcasm in her last remark. He wondered what kind of indiscretion by a member of Congress had led to a confrontation or assault of some kind. He didn't wish to entertain the thought that it could be something worse.

"When? You're sure you don't want me to come now? All right, I'll be in by six in the morning. No, no. That's okay. I'm glad you called. See you in the morning. Bye."

She stared at the far wall. He thought her face registered more sympathy than surprise.

"Robyn?"

"Tom, I'm so sorry to have to tell you this, but Marshall's dead. He was murdered earlier tonight."

•　•　•　•　•

By 10:00 p.m. all evidence of his having been in Maureen Blakely's apartment had, to the man's satisfaction, been completely eliminated. Sitting on the edge of his bed nursing two fingers of inexpensive scotch, the man replayed the events of the evening. When he entered the darkened living room at 7:39 p.m., the woman was already in the bathroom humming a familiar Broadway tune. Moving quietly toward the bathroom door, which was slightly open, he detected other sounds: the tube of her lip gloss popping open and perfume being sprayed—on her lovely neck, he imagined.

A minute later, he heard her cut something with a pair of scissors and then slide the shower curtain open, followed by the slight squeak of her bare feet stepping into the tub. After she pulled the shower curtain shut, the man opened the bathroom door enough to see her silhouette through the sheer curtain.

He watched her wrap a rope around one of her elevated wrists and turn on the water, which hit her porcelain skin between her neck and full breasts. After seemingly securing her right hand to the left with the rope, she dropped her head in what was obviously a deliberate attempt to soak her long auburn hair.

When he stepped into the bathroom, he smelled the aroma of the lighted candles and caught sight of the digital clock on the vanity. The time flicked to 7:42. His meticulous research informed him that Marshall Grayson would arrive in three minutes, and he would not enter a second before then.

The man looked on the vanity and saw the other part of the cut rope. He stepped over and took it in his hands, quickly extending it to see if it would serve his purpose. The flutter of noise prompted Maureen Blakely to call out "Marshall?" The man allowed her assumption to stand for a moment before he entered the tub.

"Is this how you wanted me, baby?" She began to wiggle her voluptuous body, as if she were trying to free her hands from the shower head high above her. The man thought her attempt to make believable her state of bondage was pathetic. "Please don't do this to me, baby." The young woman purred with delight.

It was then that he wrapped the rope around her throat. Since the showerhead prevented him from dropping it over her head, he slipped the rope around the front of her neck and grabbed it on the other side. He crossed his hands and increased the pressure of the rope around her neck. Momentarily she freed her hands but then she lost consciousness.

Before stepping out of the shower, the man retied her hands and spread her thighs several inches so her body would remain upright.

He exited the tub with his trousers and shoes soaked with water. He checked the time on the digital clock: 7:44 p.m. Moving to the interior bathroom closet on the left, he opened the door and saw a laundered man's robe, sweat suit, and expensive running shoes. He assumed the woman had planned to present them to her lover after their little sex game. He closed the closet door the moment he heard the front door open.

After the murders and double-checking the note with the numbers "20-18-11-19-07" placed in Marshall Grayson's hand, the man removed his clothes and shoes and donned the dry sweat suit and running shoes. Before leaving the apartment, he bundled up his wet clothes in one of the bath towels and again checked the time: 7:52 p.m.

Getting up from his own bed, the man walked to his mini-bar and poured himself another two fingers of the cheap scotch. He closed his eyes and recalled the image of his mother speaking to him while lying in her bed fourteen years earlier. After finishing his drink, he opened a handsomely bound journal. He reread the quotation he'd selected when he began planning the murder of Marshall Grayson in September. It was from the Pulitzer Prize-winning author Robert Penn Warren: "The end of man is knowledge, but man can't know whether knowledge will save him or kill him; whether he is killed because of the knowledge which he has got or because of the knowledge which he hasn't got and which if he had it would save him."

He closed the journal and reached across his desk for the large knife he had used to murder Grayson. He carefully rubbed the edge of the blade with a chamois cloth, removing all visible traces of Marshall Grayson's blood. It was important that the blade be clean before he used it again.

Chapter 3

"Mr. Vice President, I'm sorry to wake you, but I have terrible news."

It took a moment before Edward Malloch could read his bedside clock. It was 4:30 a.m. "The president?"

"No, sir. It's Marshall."

"Oh, God. Wait." Malloch lurched out of bed and made his way toward the kitchen of the Vice President's residence. He poured himself some Buffalo Trace Kentucky bourbon and downed it before remembering that the bottle was a Christmas gift from Marshall Grayson, a native of Frankfort, Kentucky. "Okay, Max, go ahead. Please don't tell me it's drugs or an accusation by one of his lady friends."

Malloch's chief of staff, Maximilian Nettleton, responded slowly and emphatically. "Mr. Vice President, Marshall has been murdered."

"Oh, Jesus, no."

"There was a young woman involved—also murdered."

"God damn it. By Marshall?"

"I don't know much yet, but I've been informed that based on the crime scene evidence he couldn't have killed her."

"My God, Marshall's dead?"

"Sir, there's one more thing. Cocaine was found in the bathroom where the murders took place."

"Oh, Christ. All right, Max. You need to prepare a statement for the morning."

"Already on it, sir."

"It might be wise to add something about how much we've all been worrying about Marshall these past several months. That we just assumed it had something to do with his recent testimony to the grand jury."

"I understand, sir." Nettleton had warned Grayson not to come forward in the case against Patrick Sims of the Justice Department, doubting that Grayson fully appreciated just how dangerous Sims could be. Sims had a childish petulant streak and a reliance on alcohol that quickly unharnessed a violent temper, which Nettleton believed was characteristic of an increasingly unstable mental state. Only a week earlier, Nettleton had seen Sims hurl a tire jack at a car coming too close while he was changing one of his tires. Nettleton paid the driver enough to dissuade her from filing a police report against Sims.

When they first met the previous spring, Nettleton soon determined that Sims wasn't a happy camper; but realizing that such disenchanted men often proved useful, he cultivated Sims' friendship. Each time they met over the summer and early autumn, Nettleton reiterated a promise to let Sims know if anything worthwhile opened up at the Eisenhower Executive Office Building. But Nettleton preferred that Sims remain at Justice where he could provide more valuable inside information, though lately the flow had trickled down to almost nothing. And now Sims' legal difficulties had placed him on "temporary leave" at Justice—although it was evident Sims wouldn't be returning. During their last conversation a week earlier, after he had hurled the tire jack, an agitated Sims hinted that he was being "courted" by someone with considerable clout in the capital, but he refused to tell Nettleton who it was. Sims also admitted that he had stopped speaking to former associates he no longer trusted, most notably Marshall Grayson.

As for Grayson, Nettleton had concluded that his rival was damaging himself and the office of the vice president by maintaining his communication with Sims, especially since he was forced to testify against him in court. But Grayson was now dead, and nothing else he knew or suspected about Nettleton was likely to surface. Then again, what if he had already talked to that reporter from the *Washington Post* or his good friend Tom Roper? Yes, that son-of-a-bitch Roper. Not long ago, Nettleton had taken measures to prevent one of Grayson's communications from reaching the senator.

"And damn it, Max, do what you can to suppress a public statement by the police or the press about that cocaine."

"I'll see what I can do, Mr. Vice President."

Nettleton heard the half-mutter of a thank you before Malloch hung up. Times like this he understood how unappreciative the V. P. was of having someone with such talent and Machiavellian know-how serving as his chief of staff. Yet Nettleton appreciated the advantages of the Veep's lack of recognition. Indeed, Malloch seemed oblivious to what Nettleton was capable of in areas outside the sphere of the vice president's immediate interests. In any event, Nettleton understood that he would be adequately rewarded for getting Ed Malloch dumped from the ticket in the next election.

•　　•　　•　　•　　•

"Tom, I appreciate your coming in this early on a Monday morning. Coffee? You look like you could use it."

"Yes, thanks." Roper smiled in a vain attempt to disguise his shock over the loss of a friend. He understood that the news of Grayson's death had not yet reached everyone on Capitol Hill; therefore, he didn't want to be the one to break it to Carol McCrimmon if she didn't know. But then she'd probably offer only a quick "I'm sorry to hear that" and get on with Senate business.

The new majority leader called to someone on her staff to bring two cups of coffee "sweet and light," as both she and Roper preferred it. She stepped from behind her desk and sat in the chair directly across from his. This was one of the several ways she wished to distinguish herself from her predecessor Vince Galino, who liked to pronounce *ex cathedra* from behind his weighty and ornate desk. The former leader preferred to position his ample carcass in his chair as though he were hurled into it by some force mighty enough to toss his 285 pounds. Carol McCrimmon, on the other hand, carefully placed her 115 pounds primly into every chair and sofa she sat on.

"Are you still seeing Robyn Meadows, Tom?"

"Yes."

"I like her. Fascinating career she's engaged in."

"Far more fascinating than mine, I think."

McCrimmon frowned. Roper could see she wasn't pleased by his half-facetious remark. The leader's staff person interrupted with the coffee.

"Thank you, Robert. You know the senator, I assume?" The men exchanged pleasantries.

"You bet we do. I tried to get him on the diamond this fall, but to no avail. As I said, I see center field in your genetic make up, Bobby."

"I have a weak arm and only average speed, Senator. Anyway, there were..." Robert Gleeson looked at Senator McCrimmon and raised his hand to his mouth as if to stifle what he wanted to say next.

"Bobby, close the door as you go out. Thank you."

"Good kid." Roper paused. "What do you think he was about to say when he cut himself off?"

"Oh, that this past fall there were 'lots of *changes* going on in this office.' Meaning, I assume, that he took Vince's death hard and wasn't sure he wanted to work for the first female majority leader of the Senate. But I like Bobby. No way I was going to let him go. And I think he'll soon come around to the new reality here."

Roper knew the transition must be difficult—going from Vince Galino's back-slapping to Carol McCrimmon's hand-wringing approach to the office.

Roper expected that the new leader would stare at him for several moments before launching into her well-outlined and rehearsed lecture. He met her gaze with one that conveyed bemused anticipation.

"Tom, what the hell is wrong with you?"

"I'll assume you're about to tell me."

"I don't know anyone in my political lifetime who's come to the Senate with as much going for him as you did when you took the oath last year. Your father's reputation, your impressive personal history, and your act of heroism on behalf of Senator Eldridge's child. Yet since then you've managed to completely alienate or at least temporarily tick off over half of your own party, not to mention the president."

"And the new majority leader?"

"Yes, and the new majority leader. I find that I can't depend on you, Tom. At first I couldn't be sure where you were going half the time, but now I can't help assuming that you're going in a direction detrimental to me, to your party, and certainly to yourself."

Roper wondered if she would bring up the disturbing information provided by Capitol police that in December two anonymous threats had been made against his life.

"Carol, I'm not that bad, am I? I mean, the vice president still likes me." In spite of his grief over Marshall Grayson's death, Roper still exuded enough charm to force a reluctant smile from McCrimmon.

"Just about that bad. I still don't believe that stunt you pulled with the deputy director on Thursday. You weren't given a seat on the Judiciary Committee to act like that. And right when we had just returned from the holiday recess. Damn it, Tom, you've been in Washington long enough to know that despite popular impressions to the contrary the nation has tremendous respect for the FBI and what they do to keep us safe—especially in these times. *Both* parties have to tread very carefully on oversight. Do you know what you said to the deputy director when you were told by Chuck Hefferen that your questioning would have to wait until today?"

"Of course I know what I said, Carol." Ever since high school, Roper had given in to the incorrigible urge to answer rhetorical questions directly. "I said that when we met today I would offer a suggestion to the American people that might wipe that smug expression off Sheridan Browning's face."

"Tom, we all agree that he's an insufferable jerk—almost everyone in the Hoover Building thinks so—but you don't use an open and televised hearing of the Judiciary Committee to tell someone what you think of him. That's what the Senate hallways are for. I'm asking you nicely to pose your questions professionally and challenge the answers professionally. You don't have to bring up what you said on Thursday."

"You know Browning will bring it up, Carol. I've challenged him, you see. He's not used to being threatened—that is, if he sees what I said as a threat, which I know he does. Carol, can I have more coffee? And my compliments to whoever brews it."

The leader punched keys on her phone. "Bobby, more coffee for Senator Roper." McCrimmon stood and began to pace. Roper hadn't seen such nervousness from her before. He knew she was determined always to show herself as strong and imperturbable. "Would it do me any good to order you to refrain from saying what you intend to say, Tom?"

"Carol, don't do that. You know I have great respect for you—and I like you very much. I wouldn't want to disobey a direct order from my commander."

Again she couldn't help smiling. "And what am I commanding? A brace of my party's senators who think I am of the wrong gender to be majority leader. A handful of female senators who think each one of them should have been the first woman chosen as our party's leader. And then there's you—a charismatic and talented man who probably hasn't followed any commander since he left the service."

"That's only because I served under the best commanding general who in my humble estimation ever lived."

"Right. General Nathan Roper. And every other 'general' under whose command you've been placed has just not been able to measure up to your brilliant father, the master tactician."

Gleeson entered with the coffee.

"Bobby, Senator Roper would like to compliment you on your splendid coffee."

"Indeed I would. Good job, Master Robert."

"Thank you, Senator. I spent two months working in an upscale French café when I was in grad school."

"I see. Well, keep up the good work. And oil your glove. I'm comin' to getcha for summer ball."

"We'll see. Excuse me, Senator. Madame Leader." Gleeson closed the door behind him.

"Tom, I want you to know that the new majority whip seemed almost grateful when I told him that I would talk to you myself. Any idea why he felt that way?"

"Oh, it may be because the last time Bill Devonshire poked his finger into my chest, I grabbed it and bent it back until he dropped to his knees."

"Oh, Jesus. In front of anyone?"

"Did it in the restroom outside the Senate Chamber. Just the two of us. Don't worry, I checked the stalls to be sure there were no witnesses. My father taught me not to put up with any crap from little bullying martinets flaunting their supposed authority."

Having little patience with the new majority whip herself, McCrimmon laughed. "Tom, you do know, don't you, that you have *your* finger on the self-destruct button? You may well be blowing up your career."

"Carol, I told you last month that I'm one and done."

"Do you know how many senators have said the same thing over the past two centuries? Tom, listen to me. You need to be careful about whom you insult. There are men—and a good number of women—in this city who live only for political revenge. I don't have to remind you that there's very little they wouldn't do to get it."

"Excuse me again, Senator." Gleeson poked his head in.

"What is it, Bobby?"

"Terrible news. We've just been informed that Marshall Grayson was murdered last night."

McCrimmon looked at Tom Roper, well aware of his

friendship with Grayson. She saw in his face that he already knew. "Robert, see if you can get the vice president on the line."

"Yes, ma'am."

•   •   •   •   •

Returning to his office, Roper went straight for the portable safe on top of his file cabinet. The moment he heard the news of the double murder the night before, he became anxious to retrieve the envelope Marshall Grayson gave him for safekeeping weeks earlier. After opening the safe and taking the large envelope to his desk, he reached for a letter opener and broke open the heavily-taped seal. Inside was a smaller envelope, which he opened as well. He paused and took a full breath before pulling the contents out. Roper unfolded and fanned out the six 8 ½ by 11-inch pages. They were all blank.

Chapter 4

The man felt no physical effects from the night before, except for slight tingling on the palms of both hands, the consequence of the forceful grip he had had on the rope that strangled the beautiful Maureen Blakely. He recalled the first time he studied Marshall Grayson, when the political advisor rubbed pine tar on the palms of both hands during a softball game.

After getting dressed, the man went to his kitchen table and examined a 2014 calendar opened to the current month, January. On New Year's morning, he had circled the 16th with a green marker. Sixteen. The number was all important to him—the significance of that birthday "celebration" years earlier for one thing. The horrifying truths he had discovered at the time about who he was and what he would have to be as a result of what had been done to him that night.

The actions to validate the claim of his parents—that he would make his mark by this coming birthday—had begun. And he had until the end of the day on Friday to meet the deadline set by his mother and father all those years ago. He couldn't have started the process until now—though he had begun his preparations in late August—and he would have to complete everything by the end of the week. But he was confident he would. The numbers had finally aligned.

Reaching for his brown leather journal, he wrote down the words of James Thurber: "There is no safety in numbers, or in anything else."

After closing his journal, he jotted down the string of numbers on his calendar. "20-18-11-19-07." He nodded and began tapping his finger rapidly on the number 18. The past several months had been devoted to learning all he could about those whom he would kill. In truth, the accumulation of this information came much easier than he had ever expected it would.

The man ran his finger in a circle around the number 18. He sighed. "Poor Ian."

•   •   •   •   •

"Tom, that's what we have at present. I'm sure I'll have more before the day is out. We can talk about it tonight." Roper sensed the excitement clashing with the professional tone in Robyn's voice. "Just remember not to say anything. I'd be out of work if they knew I was sharing this with you."

"All right. Tell me those numbers again."

"20, 18, 11, 19, 07."

"Robyn, was the '7' typed with just the single number 7?

"No, there was a zero before the seven."

"Okay, I see. Look, when I get some time today I'll do some work on the sequence."

"We obviously have perfectly qualified adult boy-scout decoders working for the Metro force—not to mention for the Bureau—so it's not necessary that you devote any of your time to this."

"You're right, Robyn. But puzzle-solving is my life. So I must." He couldn't believe he could be so playful in the wake of Grayson's death.

"Tom, I've got to go. And you have your hearing in a few minutes." She grinned mischievously. "Promise me you won't be too rough on old Sheridan Browning."

"I don't think it's possible to be *too* rough on Sheridan Browning. I'll talk to you tonight."

"Wait, wait. I almost forgot to tell you." The altered inflection of her voice left him uneasy. "On the buttocks of the young woman were the initials 'M.T'—printed with blood."

"Marshall's blood?"

"They're pretty sure, even without the lab report. The rope that strangled her had blood dipped on the edge of it. It's what the killer used to print the initials on her skin. The woman wasn't cut. Nor was she menstruating." She paused. "Sorry for that little detail."

"'M.T.' All right, I'll think about that as well."

"Tom, are you all right?"

He knew she was concerned that Grayson's death might affect his performance at the Judiciary hearing. "I'll be all right. With me, full grief is invariably a delayed reaction. It was the same with my father. In a week I'll grieve as I should."

"I'm so sorry, Tom."

"I always believed Marshall was too irresponsible in his private life to last long in this business, Robyn. Still, I really loved the guy. We never had a bad word between us. Thanks for being so concerned."

"All right, then. Well, this isn't likely to help much, but I'd like to tell you that I love you, Tom."

"Helps a lot more than you know."

• • • • •

"Oh, come on, Natalie. You can't expect me to tell you everything that happens with the Deputy Secretary of State. As much as I love you, I couldn't betray him like that. He was kind enough to bring me over from Commerce. He was my father's roommate at Dartmouth, remember?" At times like these, Ian Arrington wondered if Natalie Yarrow was dating him only because he was the kind of research source she couldn't get anywhere else.

"Ian, whatever you tell me, I'm not going to cite you in one of my footnotes." She was presently writing a dissertation to complete her Ph.D. in Government at Georgetown.

"Natalie, I've introduced you to him as my significant other. He'd know how you got the information."

"As if he would even read my dissertation."

Arrington's feelings for Natalie Yarrow led him to provide her with selected information he'd heard about the secretary of state's inner circle. But Natalie wasn't the only one with whom he shared such information. There were, for example, members of the D.C. softball team he played on in the late summer and early fall.

He sensed her anger. "Natalie, can we meet and talk?" She said nothing. "I think I can give you something in a way that won't get me fired or thrown in jail."

"Where do you want to meet?"

"You know I work late on Mondays."

"Yes, I know that, Ian. Till 8:30 p.m. Everybody knows that, don't they?"

"Look, Natalie, I just want to please you, so I thought I could leave the Truman Building and come up to Georgetown and meet you in front of St. Clare's."

Natalie's voice altered, reflecting her surprise and delight. She was a devout Roman Catholic who chided Arrington for his seeming indifference to religion. "Ian, are you sure you don't want to meet at my place?"

"You've wanted me to see the church where you go, right? So now I want to. Who knows? I might even go to mass with you next weekend." Although born a Roman Catholic, Arrington hadn't stepped inside a church since he left northern Ohio when he was eighteen.

"Ian, call me when you're almost there and I'll leave my apartment and meet you in front of St. Clare's."

"Great. I'll see you tonight. Bye."

Arrington was slightly stung by her remark about his predictable habits. Did "everyone" really know he worked until 8:30 on Monday nights?

• • • • •

The men had just finished their lunch at the Café du Parc in the historic Willard Hotel, just a short stroll from the White House. Sheridan Browning had tried something new this time, the *St. Jacques rôties à la ventrèche.*

"How are the scallops, Sheridan?"

"Ever eat a dog's testicles, Devin?"

"Haven't had the pleasure."

"Well, this must be what it's like. Remind me never to order these again." Browning reached inside his mouth with his fingers and removed the masticated piece of scallop. "Christ, they can give it a French name but that don't make it taste worth a shit."

Browning's breakfast companion Devin Cassell, nominally an FBI special agent though in truth Deputy Director

Browning's jack of all trades, maintained the pleasant though non-committal expression on his trustworthy face. In truth, he'd finally had enough of Browning's boorishness and wished only that he had the guts to give up his lucrative position and try his hand at something else. Foreign Service, perhaps. In any event, Cassell, who was fluent in French, knew that in spite of Browning's reaction to the scallops, French food was the only aspect of European culture the man found appealing. Otherwise, Browning stuck to one brand—prime U.S.A. Too often he had "assisted" those politicians who warded off the chill of scrutiny by wrapping themselves in the flag.

"Hell of a hotel, Devin." Browning glanced around the Café du Parc.

"Yes, sir. Hard to imagine that the Willard hosted both Dickens and Twain."

"And Buffalo Bill and P.T. Barnum."

Cassell thought Browning's references most apt. Soon they would step inside yet another ring of the three-ring circus at the Dirksen Building. They were scheduled to be there in twenty-five minutes, but Cassell knew that Browning would delay his arrival just long enough to get committee chair Chuck Hefferen's blood pressure boiling.

"Devin, tell me what the fuck Tom Roper is up to."

"I'm not sure, sir, but I would be prepared for something unique."

"Another hand-wringing senator making points with the folks back home, implying that he'll single-handedly see justice done and protect the civil liberties of every citizen in his state. The usual bullshit."

"No, I'm guessing he's going to say something we haven't heard before."

"I've been around long enough to hear everything those

senatorial pricks have in their arsenal."

Cassell winced at yet another clumsy metaphor coming from his boss. "As I said, Sheridan, I'd be ready for something different. Thomas Roper isn't your typical loose canon. From what we've been able to find out, he appears to accept the fact that he'll have only one term."

"If he shows me even the slightest hint of disrespect this afternoon, he can bet his sweet ass he'll only have one term." Browning suddenly couldn't get comfortable in his chair. "I need a fucking drink." Cassell slightly shook his head no. "Didn't you talk to that god-damned party whip? Can't he rein in the son-of-a-bitch?"

Cassell smiled. "Can't. Bill Devonshire is afraid of him."

"What? Of a first-term senator just beginning his second year in office? So, tell me, Devin, what is it about Roper that got him so easily into the Senate? I assume being Nathan Roper's son was mostly responsible."

"In part responsible, yes. But his father's sterling reputation, which he earned as a combat officer in Vietnam and then as a four-star general in the first Gulf War, was only part of the son's calling card. Nathan Roper made fans out of many in Washington when he ended up on Nixon's enemies list after his controversial *Time* interview in 1971 regarding the poor handling of the war by the boys in Washington. Some of his biggest fans then were some of the most senior senators and congressmen you've butted heads with the past ten years."

Browning offered a succinct dry spit to demonstrate his contempt. "Then what else was it about the son that paved his way to the Senate?"

"An All-American story."

"My favorite kind. Proceed."

"Well, after Nathan Roper's son Tom graduated from

Marquette in 1997—at the tender age of twenty, I might add—he went into the Army—basic training, then OCS, then some strings pulled. He ended up working intelligence in the Middle East in 1998 and 1999."

"The old man the one pulling the strings?"

"Obviously. But the general couldn't persuade his son to make a career in the military, so Tom Roper got out in the summer of 2000 and entered law school that fall. When he finished third in his class in '03, he was immediately offered a chance to join the White House legal team."

"Nice starter job. Jesus."

"But he turned it down."

Browning checked his watch and then straightened his tie. "Time to go, Devin, but please continue. Tell me more about wonder boy." After Browning complained about the scallops to their waiter, the men strolled out of the Willard.

"Tom Roper practiced law in Wisconsin for two years before he got into politics."

"Now I remember. He did some heroic shit, right?"

"Yes. In January 2006, Roper accompanied his father to a party given by the state's senior senator, another of your old nemeses, Parker Eldridge. I believe the party was thrown in honor of Nathan Roper's retirement from the Army the month before."

The men stepped into the waiting limousine and headed down Pennsylvania Avenue toward the Capitol. Cassell noticed that Browning's tie was stained with a dropping from the scallop he had earlier pulled out of his mouth. Without a word, Cassell reached for one for the three additional ties he carried in his briefcase and handed it to Browning, who didn't bother to look at the stain but simply yanked off the tie he was wearing, slipped the new one around his neck, and then leaned back as

Cassell tied the full Windsor and re-buttoned his shirt.

As the limousine passed 9th Street, Cassell continued. "Senator Eldridge had a young daughter from his second marriage. I believe she was seven at the time. When it came time to show her off to the company, no one could find her. Everyone still recalled the JonBenét Ramsey murder of course, so panic set in. When they headed for various rooms of the large house and toward the basement, Tom Roper went out the kitchen back door and headed toward the guest house down the long driveway. Later he would say that he initially thought the girl might have wandered off in search of the family dog, which Parker Eldridge had tied to the railing on the back patio stairs.

"Roper found a pair of adult footprints in the shallow snow leading from the door, as well as a second pair of impressions clearly belonging to a young girl. But when those smaller footprints disappeared, and a pair of larger ones became evident in the snow, Roper concluded the child had been picked up and carried—most likely by a kidnapper. Remember that Parker Eldridge was one of the three wealthiest men on Capitol Hill.

"In any event, Roper found the dog still tied to the railing at the foot of the steps leading from the patio. It was dead--poisoned. Roper made it to the guest house just in time to see the child being lifted by a man and a woman into the trunk of a running car—the little girl's hands were bound and her mouth covered with duct tape. Apparently the woman was one of the part-time kitchen staff periodically employed when the senator had large gatherings at his home. When Roper called out for them to stop, the man pulled a pistol and shot at Roper, grazing him in the arm. But Roper reached the woman and grabbed the child before the man could fire again and before the girl could be thrown in the trunk. The male got behind the wheel and drove off the property. The woman began to run, but she was immediately surrounded by others who had just come down from the house. Later, they found the ransom note the woman had taped inside the refrigerator.

"The girl was therefore rescued, and Tom Roper soon went to work in Washington for Senator Eldridge."

Browning shifted himself awkwardly. "Did they catch the would-be kidnapper in the car?"

"Easily, especially since Roper had committed the license number to memory as the car was driving off."

"As I said, he's a wonder boy."

"One thing led to another. Roper worked for Eldridge's legal team for a time, then moved back to Wisconsin in 2007 to work in the state's attorney general's office, before becoming deputy attorney general himself in 2008. When Eldridge announced that he was retiring and would not therefore run for re-election in 2012, he devoted all his energies to making a case for Tom Roper as his successor in the Senate. Only someone as rich, popular, and stubborn as Parker Eldridge could have pulled it off, but, let's face it, nothing motivates quite like gratitude for someone's having saved your child's life."

Browning touched the knot of his tie. "Do tell."

"The polls told the party leadership that Wisconsin voters were responsive to the idea of Nathan Roper's son being in the United States Senate. When the now thirteen-year-old daughter of Parker Eldridge came out in public and reminded them what Tom Roper had done for her six years earlier, it was all over. Roper took sixty-one percent of the vote."

"Well, as I've told you time and time again, Devin, this is a great country. But it doesn't change the fact that Roper is treading on dangerous terrain if he decides to fuck with me. Anyway, thanks for the oral dossier. I knew I picked the right man in you. Well, who knows? I might be able to use some of what you just told me this afternoon—that is, if Roper decides to become the little prick I just know he's dying to be."

· · · · ·

The man checked the time. It was 1:50 p.m. He would step outside from his warm and lighted surroundings into the darkening city around 5:10 p.m. He would walk on both sides of the National Mall until 5:40. Then he would go up 7th, until he entered his favorite restaurant at his usual time on this night of the week. A leisurely meal and a stiff drink—perhaps two—and then he'd head back the way he had come. He would have time to spare before he reached the State Department at 8:20 p.m. After that, he wasn't sure where he would go. That was up to Ian Arrington. Yes. Ian Arrington, native of Ohio. Marshall Grayson, native of Kentucky. He man nodded in satisfaction.

Perhaps Arrington would go straight to his apartment, where he would meet his girlfriend—the doctoral student at Georgetown. Or he might decide to go to her place. It didn't matter. Either location was fine.

Chapter 5

Roper was in the middle of a prosciutto, red pepper, and provolone sandwich—the favorite snack food of the late majority leader Vince Galino—when the door opened to his office in the Hart Senate Office Building.

"All set for your execution, Senator Roper?" It was Roper's Senate buddy Tripp Wilcox of South Dakota.

"So you've come to perform the last rites, Tripp?"

"Can't do it. I'm Methodist. But I'll be happy to collect that twenty you owe me." "Right." Roper reached for his wallet. "Oh, the agony of being a Milwaukee Bucks fan this year."

"I warned you not to bet against my team."

"You're from South Dakota. How the hell is Phoenix *your* team?"

"I graduated from little Dakota Wesleyan. I wanted a horse in the big hoops race—so I chose the Phoenix Suns. But at least we're still playing football at Dakota Wesleyan—not like some universities I could name—that you went to."

"So glad you're my best friend, Tripp."

Wilcox dropped his head and his smile. "Tom, when you get in the hearing room, knock the shit out of them, all right? I'll be rooting for you. Talk to you later, good buddy."

"Bye, Senator Wilcox." Roper's office manager Lena Roseboro stuck her head in as Wilcox left the office.

"It's getting about that time, Senator Roper."

"I know, I know. And I'm only half way through my lunch."

Lena offered an exaggerated sigh. "That's what you get for eating so close to two in the afternoon. Get with the program, Senator."

Roper enjoyed his daily bantering with Lena, whom he hired to run his office when he was deputy attorney general back home. She was the granddaughter of the building's chief custodian, of whom Roper was very fond. Now in Washington, Roper missed his daily briefings on baseball in the late '40s and '50s from Jefferson "No-Web" Stevenson. Stevenson had picked up the nickname "No-Web" for the sad excuse for a glove he carried with him when he first signed with Brooklyn in 1950, when he was a skinny hurler of seventeen.

"My granddaddy used to tell me that he had ten miles per hour less on his fast ball when he ate a late lunch."

"And how is No-Web doing, Lena?"

"He says he's still like 'a well-oiled glove,' but in fact he just had by-pass surgery to go along with his hip replacement. Other than that, he's just fine. He wants to know when you're going to get him tickets to a Nationals game."

"You give him my best and tell him he's got tickets anytime he wants to come to Washington."

"Now, you better hurry and finish that sandwich. Senator Hefferen doesn't appreciate his committee members sashaying in late."

"All right, all right." Roper shoved the last third of the sandwich into his mouth.

"Can I ask what you were doing all this time in your office

when you should have been eating a leisurely lunch and not rushing to choke yourself to death?"

"I was crunching some numbers." Lena could hardly make out what he said, owing to the bread, prosciutto, and provolone stuffed between his teeth. Roper scooped up the last piece of red pepper, which had fallen onto his desk, and at last he was finished with his meal.

"Well, Senator, now you have to 'crunch' on over the Dirksen Building. The FBI awaits your presence."

As they made their way out of the office, Roper thought better of telling Lena Roseboro what numbers he had spent so much time crunching. Perhaps it was because the sequence was tied to the murder of a close friend, but Roper couldn't stop dwelling on the order of the five numbers Robyn Meeds said were on a small sheet of paper in Marshall Grayson's hand: "20-18-11-19-07." Roper had given up trying to find a sophisticated mathematical code in the sequence. First, he didn't have a stratospheric mathematical mind; second, he was certain that they had someone at Metro or at the Bureau—or at one of the area's several universities—working on that possibility.

Roper saw first in the five numbers that the police obviously had a serial killer in their midst. Roper assumed, since Robyn had not heard of any similar "numbers slayings" of late, that the first number—20—had a connection to Marshall Grayson—or to Grayson and the woman murdered at the same time. It couldn't be that she was the prime victim to the killer—the note, after all, was placed in Grayson's hand—even though Roper wasn't sure whether she was also an intended victim or simply an unfortunate "wrong place-wrong time" casualty.

Roper also assumed that this was surely no jealousy killing, although the police investigation would do its job in tracing the woman's background. Roper feared that the next four victims—

if such indeed was the promise in the sequence of five numbers—would be those in the political sphere. Certainly the vice president's detail had already jumped to the next level of security. Could the next intended victim also be working in the V.P.'s office?

He wanted to give Robyn a call and learn what she had so far concluded or suspected about the double homicide, but it was time to leave for the committee meeting and his confrontation with Sheridan Browning, Deputy Director of the FBI.

•　　•　　•　　•　　•

Sitting at her lab desk, Robyn was intrigued by the initials painted on the woman's buttocks in Marshall Grayson's blood: an "M" and a "T." She had learned the woman's identity. Maureen Blakely. Age twenty-six. Unmarried. No apparent connection to Edward Malloch's office. The woman's background was still being investigated, but it seemed clear she was the one Grayson had referred to when he told her and Tom at a Kennedy Center reception over the holidays that he had met "the most incredible woman." Robyn remembered Marshall's remarks about the woman's height—five nine or five ten—and her long beautiful auburn hair. But neither she nor Tom knew where Marshall had met her.

During their brief phone call an hour earlier, Robyn listened to Tom dismiss the possibility that it was a domestic killing— that is, by another man with a romantic claim to the woman. Yet Robyn couldn't help wondering. If the "M" indeed stood for "Maureen," did the "T" stand for the killer's first name? Like some quaint couple's carving of their initials on an old oak, only this time the marking being done by a jilted and insane lover?

But Tom was surely right. Why would the killer leave such an overt sign as that? No, this murderer seemed too shrewd for something that plain. And that was the word Robyn kept bringing back to mind. Shrewd.

•   •   •   •   •

"All right, we have been delayed long enough. This committee prides itself *nowadays* on beginning on time." Chuck Hefferen daubed his handkerchief at the perspiration collecting in the folds of the flesh below his chin. Even so, he was the one who saw to it that the hearing room was as warm as it was.

"Fortunately, Mr. Browning, you can share part of the blame with those in the press who waylaid you out in the hall."

"You have that correct, sir." Sheridan Browning smiled at Devin Cassell. Browning had deliberately delayed his entrance. No one had stopped him in the hall.

Cassell wanted to shake his head at his boss's audacity and guile but maintained his professional demeanor. What dominated his thoughts was what Thomas Roper was likely going to say to the deputy director. Last week the senator had "threatened" to suggest something to the public that would wipe the "smug expression" off Browning's face. Surely, Roper was shooting from the hip and had by now been dressed down by the party leadership. Cassell had been informed that Carol McCrimmon had asked to see Roper, and without question she would have addressed the inappropriate remark of several days earlier. But Cassell also knew Carol McCrimmon well enough to believe she might not have pressed the issue as hard as she should have, letting let her fondness for Roper affect her handling of the matter.

"All right, we come to order," Hefferen continued, daubing

his pendulous jowls. "We had to end last Thursday before we got to Senator Roper's questioning. I ask that the senator remember his time, and..." Hefferen didn't complete his thought, but everyone in the room knew what he wanted to say: "remember his time and...watch his god-damn manners." The room was deathly quiet for once. Standing in the back was Robert Gleeson from Carol McCrimmon's office, entering a summary of events in a schoolboy's notebook.

"Thank you, Mr. Chairman." Roper offered the obligatory and strained smile of the adversary. "Welcome back, Mr. Browning."

"More pleasure than I can say, Senator." The silence in the room was broken by laughter and whispering. For the first time Devin Cassell allowed himself a smile.

Browning half raised his hand. "Can I say something before we launch, Mr. Chairman?"

Hefferen nodded. "Of course, Mr. Browning."

"Senator Roper, if you're intending to ask me why I seemingly have no *regrets* over our so-called violations in our attempt to root out members of a terrorist group in your state, then I can save us both some time and repeat what I have said to some of the committee last week and for so several years now to so many senators who came before you—Senator Parker Eldridge among them." Browning paused for a reaction from Roper, who merely looked inquisitively at him.

Browning began by explaining the need to "break some eggs" in making an omelet. "It happens in wartime, Senator— and be assured we are at war domestically—and we are the army the country depends on." Roper felt a tightening in his gut at Browning's allusion to war and its casualties, complete with the trite kitchen metaphor. Browning plowed ahead. "Unfortunate misconceptions over the years relating in our so-called abuses have been fostered and embellished by—and forgive me, Mr. Chairman—by hearings such as this one. Every few years we have to engage in dancing the same tired dance." Browning fixed his gaze on Roper. "Senator, can I request that you ask me specific questions that may shed some light on what we are doing to keep the American people safe? If you are simply going to add to the chorus of complaints merely for crass political gain, then you are not serving your constituents very well. And they should know it." Browning heaved his body back in his chair and fidgeted with the knot of his tie.

With several of the committee members staring with disbelief at the chairman, Hefferen pointed the gavel toward Roper. "Senator."

"Thank you, Mr. Chairman. I'll be brief."

Browning shot a quick smile at Devin Cassell. Clearly, he had intimidated the snot-nose young senator. He sat back in his chair, raised both hands, and opened both palms in the gesture of "Well, what have you got?"

"I am grateful for Mr. Browning's remarks. So very grateful that he has publicly expressed himself the way he has that I will only make one or two points and ask absolutely no questions." The room remained completely still. Cassell sat up, clearly concerned.

"Since you feel the way you do, Mr. Browning, I would like to read two letters from staff personnel at your Milwaukee field office. These letters mention their hearing your abusive and sexist language directed at the students and faculty at the University of Wisconsin you apparently suspected of terrorist activity. These letters also note that when the evidence just wasn't there to implicate any of them, you said to one of the field agents, and I quote--."

"Senator Roper." Hefferen quickly interrupted. "This isn't

the time."

"Roper leaned close to his microphone so that he could be heard clearly over the vocal rumbling from the audience and from other members of the committee. "My apologies, Mr. Chairman. Perhaps this isn't the time. It should however be repeated that the Deputy Director—or Acting Director, as he has no doubt considered himself since Director Tillotson's unfortunate accident—has no right to strut in here with the arrogance he has consistently displayed in front of this committee."

Hefferen banged the gavel twice. "Senator, that last remark was uncalled for."

"Again, forgive me, Mr. Chairman." Two of the other committee members stared at Roper as if they were children and he was the neighborhood ice cream man. "Perhaps Mr. Browning might better respect those he claims to serve and protect."

Browning began with a derisive laugh but soon stopped when he realized no one else had joined him in mocking Roper's accusations and lecture. Devin Cassell's mind quickly went into fast-forward. He saw there was a chance—a good one at that—that Sheridan Browning would regret dismissing the senator the way he had. Cassell knew Browning had been guilty of forcing the issue in Wisconsin, slapping aside privacy concerns, indulging in crass name-calling, and claiming that the Bureau would look bad if nothing came of his insistence that the campus harbored students and a few faculty members determined to cause serious mischief. Cassell wondered about the authenticity of the letters Roper claimed to have in his possession. He said they came from staff personnel, not FBI agents, after all—making the correspondence more easily dismissed. But the exchange with Roper was an embarrassment at the very least—for the Bureau and especially for Browning—and would likely destroy Browning's chance to be named Director when the president decided that it was the proper time to replace Matt Tillotson, who was presently lying in a coma at Walter Reed. Cassell could only hope the audience for Roper's suggestion was limited to those few watching CSPAN2. Cassell formulated which IOU's he would call in from the TV and print media to keep the moment from being publicized more fully. He would also pay an immediate visit to the Justice Department to speak with the attorney general. Finally, he would place a call to President Evan Bedingfield's chief of staff, Jerry Goldman.

Roper replied almost cheerfully. "You may laugh, Mr. Browning, and perhaps many others will as well. But it's also possible that enough of us here as well as enough citizens may wonder if you are really serving their interests as well as you have claimed. You and others play loudly the note of domestic security, but the sound often drowns out what we should hear and pay more attention to. The FBI deserves our appreciation and respect for all it has done for over a century to protect this nation. But as history has shown us, some serving in the Bureau have hardly deserved either our admiration or our respect. We need always to have in the leadership dedicated men and women who refuse to allow abuses to continue—and certainly not those who encourage them. Mr. Chairman, that's all I have. Thank you."

•   •   •   •   •

"Please, Mr. Vice President, I don't want or need anyone assigned to me. There is no connection, sir. None."

"Max, it's just until they get more of a handle on the investigation. Marshall was my chief political advisor; you're my chief of staff. There were five numbers found on the piece of paper in Marshall's hand. Logical, isn't it, that there may be five intended victims? They could *all* come from this office."

Nettleton was confident Malloch had failed to notice his subtle sliding of an unopened envelope under the loose papers on his desk. The envelope was addressed to Marshall Grayson and bore a *Washington Post* return address. Nettleton had only moments before retuned from Grayson's deserted office, relieved by the fact that he'd managed to delay a careful examination of the area until the next day. There were other papers of Grayson's he needed to look at—and when he got the passwords from Grayson's staff, the computer files and emails as well—but this envelope was his top priority and the most easily taken.

Nettleton sighed. "All right, Mr. Vice President. I agree that it makes sense to take some precautions. So, assuming that it's Grayson and me on the murderer's list, who might the other three individuals be? Never mind, I can figure the other names out for myself."

Nettleton guessed that Malloch was considering the possibility that the fifth person on the list—the fifth number— might well be himself, although the Vice President hadn't been told what that number was. Nettleton guessed that what most frightened Malloch were the possible implications in the death of the young woman slain with Marshall Grayson. What would an investigation into her background reveal? If nothing else, she was likely a recreational user of cocaine and probably shared it with Grayson.

"Is there anything else you need, Mr. Vice President?"

"No, Max. You can go home now."

As Nettleton left the Eisenhower Building, he thought further about his well-conceived plan to torpedo Malloch's chances to remain on the ticket in 2016. Getting Carol McCrimmon to run shouldn't be difficult, in spite of her recent insistence that she had made enough history as the first woman to be named Senate majority leader. Nettleton had reminded her over lunch that she won a close election to the post following the death of Vince Galino, a popular leader the Hill would continue to mourn for months to come. And who was she kidding about making history? Yes, two women had already been nominated by their parties to run for vice president, but both tickets had lost the election. Carol McCrimmon wasn't likely to be on the losing side in Evan Bedingfield's bid for a second term. The U.S. Senate, however, was less of a sure thing for the party in 2014 or 2016. A mere four-seat majority was tenuous, especially with the announced retirements of two veteran senators and early polling suggesting the party couldn't depend on keeping those seats.

With Bedingfield's chief of staff Jerry Goldman's assurances that he would only serve one term, Nettleton was confident the president would tap him to replace Goldman after the next election, as Bedingfield would be especially grateful to Nettleton for helping make the second term truly historical by having the first woman vice president.

But such pleasant contemplations were soon flushed away by Max Nettleton's lingering contempt for Malloch's deceased political advisor—he with the god-damned irresistible charm. That Max Nettleton had slept with Maureen Blakely before she began her affair with Marshall Grayson was no consolation now. As far as Nettleton was concerned, he was—to use the historical term—a cuckold. All he lacked were the horns on his head.

Even after having determined that Maureen was nothing more than a political groupie, Nettleton couldn't get past the fact that she had humiliated him even before she turned her attention to Grayson. How badly he had wanted to get back at her for that. But he could do nothing for fear she would expose him and ruin his career and his marriage—and she was well aware of that fact. They had each humiliated him—Maureen and Grayson both. But what was really upsetting Nettleton now was that someone else might know. Someone named Tom Roper.

•   •   •   •   •

As soon as Ian Arrington left his State Department office, he called Natalie Yarrow to tell her he was on his way to St. Clare's in Georgetown. When he arrived, she was waiting for him on the steps.

"Are you ready to go inside and cleanse your soul, heathen?" He was relieved that she was more her teasing self.

"Is there a mass or anything going on?"

"Don't worry. I wouldn't do that to you. No, there's no one inside. I just asked Father Renn if I could show you the church. He said, 'If there's a chance that the laddie might return to the fold, I will see to it that the door will be open for you.'"

"All right. I'm ready. Just show me what to do. It's been a long time, you know. I've forgotten the protocol."

After they entered through the heavy wooden door, Natalie grabbed his hand and led him toward the altar. Arrington couldn't help being impressed and slightly awed by the church's interior. It was far grander than his hometown church in Ohio where his dad had served as an altar boy back in the early 1960s.

When they reached the second row, Natalie entered the pew and moved to its center. She pulled down the padded kneeler and gestured for Arrington to kneel with her. The lighting inside the church was simply perfect, Arrington believed. Just dark enough to convey the proper sense of mystery and awe. The light from the many burning candles flickered across Natalie's lovely face, only enhancing her appeal. She had removed her heavy winter's coat, and her short blonde hair and the low neckline of her burgundy blouse exposed her beautiful long neck. Arrington had worn no coat—only a thick sweater, which he debated taking off as he felt the toasty warmth of the church.

Yet part of that warmth was coming from his intensifying passion for Natalie Yarrow. He was alone now in this large church with a woman he loved and desired. It was all he could do to keep his hands to himself.

Natalie sat back and smiled at him. She was about to whisper something but was interrupted by the sound of soft footsteps coming down the center aisle. Her mouth shaped a silent "Damn it." She wondered why she hadn't at least attempted to lock the front door when they'd come in. Perhaps Father Renn or the night help would come out and ask them all to leave. Natalie had promised the priest that she and Arrington would stay no more than five or ten minutes by themselves.

Someone entered the pew five rows behind them. She turned her head just enough to see where the person was sitting and began to feel apprehensive. Would this visitor strike up a conversation with them? Was he one of the city's needy? Would he ask for money? She pressed Arrington's hand and whispered, "Perhaps we should go now, Ian."

Arrington's reply was soft. "Why? I am really enjoying being here, Natalie. I think I'm falling in love with this church. I definitely want to come to mass with you. Really, I'm serious. I'm feeling so..."

He ceased when he sensed that someone had just sat in the pew directly behind them. He looked at Natalie, who had dropped her head. Just as she feared, the person had moved up four rows to converse with them.

Arrington looked straight ahead, his eyes resting on the bottom of the large crucifix hanging above the altar. He spoke louder now, but in a conversational tone. "Excuse me, but with all the pews in this church, do you have to sit directly behind us?"

"Ian, don't." Arrington heard the quiver in Natalie's voice. "Ian, let's just go, okay?"

"I mean it. Can you just move? The lady and I would like to be a--."

Before he could finish saying "alone," Arrington saw something move rapidly past his left ear and enter the side of Natalie's beautiful neck. By the time it registered that there was a surgically-gloved hand letting go of the screwdriver handle protruding from Natalie's flesh, Arrington felt his hair being pulled upward by that hand and then the burning sensation of something being rapidly raked across his throat. He instinctively brought both his hands to his neck and felt blood beginning to cascade over his fingers.

The man re-gripped the screwdriver in Natalie Yarrow's neck and pressed it deeper into her neck. Waiting just a moment, he removed the screwdriver and her body slumped in the pew. Arrington's body had lurched forward and was now crumpled downward, his head resting against the pew's rack of missals and church literature.

After wrapping the knife in parka material, the man pulled out a single sheet of paper and stuffed it down the back of Arrington's neck, between the flesh and the heavy sweater. The man took the wooden end of the screwdriver and dipped it in Natalie Yarrow's blood. He reached over the pew and grabbed her legs and lifted them up on the bench. Pulling up her dark pants, he exposed both ankles. On one he printed an "L"; on the other an "R."

Chapter 6

Carrying his overnight bag from his Arlington residence, Roper decided to drive across the Potomac and spend the night at Robyn's place, just to escape the congratulatory messages from a combination of constituents, Wisconsin and local university political junkies, and a few Senate colleagues. Without exception, each had shown admiration for what he had said to Sheridan Browning earlier in the day. Still, Roper wondered how long it would be for the disapproving and the contemptuous to come forward and outnumber the appreciative and the amused. He also wondered if he'd receive another round of death threats sent to the Capitol.

"Hello?"

"Congratulations, Tom."

"Tripp, you called earlier to congratulate me—remember?"

"No, no. I'm calling this time to let you know that you're kicking ass on YouTube tonight."

"What?"

"My wife found your exchange with Browning on the internet. It's at over thirty-five thousand views and climbing rapidly."

"Wonderful."

"That should drive half the Senate and the White House completely nuts. I'm sure you'll be called into the principal's office tomorrow."

"I've already been verbally paddled by the majority leader, Tripp."

"I'm talking about the *big* principal's office, Tom."

"The *Oval* Office?"

"Bingo. At least that's what my personal White House mole told me."

"Great."

"What? Wait, Tom. It's at forty thousand now."

Roper looked at the time: 10:40 p.m.

Twenty minutes later, Roper tossed his overnight bag in the back seat of his car for the six-mile drive to Robyn's apartment. He'd received five additional phone calls in the twenty minutes since saying goodbye to Tripp Wilcox. Two members of his family and two others claiming to be constituents. The fifth person didn't say anything but Roper could hear the soft breathing. That was it. He could imagine that person calling back and regaling him with some erotic invitation he'd rather not receive. That's when he decided definitely to "go to the mattresses" at Robyn's place.

Right before he slid into the front seat, Roper noticed someone's breath from the cold night air, visible near the street light in front of his place. The body of the person was outside the light, in the shadows. The outline suggested a man; the posture suggested an unwillingness to move from where he was standing. Roper dropped quickly into the driver's seat.

As he reached the end of the street before making a right, Roper wondered whether he shouldn't turn the car around and capture the man in his headlights. He chose instead to keep going.

•   •   •   •   •

"I knew it." Robyn was collecting her things before heading home when she heard the news about another double slaying—this time inside a Georgetown Catholic church. Her colleague Sarah Brownstein asked Robyn to hold up so they could walk to their cars together.

"Any possible way it could have been a copycat, Robyn?"

"No. Same string of numbers left at the scene. Remember, the numbers aren't public knowledge. And once more there were initials painted with blood on the female victim."

"'M' and a 'T'?"

"I don't know, Sarah. I wasn't told. Probably. We've got a team working on those initials as well as all the work being done here and elsewhere on the numbers."

"Had to be the initials of the killer's love interest—who, I'm sure, dumped his homicidal ass."

"Very likely, but..."

"What, Robyn?"

"Nothing." Robyn couldn't believe how affected she was by those initials. Earlier she had entertained the ludicrous thought that the "T" stood for "Tom." For the past hour, however, she had been annoyed by the thought that the "M" represented her last name, "Meadows."

•   •   •   •   •

Roper sat alone at Robyn's dining-room table, an open pad of plain white paper before him and a cheap red ballpoint in his hand. Preferring to do his calculating and note-taking in red pen--a habit he picked up from his Senator predecessor, Parker Eldridge--Roper knew his mentor would be extremely disappointed to know how his successor was treating his career, let alone that he'd decided to quit national politics once his term expired. But Eldridge was incapable of passing such judgment. His recent death from a sudden pulmonary embolism in October had taken away Roper's most valuable political resource.

As for his father, Roper believed that were the general still alive, he would have supported whatever decision his son made regarding his career. Roper wondered if he could even play out the string—the long string—until his term expired after the 2018 election? Perhaps his father might have advised him on when best to make the announcement. He might have recommended the "don't burn the bridge" strategy—or he might have said "blow up the god-damned bridge now and get it over with." But the general had only made it to his son's swearing-in a year ago before his cancer took him off the battlefield for good. He had no business coming to Washington considering his state of deteriorating health, but he made it, standing proudly with the assistance of Parker Eldridge as his son became a United States senator.

Getting near forty, Tom Roper still knew he needed someone in his life to offer sage counsel or merely to nod his approval to validate a decision made. Roper never really had any significant problem with his self-image, because of the kind of stability and encouragement Nathan Roper had given him. Even so, Roper wanted someone to look up to—someone he could defer to—someone he could expect to guide him at times of personal crisis. But only two men ever qualified to be that someone. And now both these great men were gone from his life.

Roper played with the numbers the killer had placed in Marshall Grayson's hand. "20-18-11-19-07." He added them up. 75. Was the killer born in 1975? Possibly. That would make him forty, about Roper's age. Next, Roper divided the 75 by 5, coming up with 15. Would the murders take place in roughly fortnight intervals? Taking the first two numbers together, he came up with the date 2018—four years from now. The second and third numbers offered another date: 1811. Was there anything that happened that year which had some direct of casual bearing on the first murder and the four others to come? Roper dismissed the possibility that the numbers were part of a highly sophisticated series of clues. It was obvious to him that the killer wanted the code to be solvable but perhaps was taking much delight in the wasted efforts of the best mathematical minds at Metro and at the Bureau.

He considered the fifth number: the 07. That it had the zero in front of the three pushed him further toward seeing the numbers as dates. But which one did the last number suggest? 1807? 1907? 2007?

Roper started doodling with the red pen as he pondered the five digits and the seemingly inexhaustible possibilities they permitted. He shook his head at his inability to let any kind of puzzle rest until he'd tried his best to solve it. He remembered sitting at a table such as this when he was a boy, working on a special code breaker game his father had secured from an acquaintance at Langley. His father would leave him to his task but periodically would come back and rest his hands on his son's shoulders or smooth his hair as the boy tightened his facial muscles and made progress in his efforts—finally breaking the code and receiving his father's crisp salute.

Roper heard the faint sound of the doorknob being turned.

He tossed his pen down and moved hurriedly to the kitchen. He didn't see what he was looking for but quickly realized he had put it down on the other side of the living room. Stepping back into the living room, he heard the doorknob wiggle again.

He grabbed the champagne that he had just brought with him from his place. He wanted to surprise Robyn with a small gesture in order to refute her assertion that he was a typically unsentimental male when it came to acknowledging the romantic anniversaries important to most women. Today made exactly six months since they had first made love.

"Coming." With a kind of dexterity that surprised him, he opened the bottle and poured enough in a glass to make the presentation satisfactory. "Here we go." He unlocked the door and pulled it open. There was no one standing in the hallway.

•   •   •   •   •

No, he wouldn't dispose of this knife the way he had the screwdriver—in a dumpster inside the District—because it had been in his possession since he was a boy, an item he'd stolen from the workshop of a friend's grandfather—an elderly man whose lifestyle and interests were diametrically opposed to those of his own father. His friend's grandfather was a sportsman but of a different kind. The old man cared little for games played on a diamond or gridiron but was instead an avid outdoorsman, owner of several rifles and other firearms and hunting knives of various sizes. The man recalled the first time he stood in the workshop and beheld the collection of knives— right after his catastrophic sixteenth birthday.

The man had stolen the knife when he was sixteen because he was searching not only for something tangible to mitigate his humiliation but for some kind of antidote to the other symbols then being placed before him by his parents as guideposts for a life well and lucratively lead--especially the books and diplomas he was forced to read and admire by a father who had not the slightest clue as to what stimulated his son's imagination.

Once more, he gently wiped the knife with the chamois cloth. It had now killed two men—Marshall Grayson and Ian Arrington. He understood he could only use this weapon in four of the five killings, but that would be enough to add another bit of singularity to a plan that demanded careful adherence to symmetry.

He put the knife down on a table and walked to his two wooden bookshelves. In the recess between them was the very diploma he had been forced to admire as a boy—his father's B.A. Degree with High Honors—which had been presented to the boy the day he left for college as a reminder of what was expected of him. Flanking the diploma were scholarly books his father had read in preparation for his Master's and Law degrees and the framed engagement portrait of his parents. His father's expression as he gazed at his fiancé matched the protective and adoring look he always gave his wife—a look she was deeply unworthy of following the events of his sixteenth birthday. In all the years since, his father never learned what she had done to her teenage son.

The man looked at his hands, spreading his fingers and holding them before him. He smiled. They were steady, not the slightest motion detectable. He said the five numbers, "20-18-11-19-07," repeating the third number—"11." He finally dropped his hands to his side, closed his eyes, and uttered a quotation to no one there. "Numbers constitute the only universal language."

•　　•　　•　　•　　•

"Yes, Tom, I'm sure. I didn't come to the door earlier. I only just now stepped off the elevator."

Roper decided not to alarm Robyn by mentioning the

doorknob turn. "Sorry, it was just my heightened anticipation of your arrival."

She scrunched her forehead. "Okay, what's going on?"

Roper retrieved the glass of champagne. "Here. Happy Anniversary!"

After clinking her glass against his, she dropped her smile. "Tom, I truly hate to interrupt this special treat, but there was another murder tonight."

Roper turned his face away. "Same as before?"

"Mostly. A male victim. Throat cut."

"And?"

"Female companion also murdered. Puncture of her carotid. Probably a different weapon than the one used on the male."

"The same five numbers, right?"

"Right."

"Same order?"

"Yes."

"Initials?"

"Yes."

"Same as before—'M' and 'T'?"

I don't know, but I'm assuming so. They promised to give me a call sometime tonight to let me know."

"Victims' names?"

"Don't know yet."

"Robyn, I've been playing with the numbers some."

"Anything?"

"Just some possibilities."

"Tell me." Her request was followed by the chimes of her cell phone. "Hello?" She nodded to Roper to say that it was the call she had been expecting. "Right, right. I have that much. Umm, wait."

Roper brought her a pad of paper and a pen.

"Repeat that. Two *r's* in the last name? And hers is? Uh, huh. Okay, okay. Thanks, Danny. All right, I'll see you...Wait." She could see Roper signaling to her.

"The initials, Robyn."

"Oh, God yes, I forgot. Danny, do you have the initials the killer left on the woman's body? Where? On her ankles—right. An 'M' and a 'T', I assume? No?" Roper could see her face relax and begin to open as she sat back on the sofa. "Thanks, Danny. Good work. Bye."

"You seem relieved, Robyn."

"To be truthful, I am." She saw the confusion on his face. "I'll tell you later. But the initials were 'L' and 'R.'"

She dropped her eyes and didn't see the concerned look on Roper's face. If she had she would have asked him why the initials struck a nerve. Instead, she continued in a matter-of-fact tone.

"The woman's name was Natalie Yarrow, Tom."

"Sounds vaguely familiar, but..."

"The male victim's name was Ian Arrington."

"Jesus."

"Tom?"

•　　•　　•　　•　　•

Patrick Sims had never done anything like this before. He had never gotten out of bed, dressed, and taken a walk at four in the morning—and certainly not in the middle of winter. But he had never been subjected to as much uncertainty and pressure as he was presently undergoing. The uncertainty and pressure of a man with nothing more than survival on his mind.

Even so, Sims knew he had dodged more than a bullet. To his mind it was more like a shell fired from an M115, 203mm

Howitzer, a weapon he learned about by listening to his father talk of firing the piece during the Korean conflict in the early 1950s.

Although he didn't follow his father's example of serving overtly in the armed forces, Sims had served his country covertly, if only briefly. Accordingly, he still liked to think and phrase ideas in military metaphors. It proved to him that his mind was fine, that all the concerns and hints to the contrary were unfounded. At one point he had believed he would be the new attorney general's division commander, if not his chief strategist, in the attempt to become this generation's Bobby Kennedy and defeat the enemy within—with the war now being fought on the environmental front rather than on the more familiar battlefield against organized crime.

Owing in part to Sims's careful preparation before the new administration assumed office in January 2013, the new attorney general, Leon Johnson, had in the past year made considerable strides in countering the trade in ozone-depleting substances and the illegal treatment and disposal of hazardous waste. That Evan Bedingfield promised to make as his attorney general a man ready to hit hard against those polluting the air, land, and water ways—as well as those endangering wildlife—sold well to the voters. Political observers credited the gain of two states to Bedingfield's early-announced choice of attorney general, a man who vowed to protect the biological integrity of the United States.

Patrick Sims had assumed that he'd be a leading candidate to be Leon Johnson's deputy attorney general—hell, he was the only logical choice—but in the end Johnson told Sims that he saw his scope and influence as too narrow for the post. Sims was bitterly disappointed, in spite of the significant staff position he was given as a consolation prize.

As Sims continued east on Constitution Avenue passing 21st[h] Street and the Federal Reserve Building, he wondered if his acute disappointment the previous January made him more vulnerable to temptation—to seduction by those who commiserated with his perceived slight—and laid the groundwork for the offer he would be given and then accept ten months later.

Sims stopped and looked up at the Washington Monument before checking his watch: 4:20 a.m. That night months ago it had been shortly before one in the morning when he agreed to accept the money and provide information that would allow one of the major targets of Leon Johnson's war in environmental crime to escape the field relatively unscathed. In addition, for a hefty sweetening of the financial pot, Sims promised to destroy two documents that would be needed for a successful prosecution by the Justice Department.

Crossing Constitution and walking into the World War II Memorial, Sims stopped in front of the Field of Stars—the very place where he had agreed to the terms offered by the two men in khaki pants and pull-over sweaters the previous October. He wondered then if the location of his betrayal could have been any more loathsome to him than right here—in front of the four thousand gold stars honoring the four hundred thousand lives sacrificed in the Second World War.

After that autumn meeting, he thought he'd never return to the Memorial, for there would be too many ghosts trumpeting his trespass across the Mall. But it was one person's trespass that brought him to where he was now. Marshall Grayson's.

The moment was engraved in his memory. He believed he had blacked out from all the alcohol he'd consumed one late afternoon. His billowing guilt for his crime—and the fact that his marriage had ended—could only be managed by several hours of continual drinking. He'd already agreed to seek help and had received it, though not for any drinking problem. It was this past Thanksgiving weekend. Grayson came to Sims's apartment because he'd been alarmed by the sound of Sims's voice on the phone earlier.

"Jesus Christ, Patrick, what did you do?"

Sims didn't stir until Grayson shook him awake. He snapped at his guest. "God damn it, Marshall, leave me the fuck alone."

Grayson saw the two bottles of vodka—one empty, the other three-quarters full. He also noticed two official Justice Department documents—clearly marked as confidential—torn completely in half, lying beneath the second bottle of vodka. Before he could pull the pages out and place them together, Sims swept his arm and knocked the two bottles and torn pages to the floor. Grayson could see the uncapped bottle spilling its contents on the floor, the puddle flowing across the documents.

"Oh, fuck. No. No." Sims dropped to his knees and attempted to pull his shirt off to daub the alcohol from the torn documents. Grayson knelt down to jerk his friend away from the puddle. It was at that moment that Sims broke down.

"Jesus, Patrick, what the hell happened?"

Sims had earlier trusted Grayson with the truth about his drinking, his short but tempestuous affair with hard drugs, and the deep resentment he felt over not being named Deputy Attorney General—but could he confess betrayal of his country?

"Patrick. Listen to me, god damn it. Patrick, did Leon ask you to resign?"

"Ah, shit, Marshall. I fucked up. I fucked up so bad."

"Tell me what you did. God damn it, Patrick. What the hell did you do?"

Sims told him. He told him everything before he realized what the hell he was saying.

Sims checked the time again. 4:35 a.m. He was walking by the Pillars in the Atlantic Pavilion when he recalled the conversation he had with Grayson over a month later, a few days after Christmas, when the suspicions had grown broad enough for friends of his, like Grayson, to be questioned about Sims's recent behavior and state of mind. At the Eisenhower Building they'd even interviewed Max Nettleton, who called Sims immediately and spent a full two hours commiserating with him.

When Grayson next saw Sims, he told him, "Patrick, if they ask me about the documents, I'm going to have to say that you had them and that they were torn in half. But…" Sims recalled that Grayson's pause was interminable. "But I'm not going to volunteer anything else. I'm not going to repeat what you told me you did or who you were benefitting with your actions. Or how much money you received. I'm at least going to act as though either I never heard you say what you did about the deal you made or that I chalked the whole thing up to a drunken hallucination over what you thought you did."

"But come on, Marshall, can't you just forget about the documents? I mean, it's not like we're talking about--."

Grayson cut him off. "No. Don't ask me to lie for you, Patrick. I said that I'm not volunteering anything. But if they ask specifically about the documents, I'm going to tell them what I saw."

"God damn it, Marshall. I admit I fucked up, but this is my career, my life, we're talking about. I'm trying to build back my relationship with Janet and the kids. Can't you see that? I can't have my boys thinking their father was a fucking traitor as well as a…oh shit."

Grayson refused to listen to the maudlin appeal. "Look, Patrick, if I were you or your lawyer, I'd make them understand how disappointed and bitter you were over not getting the post you thought Leon Johnson had promised you in December 2012. It'll be embarrassing but you can say that you took the documents and ripped them up while under the influence of alcohol—which seems to me exactly what happened. Point out that you acted like a petulant nine-year-old. That you deeply regret your display of childishness and now fully appreciate the job you did get and the contributions you have made to the Justice Department and to the country. Tell them you're still getting help and commit yourself to getting more of it. Spin the fucking thing the right way and the fall won't be as hard." Sims was silent. "Patrick? Do you see what I'm saying?"

"Yeah. I see. Thanks, Marshall." Sims walked away without another word.

After testifying to the grand jury about the torn document pages, Grayson called Sims to tell him what he'd done. Sims didn't answer his phone, nor would he take any of Grayson's calls at Justice. Accordingly, the next day Grayson wrote Sims a registered letter informing him that he had typed up what in essence was his testimony to everything Sims confessed that night. Grayson added, "After learning that you've been cursing me in front of others, a breach of professionalism and of my trust, I have to be concerned about what you might attempt to do to pay me back for testifying about the documents or perhaps to give me a warning to keep quiet about the serious crime you confessed to me. Therefore, I've written out everything you told me and I'm delivering it to a mutual friend for safe keeping, with the instructions to open only if something happens to me. I deeply regret having to communicate with you like this, Patrick, but frankly I don't think I have any choice."

Sims stepped from the World War Two Memorial and headed west, walking north of the Reflecting Pool. As he looked to his right toward the Vietnam Wall, he thought again of things military. Part of the battle had been won. Marshall Grayson was dead and would give no further direct testimony. But the holder of that sealed letter could still turn the tide of the war. And Sims had no doubt as to the identity of this "mutual friend."

As Sims reached the bottom step of the Lincoln Memorial, he felt he was right in concluding that Grayson's letter was already opened—or that it would at any moment be opened by the recipient, Senator Thomas Roper. Perhaps Roper was too busy right now with his Senate work or still in shock over Grayson's murder—of which everyone in Washington now knew. But it wouldn't be long, if he hadn't done so already, before he opened the envelope and read what his occasional softball teammate had admitted doing to his country.

Suddenly, Sims couldn't remember in which direction to head—or for that matter from where he had just come. He turned his head left and right before regaining his bearings. This temporary "blanking out," as he termed it, had become more prevalent in the past few weeks. He attributed this condition to the understandable stress he was feeling over the unsettled state of his life, but in truth he feared it was something more than that.

"Patrick."

Sims wondered when the man would appear.

"Are you ready to assist us full-time?"

"I'm damaged goods, for Christ's sake."

"We can get you out of the country with a very full wallet, Patrick."

"Not sure I can be reliable. I'm having trouble thinking straight. Can't remember what I did an hour ago."

"You just have to concentrate, Patrick. We have faith in you.

Besides, it's really your best option. You know that, don't you?"

"God damn it, all right—just tell me what you want me to do."

Chapter 7

"Well, look at you. Five minutes after eight on a winter's morning and you're actually in your office with a fresh cup of coffee in your hand. You didn't sleep here all Monday night, did you?"

Roper found it difficult to smile at Lena Roseboro's sassy jab. He felt like he'd been on a carousel all night. He'd spend a few minutes on one topic and then spin around to another—then on to yet one more. Now the carousel had stopped before the initials written in blood on the ankles of the woman at St. Clare's Catholic Church. "L" and "R." He thought of Lena Roseboro last night and was thinking of her now. He wanted desperately to believe that it was a simple coincidence and not an indication of who would be the next—the third—female victim of this serial killer. Roper took only slight comfort from the fact that the initials on the first victim were an "M" and a "T" and that the second female victim's name was Natalie Yarrow. Still, he wasn't ready to trust in the killer's stream of logic or strict adherence to some plausible pattern. He looked with concern into Lena's inquiring eyes.

"Are you all right? Can I do something, Senator?"

"No, no, Lena. It's the coffee. That's what I get for making it myself."

"I'll get you a fresh cup." She tried her best to cheer him. "Now, let me tell you that everyone in this office and within a square mile radius of it is all wigged out on what you said at the big hearing yesterday. Already this morning I've heard at least ten times, 'I'm really proud of Senator Roper.' And I'm proud of you too. I'll get that coffee now."

"Thanks, Lena." Roper realized that after hearing about the second slaying he hadn't given a single thought to his confrontation the previous afternoon with Sheridan Browning. Now the carousel spun to the second male victim, Ian Arrington.

Although Roper hadn't seen him since October, Arrington had been a casual friend and a teammate. A number of young government employees—from State, Interior, Justice, and from the staffs on Capitol Hill and other governmental offices— organized an *ad hoc* late summer/early fall softball league. There were six teams in the league, with several members of Congress playing in some of the games when they returned from their home states and had a few hours free in the evening or a Saturday or Sunday afternoon. On three occasions, Arrington had played first to Roper's second base, with Marshall Grayson at shortstop.

The fact that he had known both male victims of the killings and that both men were on his team made Roper anxious. He tried to recall the other members of the "Filibusters"—the jocular moniker Roper himself had suggested for the team: Grayson, Arrington, Thompson, Genesee, Lloyd, Sims, Delacroix, Spears, and that reporter from the *Post*, Kendall Livingston. There was also the Indian fellow named Prem something, a few other young men, and two women—twin sisters working at Interior.

Was it merely a tragic coincidence that the first two male victims in the killer's numbers game were members of the Filibusters? Roper was inclined to believe so, especially when recalling that a month ago Grayson had said he thought that there were several men in the District who wouldn't mind taking his life, though he didn't name anyone in particular. And now Grayson had proved prophetic. Yet, what of Ian Arrington? Roper hadn't socialized with the younger man from the State Department. Who could have wanted him dead? Had Arrington a connection to Grayson of which Roper was unaware? There was no doubt that the crimes were related—but how? Simply being members of the Filibusters surely had nothing to do with either man's murder.

But memory of Grayson's concerns opened Roper's mind to the number of men in Washington he had upset with his vigorously articulated views—many of whom were not anonymous. He had taken the lead from his father and spoken out against Pentagon waste, and he'd even warned that Evan Bedingfield's decisions regarding Afghanistan and Iraq seemed to deviate little from the mistakes already made there and fifty years earlier in Vietnam. Following Nathan Roper's death, the chorus of criticism from the Defense Department and the military grew from mere innuendo to specific complaint, with one of the Joint Chiefs speculating openly whether the "inexperienced and undisciplined freshman senator had his little bitty toes across the line separating free speech from outright treason."

Then there were two openly antagonistic members of his own party who held several of his contrary votes against him, lobbyists for whom his doors remained firmly closed, and now of course the Deputy Director of the FBI. But since Grayson was murdered before the confrontation with Sheridan Browning, Roper rejected any thought that Browning might have had anything to do with the first two killings. Besides, he reasoned, serial killers leaving numbers and initials at the crime scene wouldn't be working for men like Browning, nor for disgruntled senators and military officers. Still, Roper couldn't clear away the nagging thought that he was intended as one of the three remaining victims on the numbers list. He understood that the man standing outside his residence in the streetlight's shadow had stimulated his suspicions and something worse—his imagination.

"Excuse me, Senator." Roper raised his eyes and saw Lena at the door.

"That's all right, Lena, I'll introduce myself." Looking as tailored and attractive as always, Carol McCrimmon stepped past Lena and entered Roper's office.

"Please sit, Carol. I'll admit I was expecting your call this morning. I just didn't think you'd wish to strangle me in person."

McCrimmon sat down and crossed her still remarkable legs. "Strangle you, Tom? Oh, no, my dear boy. I'm more likely to kiss you instead."

"I'm sorry. There's a humming in my ears. What did you say?"

"Don't make too much of it though, Tom. Had the public reaction to your rude behavior yesterday been in any way negative, I would have come in with a scimitar and demanded your head, which I would have returned to you forthwith on a decorative platter. But you're fast becoming a legend—a hero—a 21st-century Davy Crockett. I'm told you're the hottest thing on YouTube.

"Imagine that."

"Your smirk suggests you're already aware of your 'phenom' status."

"How's Bill Devonshire taking it, Carol?"

"The majority whip looks as though he just had his bicycle stolen."

"Well, it was all worth it then."

"Tom, during your Warholian fifteen minutes please keep in mind that you're a United States senator and a member of a party that would like to maintain control of the Senate in the fall elections. And yes, the woman sitting in front of you would hate to think that her historic tenure as majority leader will come to a premature end."

"Carol, what are you afraid I'll do to put all of that in jeopardy?"

"Tom, we've had a few chats over the past year in which you spoke plainly, and may I say suicidally, to me about how you see things—politics and all its more unsavory aspects. You've also challenged the former leader's and now my patience with a few of your votes. Had those been close votes, Tom, I'm afraid that your standing might well have been... Well, you get my point. Even so, you've made enemies of two of our party's most powerful senators, let alone their close allies in the House."

"Yes, but what is my temporary YouTube status going to lead to again?"

"I'm surprised you haven't yet been approached by the news and assorted cable shows or the print media for interviews. You haven't agreed to any yet, have you?"

"Haven't heard a thing so far."

His puckish expression made it difficult for her to keep her smile contained. "I just want you to think before you wilt in the face of the enticements you're about to receive. Think about the party that has been *very* good to you—and very *patient* with you. Think of me and what I'm asking you. Think of the legacy of your mentor, Parker Eldridge. And for God's sake, think of your own career. You may dismiss this out of hand, but you could be looking at a run for the presidency in twelve or sixteen years. Or a place on the ticket much earlier—in 2020, for example."

"As your vice president, you mean?" Roper's grin belied any inherent criticism of the leader's ambitions.

McCrimmon's smile was subdued but genuine. "In fact, I *have* fantasized about such a thing, Tom. And if I were to agree to the suggestion that I..." She pursed her lips as if she had been pinched. "Never mind."

"Excuse me?"

"Now if you will excuse me, Senator Roper, I have important work to do."

After McCrimmon left, Lena stepped into the office. "Senator, you have a call. It's the White House."

"Really? Well, well, what do you know? Thank you, Lena."

Roper hesitated for a moment before picking up the phone. "Hello, this is Tom Roper."

"Senator, this is Jerry Goldman."

Roper was quite surprised. The president's chief of staff never made calls to the Hill. That chore was reserved for Evan Bedingfield's official liaison to Congress, Marta Taubman.

"Yes, Mr. Goldman, what can I do for you?"

"Senator, the president would like to see you."

Another surprise. If anything, Roper expected Goldman to visit him and offer Bedingfield's estimation that Roper was a poor team player. "Of course. When is it convenient for him?"

"This afternoon. 3:15."

"Let me check. I may have a Tuesday afternoon appointment already on my--"

Goldman raised his voice several decibels. "3:15 *this* afternoon."

Roper took a moment to allow his flash of temper to dissipate. "Got it."

"They'll be expecting you when you arrive. Have a pleasant morning, Senator."

The line went dead before Roper had a chance to respond in kind.

•　•　•　•　•

"Can we drop the extra security on me now, sir? Just got word that the second killing involved someone who worked at State."

"State? Jesus Christ."

Nettleton saw that Ed Malloch was far more relieved than upset. "So, is there anything else, Mr. Vice President?"

"Hmm? Yes, Max, there is. My wife asked how your talk on the Columbus bust went with your history group. Forgive my not asking you earlier."

"The talk went very well, sir. Thank you."

"You know, I really admire your knowledge of the past, Max."

The previous spring, Nettleton had formed a history club with some eight to ten other government, library, and museum employees, meeting every three weeks for a brief presentation by one of the member's, followed by a group discussion. But Nettleton was impatient to leave and didn't wish to talk about the Columbus bust in the V.P.'s ceremonial office.

"Thank you, sir. So, can I ask again if you can do something to call off the dogs? My wife has lost all patience, I'm afraid. Wants things back to normal at home."

"It seems as though the killer may be targeting his victims

from various governmental offices, don't you think?"

"My thought exactly, Mr. Vice President."

"Then you shouldn't have anything to worry about, Max. None of us here need to worry."

"Exactly right, sir."

Still, Nettleton had his concerns. He hadn't yet been interviewed by the FBI or the Washington police. His disdain for Marshall Grayson had been a fairly open secret, to say the least. But he had three other men on his mind as well as the deceased Grayson—three men who, based on what they already knew or would soon know, could impede Nettleton's plans for orchestrating a change in the ticket for the next election. But more than that, these three men could destroy his reputation and even place him in legal jeopardy. Patrick Sims of Justice, Kendall Livingstone of the *Washington Post*, and Thomas Roper of the United States Senate.

•   •   •   •   •

Roper sat alone on the sofa in the Roosevelt Room, across from the Oval Office. From anecdotal evidence at least, Evan Bedingfield was just the latest of a line of presidents who liked visitors to cool their heels in this impressive room, named by Richard Nixon in honor of cousins Teddy and Franklin. The former's "Rough Rider" portrait above the mantle of the fireplace particularly commanded Roper's attention.

Tripp Wilcox had warned Roper that men like Evan Bedingfield believed their political opponents or those even with legitimate complaints would be de-fanged while sitting in the Roosevelt Room. Roper could understand why. The seven standing flags and the large sixteen-person conference table in the center of the room reminded everyone of the monumental decisions and responsibilities of the presidency. That the room was windowless—the false skylight providing illumination— added a sense of claustrophobia, if not incarceration, to anyone waiting alone in the room.

At 3:25 p.m., ten minutes past the scheduled appointment with the president, Roper turned his thoughts again to the two murders. Robyn had called to say that an FBI profiler was at work coming up with a preliminary character sketch—but nothing shared as of yet. Investigations of both crime scenes had netted little of significance so far. As for his own "investigation," Roper kept dwelling on the last number in the killer's series— "07." He refused to let go of his belief that the number referred to a date. He tried to remember the major events of 2007, 1907, and 1807. 2007 saw the launch of the Phoenix Mars Probe, thirty-two killed at Virginia Tech, and in January of year, the swearing in of the 110th Congress, which included his friend the then freshman Senator Tripp Wilcox.

1907 only brought to mind Marconi's transatlantic radio transmission, the admission of Oklahoma as the forty-sixth state, and the Cubs beating the Tigers in the World Series. 1807 was the year Napoleon attacked Russia, the indictment and later acquittal of Vice President Aaron Burr for treason, and the birth of Robert E. Lee.

Was the tragedy at Virginia Tech related to the killings? A mentally unbalanced survivor of the shootings seeking some sort of revenge against the government? A father who lost a child on that day? Given Lee's birth year, was the perpetrator from Virginia? His recollection of Aaron Burr's legal difficulties seemed to offer the likeliest clue. Marshall Grayson worked for the current vice president. Could the murderer be someone with a law or prosecutorial background? Burr had also killed Alexander Hamilton in a duel.

Agitated by these many possibilities, Roper stood up from the comfortable sofa and walked toward the fireplace over which hung the portrait of Teddy Roosevelt. He felt foolish hoping that the Rough Rider might give him some kind of indication as to which of these avenues he might pursue. And what was he doing thinking about all this anyway? Simply because a good friend and a casual friend had apparently been slain by the same hand? Or because his lover was working on the case? Or was it because he couldn't quite shake the possibility, no matter how remote, that he might also be a target of the serial killer?

"Senator? The president will see you now." Roper didn't expect to see Jerry Goldman standing at the door.

"Thank you. I've just been--."

"I know. It's an impressive portrait, isn't it? Many who view it swear old TR speaks to them."

"I'm not surprised."

"That's the power of the presidency, Senator."

•　•　•　•　•

The man left work early—he had gotten permission to do so. He crossed I Street and stepped into McPherson Square, where he saw a handful of college types preparing for some kind of late afternoon protest. They'd probably gather a few more eager souls and march down to Lafayette Park in the hope that Evan Bedingfield would emerge from the White House to see what they were bitching about.

The man frowned at the thought of the time and energy wasted on mere rhetoric. He recalled his visits to the highly attractive though patronizing woman psychologist when he was twenty—all without his parent's knowledge. His admission to her about what he had been fantasizing about—after her incessant prodding—put an end to their professional relationship as well as an end to his half-hearted attempts to be understood. After that, he accepted that he had to work out for himself the lingering effects of what he saw belonging to his mother in a bathroom wastebasket and what she had forced him to endure when he turned sixteen.

He just had to discover the proper way to resolve for good his humiliation and to act on the powerful, vengeful promptings that had lain dormant while he went on with his life. Still, his intelligence and instincts had only been sharpened over the years, and somehow he knew he'd experience the epiphany as he approached his important milestone birthday. And in late August of 2014 the answer came to him when he pulled from storage a gift his parents had given him when he was a teenager.

Disturbed by the noise of people exiting the McPherson Square metro stop, the man broke into a jog until he reached K Street. He looked at the *Washington Post* building a block ahead. Yes, the *Post*. Right after he turned sixteen, his mother insisted he spend more time on word games and crossword puzzles rather than with the numbers, percentages, and averages he loved to ponder and formulate. With tears welling in her eyes, his mother had handed him one of the *Post's* Sunday crossword puzzles and demanded that he do the best he could to solve it. "Remember—words, not numbers," she said and repeated incessantly over the next several weeks. She urged him to become an English major in college, a goal his attorney father supported because he knew that many English majors went into law.

As he went through the rest of his adolescence and developed his impenetrable shell of bitterness and hatred, the man was amused that his parents never fully realized how soon and how often their boy subverted their best laid schemes for his future. He took great pleasure announcing at the beginning of his sophomore year in college that he would in fact not be majoring in English. He also took delight in seeing the panic on his mother's face followed by a flood of immense relief when he said that he wouldn't be majoring in math either.

The man walked into the *Post* building and made his way to the reception area, where he was told that Kendall Livingstone was still on leave. Livingstone had already been hailed by many as "the political reporter the White House despises most," just the latest star journalist wanting to be known as "the next Bob Woodward." By asking a few innocuous questions, he learned that Livingstone was out at his Southeastern Maryland farmhouse completing the last chapter of his book on Evan Bedingfield's first year in office. The man was not the only person who believed that Livingstone was a far better writer than softball player.

He left the *Washington Post* and walked back through McPherson Square, which was much quieter now—although the young protesters had added four or five to their number. Retracing his route, he reached the Marriott and stepped inside for a cocktail. Why not a leisurely drink before returning to his place and preparing for the drive over to Maryland?

"What can I get you, sir?"

"Manhattan. With Canadian whiskey. And leave out the cherry. I'll donate the cherry to charity."

The bartender chuckled at the alliteration. "Got it."

"It's just that I don't care for garnishes of any kind. Hate all those fancy touches."

"I understand completely, sir."

Chapter 8

"Senator, to be blunt, you question witnesses as though you're a member of the other party, not ours."

"Mr. President, I just ask questions I think need to be asked."

Evan Bedingfield sighed. "You want something to drink, Tom?"

"No, sir, I'm fine. Thank you anyway."

"Well, as for your independence—or is it stubbornness? Whatever it is, it suggests to me that you're actively courting more difficulties than perhaps you're aware of." Bedingfield paused to allow the point to sink in. "Regardless, I want to talk to you about something much more specific."

Rather than directing Roper to sit on one of the plush Oval Office sofas or in one of the two chairs flanking the fireplace, Bedingfield had asked him to pull up one of the chairs next to the Oval Office desk and sit directly across from the middle window that looked out to the south lawn. Bedingfield was seated squarely and almost regally behind the famous Resolute Desk, looking as though he were about ready to address the nation.

"So, Mr. President, you said you wanted to talk to me about

something more specific."

"Senator, I understand that your exchange with Sheridan Browning yesterday afternoon has become quite a popular topic on the blogs and the political shows." Roper wasn't surprised; he knew Bedingfield had called him to the White House specifically to discuss the events of the previous afternoon. "Many YouTube hits and comments on Twitter as well. Am I right?"

"So I've been told."

"But, Tom, this acclaim isn't going to last, as I'm sure you're well aware."

"Can't disagree with you there, sir."

"It may be failsafe popular to paint as a villain someone with the bedside manner of Sheridan Browning, but I need to remind you that he is the deputy director of the FBI, and although a lifetime member of the other party, Browning has been a friend to this office and to me personally."

Roper knew of the men's long association and the problems their relationship caused the party base during the 2012 primary season, but he was curious to know exactly how Browning had been a friend of the office. Indulging his curiosity, he asked.

Bedingfield's shoulders sagged. He closed his eyes, apparently to control his rising anger. "Let's cut out the bullshit, Tom. We don't need—that is, our party doesn't need—to make Sheridan Browning the whipping boy for the public's frustration over a few missteps the Bureau occasionally makes. No one went to jail in Madison, Tom. I don't approve of what you call abuses in the investigation there or of anything Browning may or may not have said in a moment of frustration, but this administration isn't ever going to criticize the FBI. That wouldn't do politically." As Roper shook his head, Bedingfield slammed his hand on the desk. "Damn it, Tom, get off your idealistic high horse and start coming to terms with the business you're in. You're not *that* much of a god-damn political neophyte. You should know what the hell I'm talking about."

Roper certainly did, but he refused to acknowledge the validity of Bedingfield's observation. "Then what are you asking me to do, sir?"

At that moment the door opened. "Jerry, pull up a chair. I was just explaining to the good senator that we might do a little fence-mending with Sheridan Browning."

"I think that would be wise, Mr. President." Goldman could see the cloud forming on Roper's face. As he moved his chair close to Roper's, Goldman touched him on the shoulder. "Senator, don't worry. We're not asking you to issue a public apology for what you said—for what you *concluded* during an open hearing yesterday. Look, you're going to be interviewed plenty these next few days, but all you have to do is answer all questions about what happened yesterday with something like 'I was having a little fun with the deputy director. I wanted him to know how frustrated and disappointed many of us were with the way things went down in Madison. I thought a mock-dramatic pronouncement would get all of us thinking of better ways to avoid such a mishap in the future.' Then end with something along the lines of 'We all appreciate the efforts the Bureau has made to serve and protect us. We can't imagine what it would be like in this country without the many dedicated and hard-working men and women of the FBI. I certainly wouldn't want anyone to misconstrue what I was trying to do yesterday.'" Goldman offered the potential script without looking at any notes.

Roper kept his eyes locked on Goldman's. Finally, he turned his head and looked at the president.

"Tom, I understand you wouldn't want to call Browning

with an explanation or an apology. He's not expecting that—nor am I. I'd just like to get things back to normal with Sheridan and still take some advantage of your burgeoning popularity with the American people. I think if you proceed along the lines Jerry just outlined, we can make this a win-win—for you as well as for this office."

Bedingfield paused for Roper's reply.

"Senator?" Goldman looked at the president, who seemed as perplexed as his chief of staff.

Roper stood up. "I thank you for this opportunity to spend time in this most special place. You may not know that this has been my initial visit to the Oval Office. I truly appreciate the invitation. Good afternoon, sir. Mr. Goldman."

Goldman waited until Roper had closed the door behind him. "What the fuck did he mean by that?"

"I know what he meant, Jerry. The good senator has been talking to that cocksucker Kendall Livingstone. Couldn't you see it on his face? Tom Roper has decided to betray the President of the United States." Bedingfield stood and turned toward the Oval Office window. "Tell me. Is there anything you can do about that, Jerry?"

●　　●　　●　　●　　●

Devin Cassell helped Sheridan Browning off with his coat as the two men entered the deputy director's favorite steakhouse on the south side of the Potomac. Browning was well aware of the runaway interest in his exchange with Tom Roper at yesterday's Senate hearing. So far he'd refused all interview requests and promised to wait, on Cassell's advice, until the initial hoopla died down. Yet Cassell understood that once Browning came out of the steakhouse—well fortified with his favorite cut of bison, gin, and vermouth—he'd forget his promise and start talking to the press. He'd launch into the familiar talking points. Protection from domestic terrorism demands vigor and speed. History replete with tales of tragedies thwarted by the Bureau. Too many unheralded successes. Too few of the very few excesses considered in context. The need for the public and the damned Congress to give the Bureau the benefit of the doubt—and so on. But Cassell knew as well that Browning would give him a look that demanded he do something more than merely recycle rhetoric—something that would not only address matters politically but also, for Browning, personally.

During the meal, Cassell assured Browning that he was working on getting an appointment the next day with Carol McCrimmon but said he'd already spoken with Jerry Goldman and expressed Browning's "deep disappointment" with two members of the president's party: committee chair Chuck Hefferen for not checking Tom Roper more aggressively and of course Roper himself for a juvenile stunt that could only cause the Bedingfield administration serious problems in months ahead, and by "months ahead" Cassell was of course referring to the president's reelection bid in 2016. Goldman, Cassell added, had promised to speak "immediately" with Bedingfield and assured Cassell that before the day was out he'd be "hauling Roper's ass into the Oval Office for a dressing down by the president."

Cassell didn't mention to his boss that he'd also considered speaking with Ed Malloch's chief of staff, Max Nettleton. As he had learned the previous spring, Nettleton was more than willing to share information of interest to Browning, provided he received the expected *quid pro quo*. Cassell knew that Nettleton was hot to get Carol McCrimmon on the ticket in 2016 and to replace Goldman as Bedingfield's chief of staff in the next administration. He had assured Nettleton that Browning would do what he could—within reason, of course—to make such a transition smoother than it might otherwise be. And Cassell was also considering how he might use the possibility of McCrimmon's elevation to V.P. as leverage with her. It would take a delicate touch, but he was confident that the majority leader could assist them in this Roper business.

As for Browning, Cassell knew his boss's anger wouldn't be mollified by any "private woodshed paddling" President Bedingfield might give Roper. Especially now, given the public's positive response to Roper's confrontation with Browning, it would be impossible to remove Roper from the Judiciary Committee or punish him in any way politically. Also, Roper was still over four years away from a reelection campaign. But Cassell knew nevertheless that Browning would insist that he come up with some smart way to make the senator pay now. Accordingly, Cassell anticipated the marching orders he hadn't yet received, and he'd already begun the process without Browning's knowledge. What most concerned Cassell right now, though, was the possibility that Browning would issue different marching orders to others and not keep him in the loop. Perhaps Browning had already done so.

•   •   •   •   •

After he left the White House, Roper stopped briefly by his office to check his messages. His email box was stuffed with congratulations and praise from all parts of the country as well as eight foreign countries.

Sitting at his desk to read an unrelated message from the governor of his state, Roper's eye caught the opened envelope and blank pages that he'd taken from his electronic safe. He reached for the larger envelope that held the sealed envelope from Marshall Grayson, with instructions that Roper should keep it for him until he asked for it back. These instructions were in a block-print hand that certainly didn't belong to Grayson. Roper had simply assumed the instructions were written by one of Grayson's staff. Grayson had called to ask if Roper had received the "important papers," but that was all.

At the time, Roper simply guessed that his friend was indulging in some of his characteristic melodrama. Indeed, part of Grayson's appeal to the press was his tendency toward flights of rhetorical fancy.

When he first received the package, Roper had also assumed the envelope included something Grayson had written about his relationship with Maureen Blakely, perhaps some indication that a man in her life—an ex-husband, for example—was prone to violence and had vowed to kill Grayson if he caught him with his former spouse. But Roper now believed such a theory wasn't plausible, given the connected murders of Ian Arrington and the young woman with him at St. Clare's Catholic Church in Georgetown. If Grayson's written remarks had anything to do with Maureen Blakely, they were likely evidence to be used against her in case she turned against him in some way.

He had also thought it possible—though he didn't want to believe it—that the letter contained some information about Edward Malloch. More likely, Grayson had written up something or included a document that reflected badly on the V.P.'s omnipresent chief of staff, Max Nettleton. Roper knew that Grayson and Nettleton were widely perceived as the vice president's cobra and mongoose. Given Nettleton's intelligence and ability to ingratiate himself with others, Roper understood why the Veep's chief of staff had so many friends in the District, but he was glad he wasn't one of them. Regardless, Roper was uncomfortable with the possibility that the note was a private confession of some kind.

Roper decided to put the envelopes and blank pages back in his safe. When he picked up the sheets, he pricked his index finger on the letter opener. He chuckled when he looked at the utilitarian opener, measuring maybe six inches—quite different from the ornate letter opener cradled by an ebony holder that he had just seen on the table behind Evan Bedingfield's Oval Office desk. Months ago Grayson had mentioned the brassy instrument with the red tassel, smirking at the president's opulent tastes. But now Roper didn't have time to contemplate the vanity and peculiarities of Evan Bedingfield. He had to meet Robyn in less than an hour for a quick dinner, and then he was scheduled to drive over to Kendall Livingstone's farmhouse in Maryland.

After several weeks of requests from the *Post's* hottest political writer, Roper finally called him back soon after he left the White House and said he'd drive over in the evening for a chat. Roper didn't promise Livingstone he'd give him anything he could really use, though. Nor did he say whether he'd allow himself to be quoted by name or only anonymously as "a member of Congress." He'd just have to see how their talk went.

He already knew Livingstone from the unofficial softball league and bantering about sports teams, especially the Cleveland pro franchises, so he expected he'd actually enjoy an hour or two with the reporter. In fact, Roper recalled how excited Livingstone and Ian Arrington got last fall as they went on about the Indians and the Browns, both men having been devoted fans of the teams since boyhood.

•　•　•　•　•

"Just let it ring."

"No, I need to get it. Don't. Just stop. Stop!"

"Come on, not now. Let it ring. Let it ring."

"Get off me. Off!" The woman pinched the loose flesh above the man's hips, forcing him to pull out of her and lurch his torso to the left side of the bed. Through their sighs, both partners expressed disgust with each other but for different reasons.

"Hello? Just a minute, please." The woman pressed her hand over the receiver and looked at the man lying frustrated in her bed and indicated with her expression that she wanted to take this call in private.

"All right. I'll call you later. Dinner, Alyona?" She looked away, ignoring his request. "Fine. Fuck it." He scooped up his clothing and shoes and headed to the living room, where he would change and then leave the apartment.

She waited a few moments before taking the palm of her hand off the receiver. "I'm sorry. Are you calling from Brodie and Levine?" Her voice was hopeful and her breathing began to accelerate.

The caller's voice was female. "Not directly, Ms. Novikova, but I would say that this call is certainly related to your career."

Alyona's voice emitted an involuntary and awkward giggle. "All right. Then what can I do for you?"

"Alyona—can I call you Alyona?"

"Of course. Of course. And what is your name again?"

The caller hesitated. "I'm...I'm Brenda Laughton. How are you, Alyona?"

She frowned. There was so much scam activity directed toward out-of-work actors in the greater Los Angeles area. Or could this instead be someone with a connection to that period of her life she worked so hard to leave behind? She checked the caller's number. She didn't recognize it. A 703 area code. Somewhere on the east coast. Virginia?

"Alyona?"

"Yes, yes, I'm here. Can I ask who you represent?"

The woman on the other end sighed. Alyona heard a muffled reply, which sounded like "Here, please talk to her." Immediately, a man's voice came on the line.

"Hello, Alyona. My name is Gary Hendrix. I'm an agent with the Bureau."

"Oh, I..."

"No, no. This has nothing to do with anything you did. Look, I didn't want to startle you by announcing whom I'm with. That's why I had agent Laughton speak to you first. Please let me explain my call. First, you have nothing to fear. You only have something to gain. Something you want very much."

"I don't believe I should be talking to you because I can't tell whether you are really... well, I should go."

"No, no, don't hang up. Please don't hang up. This is no hustle. And, again, it has nothing to do with anything you've done. What's important is that as peculiar as it may sound I have connections in your business—connections that can get you that break that you're seeking."

Alyona hesitated before continuing. "But I still don't understand why your partner talked to me first instead of you."

"I just asked her to speak first because I thought you'd trust a woman more than a man calling you up and promising you a break. I'm sure you're sensitive to the fact that there are many bogus calls made to unemployed actresses. In fact, such fraud is part of what we're looking into, along with our colleagues in California's Bureau of Investigation."

She pressed the phone more fully to her ear. She decided not to hang up. "Yes, I am very much aware of that."

"Look, Alyona, just know that I can at least help you get to the front of the line. Film or television. You'll get a chance to do something substantial. A good role. But I have to be honest and say that after that, it will all be up to you."

She pulled the covers over her nude body. "Well, that's all I want. Just a fair chance." She felt the tears welling in her eyes. At thirty-one, Alyona Novikova knew her opportunities were rapidly dwindling. Although assured by her fellow unemployed actresses and a handful of male lovers eager to please that the roles for woman out of their twenties had increased tenfold in the past two decades, Alyona knew it was still a young woman's game—especially for those who had no major solid credits on their resumes.

Besides, there was her eight-month stint as an actress in adult films when she was twenty-two and twenty-three—a regrettable episode in her life she was almost certain had stood in the way of legitimate roles in the years that followed. What she knew for certain was that her revelation of this phase of her career had cost her the man she loved. A handsome lawyer and up-and-coming name in Wisconsin politics. A man who was currently the junior senator from that state—Thomas Roper.

"Are you calling me from Virginia?"

"Yes, we are."

"Then how can you promise me something like a role out here?" She was fighting against the conclusion that such a call made absolutely no sense. Why didn't an FBI agent working in California call her? Why was this man being so generous? Was he acting without knowledge of his superiors? Did federal agents get involved in making promises of such kind? Who was he exactly to have such connections in the entertainment industry?

"Power in any field of endeavor is not exclusively geographical, Alyona. I assure you I spend a considerable part of my time in Southern California, and I know important people in the field you're pursuing—people out there in the L.A. area. Without sounding too 'Godfatherish,' some owe me favors they will be very happy to pay back by giving you a small break— which can be a highly significant opportunity for you."

"May I ask you specifically who owes you favors?"

"Good question. Several casting directors to be specific."

"I'm not sure I understand how they owe you favors. It does sound 'Godfatherish,' as you say, and that makes me uncomfortable."

"Perfectly understandable. All right. I suppose the unusual nature of this call demands that I be a little more forthcoming. The favors are owed me because these individuals are very much committed to assisting law enforcement."

"I don't--."

"Think of it this way. If you were in the producing or casting end of the business and you had violated a certain law regarding, say, the possession of illegal substances, you might— in return for giving information on more serious illegal activities in the industry—wish to assist those in my profession when you can. And remember, I won't tell them that you'll *have* to be cast—only that they should give you a fair opportunity to be cast. I'm not about to do anything illegal myself—see?" He briefly paused. "If you want I can have someone from the industry call to assure you that it's all on the up and up."

Alyona kept waiting for the proverbial other shoe and kept kicking away the warning that this was some kind of con, practical joke, or worse. Yet she had to be certain that the caller wasn't really some part of state or national law enforcement before she hung up on him. She decided quickly, however, that the moment he said anything about doing another adult film she'd remind him that she had his phone number and would be sure to give it to the real police if he called again. But for now, she had to ask, "What is it you'd want me to do? I'll tell you right now I refuse to be involved in anything other than legitimate film or television acting." If he was legitimate, she assumed he'd ask her to provide information about what she had observed relating to pot, cocaine, meth, and heroin. She had much to tell him if she so chose.

"I'm afraid I don't know what you're assuming about me, Alyona." The man paused. She pulled the covers up higher—touching the bottom of her chin. "But you are of course right. There is a 'scratch-my-back—scratch yours' expectation here. What we'd like is to talk to you about your past relationship with Senator Thomas Roper."

Alyona uttered a soft, almost imperceptible gasp. Her hand quivered. She shifted the phone to the other hand—which, oddly, was steady.

"Alyona, I realize you might not wish to speak of a painful time in your life. But for reasons I wish not to explain, it is important that we interview you about the senator."

Alyona was perplexed. "How did you know about my relationship with...my God, what did he do?"

"You need not worry about that. Just remember that we will reward you—not with cash, for that's a bit sordid, I think you'll agree. Or any kind of immunity—because you've done nothing wrong. But we can see to it that you get that break you've been so actively seeking. That way, it's not a payment behind a closed door but rather a mere opening of that door. The rest you'd have to do for yourself."

"But I'm still confused. What are you hoping I'll tell you about him?"

"Hoping? Nothing. We just want you to be honest. And as you can tell from our offer to help you get a serious audition, we are not about to compel you to testify against the senator. So, what do you say, Alyona? It's a good deal, I think you'll agree. For about a half hour or so of your time, you'll get that chance to show what you can do in front of legitimate casting directors. And you won't be treated like a mere number—the two hundredth hopeful standing in front of three or four greatly fatigued men and women who've already made up their minds. Excuse me for saying this, but I think now is the time if you're going to make a move in the profession. I've been working your neck of the woods long enough to understand that."

Her voice sounded both hopeful and vulnerable. "I understand. If I decide to talk with you, where would I go to...?"

"We'll send someone to you. There's no reason to have you fly to D.C. Let's see, it's 6:45 here—so 3:45 there. Can you meet with one of our field agents tonight? How about 11:00 p.m. your time? I wish I could be there to meet with you myself, but that's impossible, I'm afraid. I assume that 11:00 p.m. wouldn't be too late, would it?"

"No, I'm almost always up then." She dropped her head, feeling the effects of an overwhelming sense of caution. "But can I have another day to think about this? It's Tuesday. How about calling me back tomorrow and I'll give you an answer."

The caller was silent for a few seconds. "All right."

"Thank you. Thank you so much. I'll look forward to your call. I'll be here from 3:00 on—that's 6:00 p.m. your time." She pulled the covers away from her body and sat up in the bed, once more dropping her head forward, but this time in a gesture of gratitude and relief.

"Oh, Alyona, one more thing—and this is very important. Please keep this call to yourself. If it got out that you're making some kind of deal with me to get a good role or any role—even though, again, you're only getting a good shot at a role—then the Bureau will be embarrassed and they'll renege and you'll have lost your chance to get that break you've been looking for. So please say nothing to any of your family or to *any* of your friends—even your closest confidants, okay?"

"Yes, yes. I understand. I won't say anything to anyone."

"Fine. Then we'll talk tomorrow. Goodbye, Alyona."

"Goodbye."

Almost nine years younger than Roper, Alyona Novikova first met him when she returned to Wisconsin after her disastrous initial residence on the West Coast. After appearing in her fourteenth and last adult film, she remained in L.A. for another nine months, hoping to enter mainstream productions. The few jobs she landed were commercials, from high fashion shoes to hair products. She did manage to get two good movie offers, but both were pulled when those in charge learned of her work in adult features. She couldn't prove it but she was sure that the man purporting to be her agent betrayed her after she refused his sexual advances. In the months that followed, Alyona couldn't secure a legitimate film role or a reputable agent. The only thing she had in her favor was that her adult-film "stage name" was nothing like her distinctive real name.

Roper and Alyona began dating when she was twenty-five and he was thirty-four. Roper had become friends with her émigré father, the former Soviet decathlete Tolik Novikova, and before long the men were handball and golfing partners. At first Roper was cautious with the much younger Alyona, as her father wanted him to be, but the pace of her emotions was far more accelerated, with her passionate nature leading to frequent displays of frustration at his more steady stride—which restricted their lovemaking to kissing and embracing. Having by now begun to write him love notes and signing them with a girlish "Alyona Roperakova," she'd come to the conclusion that he wanted her to be the aggressive partner in their relationship. She falsely assumed that he couldn't believe she was truly as sexual as her stunning physical appearance suggested. Following one evening's second bottle of champagne, she made the mistake that lost her his affections. She told him about her recent film "career" in Los Angeles.

Moving back to Los Angeles to renew her quest to make it as a legitimate actress found her in varying states of mind about Tom Roper. From placing all the blame on herself to blaming him entirely for the breakup. From respecting him for making the decision he did to almost hating him for doing exactly that. From painful self-castigation to bitter thoughts of revenge. In the past three years, she had several appointments to seek counseling about this relationship with Roper and about the generally self-destructive manner in which she was leading her life, but each time she failed to show.

Alyona got off the bed, slipped into an oversized powder blue UCLA football jersey and headed to her kitchen. She sat at the table and poured herself a glass of Pinot Grigio. It was almost four in the afternoon. She hadn't finished the first sip when she made up her mind—she'd take the chance for the chance. Why wasn't it possible that the FBI had influence in the film world? They probably had agents in every facet of American business. Surely law enforcement as well as organized crime had chips they could always cash in. Agent Hendrix wasn't promising her a career or even a part. That would be what a scam artist would have done. It was just what he said it was—assistance for her assistance. Tomorrow she'd tell Hendrix that she'd be happy to discuss her relationship with the senator. What did she owe Tom Roper anyway?

Chapter 9

As he crossed into Maryland on the Suitland Parkway, Roper prepared himself for the turns he'd have to make to reach Kendall Livingstone's farmhouse—or faux farmhouse, seeing that there were no sheep, chicken, or cows on the premises as far as he knew. From what Livingstone told him, he had renovated the house on the three-acre lot to look as much as possible like the family's Ohio farm on which he spent most of his boyhood.

Roper was in a better mood now that he'd been able to spend forty minutes alone with Robyn. She had looked terrific. Her hair was up, but a section of it looked as though it was about to fall to her shoulders. Roper had always enjoyed unpinning her long black hair and feeling it fall on his hands, wrists, and forearms. He knew he'd want her when he returned from Maryland. She'd promised to be back at her place by 10:30.

They had also found time at dinner to discuss the serial killings. A few decent leads were being pursued. Almost three dozen persons, male and female, with the initials "M.T." and "L.R." had been contacted, Robyn told him. "Lena Roseboro?" he asked. She shook her head no and made a note for Metro to touch base with her. Robyn continued by noting the conclusions reached so far about the knife wounds to Grayson and Arrington, the wet footprints on the carpet at Maureen Blakely's, and the male clothing found in her bedroom closet—none of which could have been Marshall Grayson's.

"Know who the man was?"

"*Men*, you mean? We think so. Seems Maureen might have been 'screwing the field.' Whether Marshall knew that little fact, we're not sure."

"It's not a love-triangle—or quadrangle—thing, Robyn."

"I know. The Arrington murder tells us that. But someone up the food chain at Metro wants to pursue it as a crime of passion a little while longer."

"I'm sure it is a crime of passion. Just not that kind."

"Did Marshall ever tell you that Maureen liked role-playing—with him as the dominant male?"

"I made it a habit never to believe what Marshall told me about his lady friends and what they did to or desired from him—but no, he never said anything about that specifically." For a brief moment, Roper recalled what young Alyona Novikova told him six years earlier about one of the "specialty" films she had appeared in.

"Tom, I'd like to think that the killer tied her up and made it only look like a sex game between her and Marshall."

"Didn't you say that her hands were only loosely bound?"

"I did. Damn. Tom, tell you what. When you leave the Senate, let's rent ourselves out as the Nick and Nora Charles of the new millennium. Crime investigators by day; martini and caviar chugging social types at night."

"Watching old movies again, Robyn?"

"Is there any other kind?"

"Well, if we're going to be Nick and Nora, we'd have to get a dog."

Roper smiled recalling every word of their discussion. But as he made the final turn down the road that would take him to Livingstone's, he again pondered the four initials—"M.T." and "L.R." He entertained a new thought: the killer obviously planned three more murders, given the five numbers he left for all to see. Therefore, if he killed again, would he leave his first vowel—or perhaps two? Were these initials forming into the man's name—or rather an anagram of his name? Could that be it? Still, Roper couldn't square the numbers with those letters. The numbers seemed the most important indicator. And they were left on the male victims. Then again, in both killings the blood was on the woman's body—the buttocks and the lower legs. Yet that blood was surely from the wounds on the male. It was clearly so in the first murder, since Maureen was garroted and not stabbed. But both Arrington's and Natalie Yarrow's wounds were in the neck and throat. Had the blood work come back on the initials left on Natalie's ankles? He'd forgotten to ask Robyn.

Roper was about to begin working on the four initials and a possible anagram when he saw just ahead Kendall Livingstone's mailbox and farmhouse.

•   •   •   •   •

"Mr. Sims, I can't meet with you right now. I'm on the west coast—on an assignment. Just know that your situation has been evaluated thoroughly, based on the facts you have given us and what we've learned independently."

"What do you mean 'learned independently'"? Patrick Sims was naturally defensive about the details of his private life being fully ascertained. He knew he'd blow everything if he let his temper get the best of him on the phone. "Sorry. I'm just a little sensitive when it comes to..."

"Not a problem. I understand, Patrick, if I may call you by your first name."

"Sure. Thank you,...uh..."

"Barry."

"So, Barry, you think Roper's the one I should be focusing on now?"

"Yes, your concerns about Max Nettleton and the *Post* reporter don't seem to us as potentially damaging as you fear."

"I still think all three of them have the ability to ruin me, Barry."

"Listen to me. You don't know what the reporter may write about you in his book—if he's even going to mention you. Nettleton has too important a career to put in jeopardy by linking himself publicly to you in any way. Roper's the one who likely has the damaging evidence on you, which he will soon share. You can bet on that."

"Still, the other two can also fuck me up just by--."

"Patrick, I didn't call to debate this with you. Forgive my being blunt, but you're in no condition either legally or emotionally to make the best decision about all of this. Remember that we'll get you out of the country, pay you handsomely, and salvage enough of your reputation to keep your kids from growing up believing you were in any way a traitor to your country, as you put it. After some time, you may be able to come back and renew your relationship with them. Try thinking more like a father, Patrick."

Sims seethed at the patronizing tone of the caller. "You're forgetting that I did you guys the biggest fucking favor in the world by tampering with and concealing the evidence against you—remember?"

The caller responded in kind. "And you were rewarded well for that—remember? We just didn't count on your relationship with Marshall Grayson, Patrick—remember?"

Sims remained silent for several moments until he once again regained his equilibrium. "All right. So let me ask this calmly. What do you want me to do exactly? I keep having trouble getting you to tell me what you want me to do."

"I'll call you back in a few minutes. You in your car?

"Yes. I'm sitting outside a fast food place in Maryland, off 95, near Andrews Air Force Base.

"Good. Hang loose. I need to get a location report and then call you back."

"What do you mean by 'location report'? I just told you where I am." The line went dead. "Son-of-a-bitch."

•　•　•　•　•

"Senator, please come in. I'm so happy you've decided to talk with me. And also that you were willing to come all the way out here."

"Since we're across the border, Kendall, just call me Tom—as I asked you to do when we played ball."

"My pleasure, Tom. If it's okay, I've prepared something. Hope you don't mind."

Roper expected Livingstone to pull out a laminated list of questions he wanted to ask.

"It's some baked brie—with almonds and some fruit. But before that, what can I get you to drink?"

"Trying to loosen my tongue, Kendall?"

"Exactly."

"All right, what do you have?"

"Sandy has made us a pitcher of frozen margaritas. You

interested?"

"On a winter's night?"

"Yes, a little *Cinco de Mayo* on the *Cinco de Enero*—or close enough. I'm only about a week late." It was January 13th.

"That would be my cue." Sandra Livingstone entered with the drinks already poured in attractive cocktail glasses, a wedge of lime perched invitingly on the rim of each. "I left off the salt. Hope that's all right."

"Perfectly all right. By the way, I'm Tom Roper."

Livingstone threw back his head in embarrassment. "Oh, I'm sorry, Tom. I thought you two met on the ball field this past September."

"No, no. I saw her in the bleachers cheering you on, but we never officially met."

As they enjoyed the baked brie and drinks, the three spoke generally about sports and the couple's plans for a family "after the money from Kendall's book starts coming in." Upon mention of the near-finished manuscript, Sandra excused herself.

"Tom, it's a bit cold out there, but I'd like you to take a very short walk with me so I can show you my pride and joy." Livingstone opened the back door of the house and the men stepped out to the patio. Roper immediately saw the path leading toward a little cluster of bare deciduous trees, which surrounded a structure that looked like a large enclosed gazebo. He thought at once of the patio and footpath at the back of his mentor's home the day he rescued little Laurie Eldridge.

When the men reached the structure, Roper could see that it was a writer's retreat, a small office complete with some of the comforts of home, including a wood burning stove. As soon as they entered, Livingstone lit a fire while Roper admired the surroundings.

"Pretty nice, isn't it? I finished it at the beginning of fall. I've written almost all the book out here."

"I'm impressed, Kendall."

"Thanks. It's been great. Only eighty-six feet from the back door. Just perfect for getting off by myself while still being at home. It's all here. Computer, desk, desk-chair, two shelves for books, small sofa, cushy chair, mini-refrigerator and freezer, and here." Livingstone opened a cabinet to reveal a full selection of potables and mixers. "Plenty of room for three persons—or four—depending on the size of everyone. Like another drink?"

"No, I'm fine. You *are* trying to loosen my tongue, aren't you?"

Livingstone dropped his smile. "Tom, it would mean a great deal to me and to this book if you'd speak frankly about Evan Bedingfield. You know I'd love to quote you, but if you want, I can simply call you a 'United States senator.' If that's too specific, how about 'a member of Congress'? I'd of course prefer in any case to state that you're a member of Bedingfield's own party."

Roper looked out the one window, which faced the house, and listened to the wood starting to crackle in the stove. He thought of all the new enemies he would accumulate if he opened up to Livingstone. He smiled sardonically. Perhaps the number of death threats he'd then receive would rival the number of YouTube hits of his moment with Sheridan Browning.

"Kendall, it's no secret that the president has expressed frustration with me on several occasions."

"Tom, I know this is difficult for you. But I--."

"No, Kendall. It's not as difficult as you think. Tell you what. Pour me a short bourbon. I'll let you know what you can cite as coming from me by name and..." Roper hesitated, for what he was about to say bothered him and would likely continue to bother him in the days ahead. "...and what you can quote under the banner of 'a member of Congress of the president's own party.'" He wondered why he wasn't courageous enough to put everything he would say about Bedingfield under his own name—and how his father would have judged him for it. Or was it simply prudence? A way to protect the Senate? Or Carol McCrimmon? Or his family name?

What he would share with Kendall Livingstone would speak to his doubts about the Bedingfield administration and his disappointment in its refusal to undo some of the more egregious acts of previous administrations and in its commitment to a closed presidency—as well as the petty gamesmanship in its dealings with the press and the courts and the inability to communicate less defensively with Congress.

Although he realized Roper had no startling revelation to share about Bedingfield, Livingstone knew the senator was unhappy with the administration—on matters of principle more than of policy. Unhappy enough, perhaps, to step up on the scaffold, if not actually to lay his head bare for the executioner. Livingstone badly wanted something good from Roper before he turned in his completed manuscript. Besides, he hadn't gotten a single thing from anyone working at the White House. He had told his wife only half-facetiously that he was certain chief of staff Jerry Goldman was having him watched.

He handed Roper the bourbon. "You comfortable, Tom?" He looked at the wood stove. "Warm enough for you?" Both men laughed at the inadvertent joke.

•　　•　　•　　•　　•

Lena Roseboro decided to cut her workout short. She'd arrived at her gym later than usual this Tuesday evening after having dealt with constant phone calls and emails regarding Senator Roper's tussle with Sheridan Browning.

As she turned her ignition key, the high beams came on from a car parked directly in front of her. She waited a few moments to see if the car facing her would back out of her way, but it remained where it was. A year earlier she would've gotten out and told the other driver where he should stick those high beams, but too many reports on assault, rape, and murder in and around D.C. had shoved caution and prudence into her system. Lena finally backed up and turned to the right so she could drive past the idiot.

As she left the parking lot, she checked her rear-view mirror and saw that the other car had not turned around to follow her out to the main road. She relaxed and dropped her eyes to the CD player and ejected the disc. Before she could look up again, the high beams behind her reflected off her rear-view mirror and temporarily blinded her. Was this the same car?

For the next four miles, the trailing car remained at a safe distance behind—but the high beams remained on. When it was time to make the turn toward her house, she turned left instead of right toward the nearby home of a male friend who happened to be on the Metro force. The car behind her kept going straight. Relieved, she turned around in the *cul de sac* where the officer lived and headed home. But when she finally pulled into her driveway, she saw the high beams coming down her street. The car slowed as it passed in front of her house.

Somehow Lena found her house key immediately and thrust it into the lock. She bolted the door behind her and rushed to call her police officer friend. As she did so, she took a quick look out her curtained window—the car had moved on. She continued peering through the curtain, looking up and down the street, which was now dark and empty of traffic. She never gave a thought to looking through any other window in the house. She didn't hear the man come into the room.

•   •   •   •   •

From her kitchen, Sandra Livingstone could see directly into the window of her husband's hideaway office. Senator Roper was pacing back and forth, his gestures controlled but still animated. She couldn't see her husband, but she knew he was sitting on the small sofa, probably sipping on some amaretto, constantly checking his hand-held recorder to make sure it was functioning properly. Her concern was that both men might drink too much on top of the tequila they had earlier. The wind had evidently come up, for the branches of the deciduous oaks and maples were weaving, as were some of the white and loblolly pines that flanked the backyard area all the way down to and then past the office.

She barely saw it. Something that moved into her peripheral vision—to the right, about halfway between the house and the renovated gazebo.

Sandra was certain the figure moved closer to the office, disappearing into the cluster of pines. Her mind raced through the possible identities of this trespasser. There was a family of six down the road—three of the four children being teenage boys. Once before she had seen the fifteen-year-old middle brother on her property shooting baskets at the hoop Kendall had put up beyond the driveway. She'd chastised the boy and was put off by his impertinent attitude. Was this the Felton boy running through their property, perhaps wishing to break into the gazebo office?

After putting away a stack of dishes, Sandra decided to call her husband's cell and tell him. She had dialed only five of the numbers when she heard movement in the living room. Softly putting down the phone, she gently opened one of the kitchen drawers. She withdrew a .22 caliber handgun and clicked off the safety, just as her husband had taught her. The sound from the living room seemed to move in her direction. She lifted the pistol and placed her trembling finger on the trigger. She saw a shadow appear on the floor. Before she could even look up he was in the kitchen.

"Jesus Christ, Sandy!" Kendall instinctively lurched to his left, ending up in a half-kneeling, half-squatting posture. His wife dropped the pistol as she heard the sound of Tom Roper starting his car.

"Oh my God, Kendall, I thought..."

"Honey, I'm so sorry. I walked Tom to his car and then came in the front door."

Sandra rushed to her husband and embraced him. She saw the pistol on the floor. Fortunately, it hadn't discharged.

•　　•　　•　　•　　•

The moment Roper's car turned from the long dirt driveway onto the road that lead him back to the Suitland Parkway, the man was three miles ahead, returning to D.C. on the same route. His fingers were tight on the steering wheel—he had not expected a visitor to the Livingstone home. He knew Livingston had been writing haphazardly in the mornings and late afternoons, but without fail from 6:30 to 10:00 he did nothing but write and edit out in his little office some thirty yards from the house, while his wife read in the kitchen or watched TV in the den. He assumed they hadn't changed their habits since he first heard about them back in September. Funny what you could learn keeping your ears open in the bleachers at a softball game.

He looked at the knife on the passenger seat, wrapped in a bath towel. By now it should be covered in blood, but Thomas Roper had arrived before he did and stayed for at least two hours, forcing the man to conceal himself and wait. And wait. Finally, he decided to postpone the event and left.

A mile or two down the road, he calmed down. All was fine. He could wait until the next evening. He knew all along that he had an extra day worked into his planning, in case something like this happened. If Roper was a house guest, surely he wouldn't stay for more than one night, and tomorrow evening Livingstone would again be alone in his outside office for those three and a half hours. The man reminded himself that it was only victim number five—the "07"—who had to die on the appointed day. There was still some flexibility time-wise for "11" and "19."

• • • • •

"Ms. Roseboro."

Lena was too frightened to scream. The man was Caucasian but she could tell this only from his hands and the flesh under his eyes, the only part of his face visible under the black ski-mask. He held some kind of blade device in his hand. "I came in through the rear door—the one at the end of your pantry." He tapped the device in the palm of his hand to remind her that he could break into her house any time he wanted. She wondered if he had already done so earlier.

She barely pushed the words out. "What do you want?"

"Just sit down and keep your mouth shut. I'm only going to talk to you *this time*. You just need to know that I can find you all alone again and *next time* it might not be a friendly visit."

"What do you want with me?" She couldn't believe the hint of anger that mixed incongruously with her panic.

"For *now*—just that you keep your mouth shut. If you call the police, I'll find out and I won't be able to prevent you from getting hurt. And if you talk to the police, it's not going to look good for Tom Roper, either."

She didn't know what he meant, but she was too frightened to ask. "I won't talk to anybody—not even to Senator Roper."

"No, no. You can talk to Senator Roper. In fact, I hope you will."

The man turned and walked back toward the pantry. Lena remained frozen where she stood.

"Oh, Ms. Roseboro." She felt blood drain from her face. "Sorry about your door."

•　　•　　•　　•　　•

The second Roper turned from the driveway onto the paved road he felt the slight stinging sensation on the rear of his neck, slightly below ear level. The radio was on so he hadn't heard the crunching sound behind him from his left or the slight thud from the edge of the passenger doorframe next to the front windshield. There were no street lights so he couldn't yet detect any alteration of his car's appearance.

But Roper could certainly feel the small shards of glass and daubs of moisture on the back of his neck. He flipped on the interior light and saw that indeed the area was pocked with small specks of his blood. He gunned the car and drove at least five miles before he found a place to turn off. He had to be sure he wasn't being followed. It was then that he spotted the indentation on the cushioned edge of the doorframe. At first he thought someone had hurled a rock at his car. Now he was sure it had been a gunshot.

Chapter 10

"I'm leaving now. Yes, I know I said I'd be back early, but as I've told you dozens of times, when the president wants to work late, I have to work late. Yes. Just three more years, Tara. I'll see you in half an hour. Bye."

Standing just outside the door, Max Nettleton listened in on Goldman's conversation with his wife. He smiled at the further evidence that his friend would be leaving the Bedingfield administration after the first term.

"Max, you still there?"

Nettleton stepped into Goldman's office. "Right here, Jerry."

"Excuse my taking the call on my cell. Tara with her usual complaint."

"Well, she's already made more than her share of sacrifices, Jerry."

"No need to remind me, Max. Anyway, as I was saying, I appreciate your help in getting Carol McCrimmon to agree to let the president borrow the historic document for a photo op. And the president wants her to be in the shot. He'll make a big deal out of her having donated the document to the National Archives."

"Jerry, I'm not sure she'll be able. She told me that the end of this week is very bad. She's scheduled meetings and one-on-ones all day Thursday and Friday. If she loses the big vote next week, she's going to be impossible to live with."

Goldman paused for several seconds. "You mean it might make her less radiant for what you have planned for her future, not to mention for your own?"

Nettleton knew Goldman had figured out his grand scheme. "Not sure I follow, Jerry."

"Don't fret, Max. I've already informed the president that I'll be retiring at the end of the first term."

"And what did he say?"

"He laughed."

"He doesn't want to lose you, Jerry."

"I'm sure he already has a replacement in mind."

Nettleton knew Goldman was toying with him, wanting him to ask whom Bedingfield had in mind. But Nettleton wouldn't take the bait. Again, he heard Goldman's cell phone.

"Sorry, Max, I have to go. I'll be back in touch about the document."

Goldman placed the cell to his ear and waited until Nettleton was down the hall. "Yeah? Talk to me. I see. All right, let me know immediately what else you find out. Anything that has to do with Roper—*or* Nettleton. Understand?"

* * * * *

Just before arriving at Robyn's apartment, Roper pulled out his cell and punched in Kendall Livingstone's number. If indeed someone had been shooting at him, then Kendall and Sandra could be in danger. He was finding it more difficult to reject the notion that the common thread in the first two killings was the fact that both men played on the same softball team.

"Kendall, it's Tom Roper."

"Tom. You okay? You sound a little upset."

"Kendall, when I was pulling out of your driveway, someone took a shot me."

"What the hell?"

"I thought it could've been a rock from the driveway that hit my window and somehow passed through the glass—but I can see on my dash what looks like a hole from a bullet fragment. No way a piece of rock could have made it. The bullet hit the rear passenger window—the one right behind my left shoulder."

"Jesus Christ, are you all right?"

"Yes, I'm fine. But what about you and Sandra?"

"We're good. Nothing's gone on here."

"Then you didn't hear the shot?"

"No, I didn't hear anything. You said it was at the end of the driveway? Wait, Tom. What is it, Sandy?"

Roper heard Sandra's voice in the background. Livingstone came back on the line. "Tom, Sandy told me she thought she heard the shot after I'd gone to the bathroom—and that was right after you left."

"But if she heard it, why...?"

"She thought it was either a hunter or this teenage delinquent we have living down the road from our place. We've heard rifles firing at all hours this fall and winter. There's a lot of concern that someone is going to get hit by a stray shot—and it appears you came close to being that someone."

"But what of this teenage kid you mentioned?"

"He's fifteen and the little shit's already been hauled before a juvenile judge for tossing rocks at passing cars and starting fires back in the woods."

"You think this kid would take a shot at me, Kendall?"

"I can't believe he'd go that far, although it's possible, I suppose, that he thinks himself a crack shot and aimed for the window behind you, but..."

"The shot went left to right on a diagonal right behind my neck."

"Christ. Still, I can't believe the kid would do something like that, on purpose, that is. Hold on, Tom. What, Sandy?....Look Tom, Sandy and I think it was a stray bullet from some nocturnal hunter—and that could have been the kid and likely was him—but it probably wasn't a deliberate shot at you or your car."

"I don't know, Kendall."

"Tom, you're not saying that someone is trying to murder you, are you?"

Roper took a moment before answering. "No, of course not."

"You don't really think it's the guy who killed Grayson and poor Ian, do you?"

Roper was stunned that Livingstone seemed to be reading his mind. "I just want you and Sandra to be careful, okay?"

"Thanks, Tom. But I bet that if it was the kid he'd probably be scared shitless if he thought he hit your car—but then I'd bet that he or whoever it was doesn't even have any idea where the bullet landed."

"You're probably right. Okay, thanks again for the hospitality, Kendall, and thank Sandra for me as well."

"Tom, I can never thank *you* enough for what you told me tonight. Oh, and have no fear. I've already written down what I can quote you directly on and what I can quote as coming from a 'member of Congress of the president's own party.' I tell you I'm really looking forward to tomorrow night's writing session more than you can imagine. But for now it's early to bed. Good night Tom."

• • • • •

"Mr. Cassell, what do you expect me to do—really?"

"You're telling me, Madam Leader, that there's nothing you can do to force a public apology from Roper?"

"Yes, that's what I'm telling you. There's really nothing I can do." Carol McCrimmon glanced at her watch. She wanted to be back at the Capitol by 8:30 a.m. If she left now, she'd make it just in time for her Wednesday morning meeting with the opposition leader.

"I find that hard to believe, Senator. Can't you at least take away one of his committee assignments. You could give him something less significant—anything to tell him he made a serious mistake the other day."

"Mr. Cassell,..."

"Please, call me Devin."

"Mr. Cassell, you must be aware of the public's reaction to Senator Roper's remarks. All of us are benefiting. Have you checked the polls? Congress and our party are up four to six points."

"Come on, Senator. You guys on the Hill have been so far down for so long that that it really doesn't mean all that much."

"Look, you know how much I appreciate all Sheridan has done for my political career. He went out of his way to protect me when I first got to the Senate and became involved with..." She stared at Cassell, not believing she'd come that close to articulating the facts about the most potentially devastating personal decision of her life.

"Your marriage was an unhappy one, Senator. You were— and are—a very beautiful woman who was vulnerable to the attention of American Petroleum's most persuasive lobbyist. Sheridan put the fear of God in him because he couldn't see ruining a career because you were merely being human—and vulnerable."

She shook her head at the fact that Cassell knew. "And I will never forget his kindness. He knows that, Mr. Cassell. Still, there is nothing I can to do about Tom Roper and this situation." She hesitated before adding, "At least for now."

Cassell touched her hand gently with the tips of his fingers. "I understand, Senator. It's just that Sheridan is as angry as I have ever seen him. Were he to turn his back on you and your party entirely, it could have serious ramifications for next fall's elections. And don't ask me how that might happen."

"Devin, can't you see it from my side?"

He smiled at her calling him by his first name. "Madame Leader, do you think I *want* to be here talking to you like this?" She believed he didn't—that Sheridan Browning didn't, for when she was voted leader, Browning sent her a dozen luxurious pink and cream variegated roses and a bottle of Dom Pérignon 1996. She felt then that it was the most blissful day of her life. And now she hated herself for having to disappoint him.

"Devin, what if *I* make a statement of some kind. I can't repudiate Tom Roper, but I might be able to say something about..." She stopped, unable to go on. She knew that politically there was really nothing she could say—not now and perhaps not ever.

Cassell sighed. "All right, Senator. I had to try. I promised Sheridan I would. Maybe I can convince him to ride this out."

"Devin, please know how much I hate that Sheridan and the Bureau is so affected by this."

"Thank you, Senator. Believe it or not, that does make me feel a little better."

She finally withdrew her hand from under his light touch.

"Forgive me, but I have to get to the Capitol."

"I know. Don't fret. I'm sure everything will be all right and that you'll do the right thing if you can. *Au revoir et salut,* Senator. Sorry. Have a nice day, *Madam Vice President.*"

After Cassell left the table, Carol McCrimmon sat staring at her dish of half-eaten food, unable to rise from her chair and escape the implications in Cassell's final words. It was clear. He and Browning knew of her political ambitions and discussions with Max Nettleton about running with Evan Bedingfield in 2016. A public revelation now of her earlier mistake, she well understood, would cost her dearly.

•　•　•　•　•

Roper got to his Senate office twenty minutes later than usual. He'd planned to speak with a member of the Capitol Police about the shot that hit his car the previous night, but at the last minute decided against it. He wondered whether he was becoming paranoid about the serial killer's next victim. What could he have to do with that third number—"11"? He reminded himself that a rifle shot did not square at all with the nature of the first two serial killings—both being obviously well thought out and grotesquely stylized. The Livingstones had to be right. A stray shot from a nocturnal hunter—perhaps the incorrigible teenager who lived nearby. Later, he'd get one of Robyn's colleagues in ballistics to examine his car and dig out the bullet. He wanted to avoid the publicity that would come if he filed a formal complaint in Prince George's County about the incident. Besides, it would then be known that he'd been out at Kendall Livingstone's place—for what purpose the White House and the media would easily guess.

Roper once more considered why Grayson would have sent

him blank pages following the seemingly melodramatic instructions never to open the envelope unless something bad happened to him. Was it some bizarre joke on Grayson's part? Had Grayson's plan been to ask for the envelope back eventually just to see if his good friend Tom Roper had been able to keep his curiosity in check and the envelope sealed? A crude test of loyalty? If so, for what purpose then?

Roper tried to recall Grayson's expression when his friend brought the envelope to the Hart Building. But in fact Grayson hadn't actually brought the envelope to him. Lena had dropped it on his desk and only said that it came from the Eisenhower Executive Office Building. Roper reminded himself again that the well-sealed envelope was inside a larger manila envelope, which was also bound securely with tape—postal tape, Roper remembered. And the handwriting on the envelope wasn't Grayson's.

But why the blank pages? Perhaps Lena could shed some light. Now exasperated that she hadn't yet stepped into his office, Roper corralled one of his staff.

"Dominic, where the hell is Lena?"

"We haven't seen her all morning, Senator. We thought that maybe you sent her on an errand of some kind."

• • • • •

"You look terrible, Patrick. You need sleep."

"No. I'm just..." Sims reached for his coffee without completing his reply.

Sims's lawyer Ted Henson raised an eyebrow. "Patrick?"

"Just tell me what you need to tell me. I've got to get going."

"Going where? Patrick, you better face the fact that the press is about to take the story further—past the assumption that you're guilty of document theft and obstruction of justice through the destruction of other documents. I've been told that either Friday or Saturday they're going to run something on the evidence that you've also intimidated colleagues when they refused to lie on your behalf and that early in the summer you initiated the purge of three DOJ officials who dared to cross the attorney general."

"It was fucking Johnson who wanted them out at Justice, not me, Ted. Jesus Christ."

"Patrick, getting worked up over this isn't going to help."

Sims stared at his attorney, who feared his client might punch him in the mouth. Henson put up his hands, palms facing Sims, and encouraged his client to remember where he was.

Sims looked to his left and right. "All right, all right. I'm sorry, Ted." Sims quickly finished his coffee. "Maybe I should switch to decaf." The poor joke failed to alleviate his attorney's concern.

"I'd strongly suggest you take it easy tonight, Patrick. Go to a movie—watch something on cable. Hit the sack early. You just need to get a good night's sleep." This time Sims lowered his eyes and stared at the barely-touched breakfast food on his plate. Henson continued. "For some reason—based on what, I don't know—you don't want to plead so that then we can build a case for extenuating circumstances owing to your past and now present severe mental strain."

"Don't give me any of that god-damn psychiatrist shit, Ted. I've been there already." Sims tapped a butter knife on his plate.

"I don't even know what to say to you, Patrick. If you don't bend on this, I'm not going to be able to stop the worst from happening. Look, Patrick, let's check you into a hospital and keep you there a few days at least. That can at least help us establish the fact that--."

"That's enough, Ted."

"Then how about my arranging an appointment with a really good--."

"God damn it, I said that's enough!"

"Keep your voice down. I still think you're holding back on me, Patrick. Especially regarding what you told Marshall Grayson."

Sims chuckled. "Grayson's no longer an issue."

"Jesus Christ, Patrick, did you kill him?"

"Fuck you, Ted."

Henson stood up and pulled his wallet out, dropping several bills on the table. "I need to go. Call me if you want to talk." Sims said nothing. "Patrick, you probably don't believe me, but I'm working very hard on this. It's still possible that I can get a little give from Johnson about those documents. He wants to avoid as much embarrassment as possible to his office and to the president."

Sims raised his eyes but his head remained lowered. Henson noticed that his client's fingers were curled around the butter knife. "And what about the other stuff the press is about to break, Ted?"

"I'm...on that too. Remember to call me if...shit, never mind. I'll talk to you soon. If not tomorrow, Friday for sure." The attorney gently tapped Sims's shoulder as he passed.

"Friday." Sims knew he wouldn't be around to talk to Henson on Friday. Had he been right to listen to his legal counsel for so long? Or to Max Nettleton? Now Sims had a new team of gurus to chart his course and get him out of this mess. He'd just have to kill Roper, as they asked.

•   •   •   •   •

Roper received the call and immediately left his office. It was 11:15 a.m. Since 9:30, he'd been dreading a call like this. He didn't stay on the line long. The conversation was too fraught with emotion for proper coherence. He knew he'd have to deal with this in person.

Fortunately, traffic cooperated. He made it up the Washington National Pike with little problem and exited on Route 80 on the south side of Frederick, Maryland. He checked his GPS for the address he'd been given and saw he had less than two miles before making a left into an attractive residential area.

When Roper pulled into the driveway, a woman opened the front door. He checked the address on the note card in his hand. As he approached the doorstep, a car passed the house and the driver laid on the horn to get a stray dog out of his way, the noise startling the woman. Roper heard another female voice cry inside the house.

"Senator, she's in the living room."

"Thank you." Now Roper recognized the face. It was Lena's younger sister, Vivian. He'd of course seen her in the large family photograph on Lena's desk. This was obviously her house. She ushered him in to the living room.

"Lena, my God, are you all right?"

Lena trembled slightly, battling her emotions, but managed to come forward and embrace him. "That car horn scared me. I'm sorry."

Vivian interposed. "I'll leave you two alone. Can I get you anything, Senator?"

"No, no, I'm fine. Thank you." Roper waited until Vivian left the room. "Lena, tell me everything that happened."

As she told her story and insisted that she wouldn't call the police, Roper tried to figure out who would have wished to frighten her and by extension him. Was this event related to the suspicious man beneath the streetlight outside his apartment? Or the doorknob turning at Robyn's place? Or the shot taken at him as he left the Livingstone farm? If not, then who might have done this to Lena Roseboro? One of his newer political adversaries, or an older one, now further angered by his handling of Sheridan Browning? He then thought of his visit to the Oval Office and the reputation Jerry Goldman had for relishing games of political hardball.

"Please understand, Senator, I've decided to stay for a while with my other sister, who just moved out west. I have a flight for later today. I'm sorry but I have to go away. Here's her number in case you need to reach me, but please don't give it to anybody else. I don't want you to be involved. I'll call you later and tell you exactly where I am. But again, I just don't want to get you involved."

Roper didn't bother telling her it was too late for that.

•   •   •   •   •

Alyona Novikova glanced at her wall clock as the phone rang. 3:15 Pacific Time, 6:15 p.m. back east. She didn't check the number; she was certain it was the same caller from last night.

"Hello?"

"Alyona?"

"Yes, Agent Hendrix?" She felt the conflicting emotions of curiosity, hope, and anxiety affecting the way she shaped her simple reply. It didn't sound like her at all.

"Did I catch you just getting back home?"

"No, no. I've been here awhile."

"Good. So, have you decided what to do about my offer?"

"I need to be honest and say I'm suspicious about all this."

"Completely understandable. You must receive dozens of 'offers' from agencies and would-be producers and directors about non-existent film opportunities—or film opportunities of the kind you want no part of."

She felt pleased by his accurate assessment. "Yes, more than I care to mention."

"And with the hundreds—or is it thousands—of young hopefuls competing for even the slightest role out there, I can only imagine how exploited all of you feel—and how many hearts are completely broken."

The phrase "young hopefuls" slapped at her sensibilities. She was now thirty-one.

"But certainly you understand I'm not merely someone calling you with a promise. What I'm asking is that you assist us in something very legitimate and important. Remember, I'm offering you an opportunity to get what you want—though it's an opportunity much better than most."

She once again measured all that with the agent's desire to have her speak about her relationship with Tom Roper, who was obviously being looked at by the FBI for something he'd done or said. Although she never followed politics, let alone Roper's career, Alyona was well aware that he didn't fear controversy and was never shy about voicing his criticism. He'd probably overstepped the bounds of a United States senator and the Bureau wanted to know more about his background so they could make an accurate evaluation of him. She could alleviate any feeling of betrayal by insisting that her remarks remain anonymous. If they wanted to know about their love life, she could be honest without shame, for she and Roper had never had sexual intercourse.

"So again, Alyona, what's your answer?

"Yes, I'll be happy to talk about my relationship with the

senator. But you still are promising me a *good chance* to get a role, right?"

"You bet. Okay. Now I told you that I'd like to send someone from the state investigative bureau to interview you. Let me also say that after talking with my contacts in the industry, they suggested that the agent be accompanied by someone connected to one of the film projects you'd be auditioning for. This person has been helping us out in the way I hinted at yesterday—so..."

"Scratch your back—scratch mine, right?"

"Exactly. Okay, we talked about a good time tonight, didn't we?"

"Yes. Around 11:00 p.m. my time, I believe you said."

"That's it. All right, it was so very nice talking with you again, Alyona. Oh, one more thing. We will be back in touch tomorrow afternoon—that's Thursday afternoon—about exactly whom you'll need to see about that role, as well as the when and where. You're about to enter a very exciting period in your life, Alyona. I have every feeling that everything is going to work out perfectly for you."

She wanted to erupt in some exclamatory way, but she couldn't shake her nagging fears. "Yes, I so very much hope you're right. But I was wondering, couldn't you or this other person just interview me on the phone? I'm happy to talk for as long as you need." She could hear the frustration in his sigh. He took several moments before responding. She could sense that he was about to change his mind. The possibility terrified her.

"Alyona, I think it would be best to have a face-to-face. For two reasons. First, it's the best way to judge your—and don't be insulted by this—your credibility. It's of course very important that we trust what you have to say about your relationship with the senator. Second, remember the person who's coming with the agent to talk with you. So think of it as a kind of pre-audition. Getting a good sense of your looks, manner, and voice are part of the reason why we want to do this in person. I hope you'll understand and that it's all acceptable to you."

Alyona caught her reflection in the mirror. She was flushed and tired of her skepticism. "Oh, yes, it's *very* acceptable. I'll even have something ready to serve the person coming with the agent." She paused slightly. "And who will this person be, again?"

"Good idea, Alyona. Let me suggest some mid-priced California sparkling wine. I think that offering will be very well received. Good night, Alyona. I'll be talking to you again tomorrow."

She decided to leave immediately and shop for a new outfit and shoes. It was imperative that she look as beautiful as she could tonight. She'd take absolutely no chances with her appearance.

Chapter 11

"Sandy, could you bring me some hot tea. And hurry. It's been a whole two and a half hours since we've seen each other." Kendall Livingstone smiled at his wife's succinct Anglo-Saxon reply as he laid down his cell phone. His gazebo office seemed nothing short of Shangri-La on this winter's night. The predicted snowfall had yet to begin in earnest, but nonetheless he enjoyed standing in front of the lone window watching the flurries dot the ground between him and the house where his wife was making tea.

Although his softball skills were modest at best, he still liked to say that the keyboard was his bat—and a particularly effective sentence or phrase the pitch he hit out of the park. Tonight it had been like a home-run marathon with the prose he composed from the many grooved pitches thrown the previous night by Tom Roper. Livingstone looked at the tangible evidence of the metaphor hanging on the wall of his gazebo office—a wooden bat signed by eight members of the 1995 American League Champions, his beloved Cleveland Indians.

Roper had given Livingstone quite a bit on the shortcomings and oddities of Evan Bedingfield. But the senator also shared his opinions of Bedingfield's chief of staff, Jerry Goldman, of the vice president, and even of Edward Malloch's chief of staff, Maximilian Nettleton—all of which provided either corroboration of or a new take on what Livingstone had gleaned from other interviews and research. Perhaps Roper's visceral dislike of Max Nettleton surprised Livingstone the most, since he had found the V.P.'s chief of staff a decent interview and a good occasional source, even if little of major consequence was ever shared. Livingstone thought Nettleton was one of those politicians you wanted to have beer with—and on one occasion he had, along with three other members of Nettleton's history club, after their December meeting.

But Roper thought Nettleton fancied himself "a modern-day Richelieu," who bristled at the fact that he didn't have the ear of the top man in government. Having noted Nettleton's cunning, Roper wondered out loud how extensive Nettleton's "network of spies" was. How many younger men and women did Nettleton feed with appeals to party loyalty and the promise of political gain for that loyalty? The Watergate prosecutions, Roper reminded Livingstone, led to charges and convictions of those still in their early thirties. Roper also shared the view of Marshall Grayson that Max Nettleton was jockeying to replace Jerry Goldman as chief of staff in a second Bedingfield administration and that Nettleton was willing to sacrifice Malloch in the bargain—providing the president and party leaders enough good reason to drop him from the ticket in 2016. Roper had no firm idea as to what Bedingfield would point to—other than Malloch's generally bland approval ratings as V.P.—but Roper had little doubt that Nettleton would do what he needed to do to move up in rank.

Livingstone sat facing his computer screen and began scrolling to places where he might add something new from what Roper had given him. The last thing he wanted, though, was for readers and reviewers to think his book on Evan Bedingfield's first year was some kind of gossip log, so he had to be careful about which impressions he used from his "significant congressional source from the president's own party." Not wanting to allow his previous approval of Nettleton or his fondness for Tom Roper cloud his journalistic objectivity, he began to reread the section before him. Livingstone didn't hear the door to his gazebo office open.

•　　•　　•　　•　　•

"To tell you the truth, Senator, I'd have to take this slug to the lab for proper examination. But if I were a guessing man, I'd say that this came from an AR-15, or the civilian version of the AR-15, the Bushmaster Varmint. Damn good weapon, Senator."

Roper listened attentively to Matt Shanahan, the ballistics expert the senator asked to come over and extract the bullet from the inside of his sedan. "Then you think it could've been a shot from a hunting rifle?"

"Well, it certainly could have been. But looking at this, I'm wondering if it isn't a .556 millimeter cartridge, which would mean it came from the military version of the AR-15. The civilian rifle would fire a .223 Remington round—so again I'd have to check."

"A military round."

"Could be. Let me get back to you sometime tomorrow. Sure you don't want to report this, Senator?"

"No, Matt, not now." He thought of Lena Roseboro. "If you tell me that it was the Remington round, then I might call someone over in Prince George's County. But if it's the military round, it might be best to say nothing." Roper detected the confusion on Shanahan's face. "Sorry, I know that doesn't make sense, Matt. But for now I'd like to avoid any potential and sensational story about someone trying to take me out with a rifle shot."

Shanahan looked dubious but nodded his head nonetheless. "Got it. Okay, I'll give you a call, Senator, and let you know."

"Thanks, Matt."

Five minutes after Shanahan left, Roper's shoes were off and he was reclined on Robyn's plush sofa. He was trying hard not to think further of the shot that had barely missed him and the man who'd visited and threatened Lena. He was too tired to think any further about the serial killer and those damned numbers and initials. He closed his eyes and fell asleep for half an hour, only to be awakened by the soft touch of Robyn's lips on his and the feel of a cold glass against his cheek.

"Thought you could use a beer."

"I like the way you think, Ms. Meadows. By the way, what time is it?"

"9:13 in the evening, Senator. You have until 10:00 to finish that—and another one if you hurry—because at 10:01 you're all mine."

"Forgive me if I doze off before then."

"That's okay. I'll take you dead or alive."

· · · · ·

Livingstone's head was flat down on his desk. His shoulders were moving slightly, his mouth open but emitting no sound. A firm hand pulled his head back by the hair.

"Take a look, sailor." Sandra Livingstone's long winter coat was fully open, revealing her exquisite nude body—with the exception of the hiking boots she'd worn for the walk from the house to the gazebo.

Her husband began shaking his head from side to side, still keeping it on top of the desk. "I can't look, I can't."

"You prudish piece of shit!" Sandra forced his head up to her breasts. "Just for that, you can sleep out with the dogs tonight."

"We don't have any dogs. You have allergies, remember?"

"Oh, yeah. Forgot." She felt her husband's hands caressing her breasts. She never had any doubt that he'd touch them immediately. "I've finished reading my book. My hair's down. My body's full of goose bumps. Come on, sailor. Dock your craft where it belongs. Right in my slip."

His face no longer in mock horror, Livingstone shook his head as he stood up to caress her. He knew he wouldn't be working anymore right now and that if he was going to finish the writing he'd planned for the night, he'd have to come back from the warm bed after they'd made love. "Come, Sandy. I see two pillows and your great-aunt Margaret's quilt in our immediate future."

"You leave Aunt Margaret out of this." He tried to wrap his arm around her nude waist. "No, no, no. You must have your tea first. I made it special. See how hot and... steamy it is?" Her naughty smile made her even more desirable to him—if that was possible.

"You're wicked."

"As wicked as they come. But tea first."

"Your British side is showing. Okay, tea first and then we go to the house?" He thoroughly enjoyed the little scenario she'd created for the two of them.

"No, no. When we finish the tea—and you have to finish every...single...drop—I'll fuck you out here. Here in your holy outer sanctum. Where I don't think you've ever done more than peck me on the cheek before. Well, just now you did fondle my boobs, but you get my point."

"Sounds like a plan."

"Umm, how about another log or two in the wood stove? I'm still a little cold from the long trek out here. Blizzard conditions, you know."

"Your wish is my command."

"Glad you accept my conditions. Surrender is your best bet tonight."

Livingstone opened the door and stepped into the now falling snow. The wood was stacked ten feet away.

Sandra poured the tea into the two mugs she had brought out with her and pulled her coat more tightly around her body. Opening the door had let in another roomful of frigid air. Wrapping her hands around one of the mugs, she felt the comforting warmth going through her hands and arms and down to her breasts. But her neck and ears still felt the stinging cold. She turned to the door. It had not shut completely when her husband stepped out for the firewood.

Taking a quick sip of the hot tea, Sandra walked the few steps to the door in order to shut it tightly. Before she could reach it, however, the door opened outwardly.

"Hurry up, hurry up, baby. You're letting in all that cold air." But Kendall simply stood in the doorway—holding the three pieces of oak in front of him. She studied his face.

"Kendall!" Her hands went immediately to her mouth as her husband fell forward, the pieces of split wood still wrapped securely in his cradled arms. She saw the handle of the large knife protruding from his purple sweater. Staring down at him, it was impossible to scream. Her winter coat parted again to reveal her nude body. She slowly raised her head and only barely saw the flash of the cut wood before it slammed against the side of her head.

The next thing she sensed was another blow landing squarely on the back of her head. But the sensation of that blow was as brief as it could possibly be. She never felt the third blow — or the fourth.

•   •   •   •   •

Before the man placed the baseball bat back in its holder against the rear wall, he inspected it and noted the autographs and the date. "Almost twenty years ago now," he said in a calm whisper. He'd already known where the bat would be situated. He couldn't help doing the calculation. Kendall Livingston had been sixteen years of age when the bat was signed.

The man saw that Livingstone's body was no longer exactly where it had fallen. It seemed to have moved several inches forward, almost rolling over the three pieces of wood still cradled in his arms. But he was confident the reporter would remain still now. He stepped gingerly and pulled the knife from Livingstone's back.

He glanced at the hot tea in one of the mugs and regretted that he couldn't take a few swallows, as cold air poured into the gazebo from the open door. Looking around, he saw a sooty rag lying near the woodstove. This would do. Again being careful not to stand too close to Livingstone's body, he took the rag and tried to transfer the blood from his knife. He frowned. It would not be sufficient. He daubed the blackened rag on Livingstone's sweater until he felt he had enough.

Reaching down, he grabbed Sandra Livingstone's shoulder with one of his gloved hands and flipped her body over so her bare breasts were exposed. On one he daubed an "I', on the other an "S" in her husband's blood.

The man had one more act to perform. He'd already written

the five numbers on the piece of paper he had folded inside his coat, but he was intrigued by the illumination coming from the laptop. He saw sixteen lines of prose on the screen. For a moment, he recalled the image of his father sitting at the family's old PC entering the tally of monthly bills.

He pressed the enter key until he had a blank page. He shifted the font size from 12 to 48 and with his gloved finger typed "20-18-11-19-07." Nodding with satisfaction, he lifted his sooty, blood-stained rag, and brought it to the computer screen.

•   •   •   •   •

"Good Thursday morning, Mr. President." Evan Bedingfield liked to be reminded first thing each day what day of the week it was.

"And to you, Jerry. Okay, what's the status of the State of the Union address?"

"It's coming along nicely, sir. Just this morning I talked to Nat Piurowski. He's organized everything in the order you requested."

"Quotations?"

"The three you wanted—Truman, Lincoln, and JFK. Nat also has three others he's going to show you as possibilities. He thinks you should have one more about three-quarters of the way through."

"He understands I want a draft by Monday morning, right?"

"Yes, sir. That will give you plenty of time before you have to deliver it on the 28th."

"All right, Jerry, so what's on tap for Friday, other than what you have here?" Bedingfield was studying the handsome appointment calendar for the next two days. "Friday is blank from 4:00 p.m. to 4:30."

"Right, Mr. President. I wanted to make sure that the manuscript could be packaged and brought over from the National Archives at that time. They called me right before I came in to the Oval Office. It's a go."

"What's it been? A week now since we first scheduled this?"

"It's been eight days—last Wednesday—when Carol McCrimmon gave her okay to let Archives lend it to us for the photo op."

"Amazing that such a document had been in her family all these years. Now you're sure that Friday is the anniversary day of the document's composition?"

"Yes. This Friday's the date. Washington's secretary dated it January 17, 1791."

"Recording Washington's thoughts on moving the seat of government to the D.C. area?"

"Right. Carol McCrimmon received it when her mother died, since she's the last descendent of the secretary who recorded Washington's observations. Max Nettleton told me she turned town his request to display it for one of his history club lectures. She felt badly about saying no, however, so she's willing to let us have it on Friday. You'll be the first non-family member photographed with it. Part of her agreement with the Archives is that she has to sign off on its being removed for any purpose of display. They were more than happy to accommodate her wishes, of course."

"All right, Jerry, I want plenty of photographs of me studying the document. I was thinking I also might quote from it in the State of the Union—so tell Nat to leave space and prepare some kind of segue. We might not need that fourth quotation after all."

"Right."

"I'm going to preempt that son-of-a-bitch Kendall

Livingstone's big assertion in his book that I have 'no historical scope' or whatever the hell he's going to say."

"You have 'no historical *perspective*' is what I was told he's writing."

"Told to you by whom again?"

"Confidential source, Mr. President. It's best you don't know by who—or in this case by whom."

"You're right, Jerry." Bedingfield had failed to get the playful jab about his having used proper objective case. "Okay, so who should we invite to the official debunking of the Evan Bedingfield has no historical...?"

"Perspective."

"The 'no historical perspective' myth, then? I was thinking a couple of history professors, one from Georgetown, another from Maryland."

"Excuse me, sir, but we should have someone from the Ivy League. I know a Harvard professor who's spending his sabbatical here in D.C. He and a Georgetown prof I personally know would be best. The Georgetown prof's a fairly young guy who's just won one of the history prizes for his book on the post-Colonial period. He's knows a number of government types throughout the city, and I think he'd be perfect."

"Good. Then invite them both. And be sure Max Nettleton knows I want him there too. And of course the majority leader."

"Max said she might be tied up all day Friday making sure our bill has the sixtieth vote to invoke cloture."

"All right, but be sure you call her and make the invitation anyway. Tell her we can make it so she'll lose only half an hour, forty-five minutes tops."

"Got it."

"How about one or two others below cabinet status?"

"Sounds good, Mr. President. Who would you like?"

"Marta Taubman. I promised her a birthday present. She asked to be included in Friday's photo shoot. Her father recently retired as project archivist at Princeton. She wants to present him with a photograph of his daughter with the document."

"Fine. Who else?"

"The first lady."

"Of course. Anyone else?"

"Not unless you think of anyone else who'd be good to have in the shot, Jerry. Just keep a spot open for Carol McCrimmon."

"Yes, sir. You want the photos taken here in the Oval Office?"

"No, the Roosevelt Room. We can spread the document on the table. All right, anything else?"

Goldman looked around the Oval Office for a moment before answering. "The matter we talked about yesterday after Tom Roper's visit. Well, we've been on that."

Bedingfield needed no further explanation. He sat squarely behind his desk and nodded. "Good."

•   •   •   •   •

Roper stood in the Capitol rotunda with both hands deep in his pockets.

"Tony, I'm not giving interviews about what I said to Sheridan Browning—at least not for a few days."

"Senator, this is the time. Have you checked on the number of YouTube views and Tweets your little moment has received the past two days? Quite a little sensation you've caused, Senator."

"So I've learned. Look, Tony, it would sound as though I was gloating if I began talking about it publicly. Best just to be quiet and let the damned thing run its course."

"Not the cliché I would have expected from a politician, if you don't mind my saying."

Roper smiled at network political commentator and reporter Tony Braithwait. "You're right, Tony. Any other politician would exploit such a moment for all it's worth. There, another cliché."

"You don't mind if I repeat that on the air, do you?"

"What the hell—sure. I'll get a call from my twelfth-grade English teacher who'll express her horror that I failed to heed her warning about failing to avoid the commonplace."

"Look, if you change your mind about an on-camera interview, will you give me first crack?"

"That I promise you, Tony. Your network has been the kindest to me anyway this past year, so of course."

Braithwait stuck out his hand. Roper liked shaking hands with the "Brahmin from Bean Town," as the reporter's colleagues called him. His firm handshake felt much like Nathan Roper's.

"Senator, you know that Sheridan Browning will find ways to fight your reelection in 2018."

"That's four and a half years from now, Tony. Besides, I..." Roper checked himself. For a moment he wanted to give Braithwait the scoop on his decision to leave the Senate after his first and only term, but decided it could wait. He remembered the promise he'd made to himself Tuesday night that he would officially tell Kendall Livingstone first.

Braithwait raised his thick grey eyebrows. "You...? What were you about to say after that 'besides,' Senator?"

"*Besides*, I have too much important work to do for my state and the American people to worry about what Sheridan Browning might have up his sleeve. How's that for an even more traditional cliché, Tony?"

"Excellent. I can't wait to share that one with the public as well. Remember, I'm on at 10:00 p.m. Have a good day, Senator."

"You too, Tony."

"Oh, I forgot to ask. Where's Lena? She owes me twenty bucks from last week's game. She made the mistake of taking the Colts and the points against my beloved Pats."

*   *   *   *   *

Returning to his office, Roper recalled Braithwait's warning about Browning. He knew he had to be ready for any forthcoming attacks on his record by at least one of the cable networks. Surely there'd be intensified scrutiny of every possible speech he'd ever given, back home and since coming to the Senate. Browning wouldn't have to wait five and a half years to seek his revenge. The innuendos and smears would arrive soon. Roper had no doubt that Browning's minions would talk with anyone in his home state who could offer something damaging. And what if in the coming months Browning was named Director after all?

Thinking about all that Sheridan Browning might do in the name of political retribution, Roper gave only passing thought to the possibility that the shot fired at him the night before and the threat made to Lena Roseboro—and even the man standing in the shadows near the streetlight and the knock on Robyn's door—were the work of Browning's crew—whoever they might be. Then again, it was unlikely that anyone before had insulted Browning so publicly.

Roper sat at his desk in the Hart Senate Building and let names and faces flit before him—political opponents and others he might've offended since he entered politics. Soon he began going back further and replacing the sour faces of enemies with those who'd assisted him in life and his career. But he should have known better to reminisce, for stepping forward in his memory now was the lovely face of the young woman he had both insulted and deeply hurt eight years before. Alyona Novikova.

He'd fallen for her hard. He loved her athleticism and her Slavic beauty, but he also imagined her to be innocent—a young woman who'd lean on him, seek his counsel as well as his love. Captivated by this image, Roper had been hesitant to pursue a sexual relationship with her. He soon understood he was protecting her—protecting her honor, yes, but also protecting his sense of her innocence. But then she drank too much and revealed to him just how she'd been making a living in California before they had met.

He knew it had been unfair and cruel of him to end their relationship so abruptly. It probably had been a knee-jerk reaction to his wounded masculine pride—that he had so misjudged her innocence and experiences—rather than a retreat from her on purely moral grounds. Roper certainly hadn't been a saint when it came to sexual partners—in his early thirties then, he'd been with several women he didn't love. But with Alyona, it was different.

After it was over, he came to believe that he didn't truly love her, although he sincerely cared for her. Rather, he'd fallen for a pleasing image of her, one he knew he'd inappropriately shaped. That he'd played Pygmalion with such a caring, sensitive woman was a thought now abhorrent to him.

Chapter 12

At 9:55 a.m., Robyn Meadows approached Meridian Hill Park on 16th Street, up a little past Florida Avenue. It was an area she'd visited once before, and she knew it was also called "Malcolm X Park." Earlier this morning, the caller had identified himself as FBI and had given a name she recognized, someone she'd never spoken to but had emailed on two occasions during unrelated homicide investigations. He'd said he wanted to share something with her about the two "number killings"—something that was being "sat on" at the Bureau for reasons that "eluded" him. He added that he'd been acquainted with Ian Arrington and was therefore more "personally involved" than he ought to have been. The choice of this park, he noted, was "less clandestine and more practical" than she might have assumed. His "lady" lived not far from the park, and he was going to see her before meeting with Robyn. He asked her to come to the statue of Joan of Arc, which Robyn believed was the only equestrian statue in Washington featuring a female rider.

The first time Robyn visited Meridian Hill Park, she'd been with Lena Roseboro. Although she was troubled by what Roper had told her about Lena's frightful experience with a masked visitor, Robyn had no concerns for her own safety as she left her car and walked into the park.

•　•　•　•　•

"I'll be at the White House tomorrow afternoon, Jerry. Please tell the president I appreciate the invitation. Very thoughtful of him to think of me." Max Nettleton had expected the invitation and would have protested had he not received it. After all, he was the one who had encouraged Carol McCrimmon to permit the historic document's removal from the National Archives and he'd known for a week that Bedingfield was planning a big photo op. He waited for a reply, but Goldman remained silent. "Is there anything else on your mind, Jerry?"

"It can wait, Max."

Nettleton didn't mind being window dressing for Evan Bedingfield's photo op, and not just because the context of the occasion was historical. First, getting in the shot would only enhance his historical bona fides with the other members of his club. Since college, Nettleton had been fascinated by anything having to do with the history of smaller literary and political organizations—from the Kit-Cat Club in early eighteenth-century London, with its strong advocacy of Whig policy and objectives, to the formation of the Phi Beta Kappa Society in Colonial Williamsburg. Nettleton frequently wore his own Phi Beta Kappa key and was never hesitant about showing it to others. He shared the distinction with three other members of his history club so the quartet included the unique PBK handshake greeting at the beginning of each club meeting.

Nettleton smiled at the thought that his boss wasn't invited to the White House tomorrow afternoon. In the past twelve months, Bedingfield had kept his vice president at more than an arm's length—pushing him even farther way whenever he could. Goldman told him that Bedingfield was sensitive to the public's understanding of how much power previous vice presidents possessed and wished to relegate Ed Malloch to a much more ceremonial role, even though Malloch wouldn't be included in the ceremony in the Roosevelt Room tomorrow afternoon. Goldman apparently approved of the president's decision to use the LBJ-Hubert Humphrey relationship as his model.

Heading out from the Eisenhower Building, Nettleton wondered when Bedingfield would get around to letting the vice president know that he wouldn't be on the 2016 ticket. He'd been happy to learn that during a holiday gathering at the White House when the president had taken several of his cabinet members into the China Room on the ground floor and spoke about the reelection campaign seemingly so far in the future. Apparently, the president had said wistfully how nice it would have been for him to have asked someone like New Mexico Governor Inez Gonzalez or Senator Carol McCrimmon to run with him in 2012. Nettleton had been told that Bedingfield enjoyed two drinks beyond the presidential limit and went on to lament the missed opportunity to become the first president to have a woman V.P. He argued that either Gonzalez or McCrimmon would have secured two, possibly three, states that Bedingfield narrowly lost in the 2012 election.

Nettleton believed that none who were at the pre-Christmas gathering had any idea that it was the current V.P.'s chief of staff who'd twice made the case to the president that Malloch was a potential liability—even though Bedingfield needed Malloch's state in 2012--owing to his colorless personality and dipping poll numbers, and that Bedingfield couldn't pass on the opportunity to make history by choosing a woman to be his next vice president. In addition, Nettleton already knew, though the president did not, that Inez Gonzalez's husband had been diagnosed with early onset of Alzheimer's, and that the governor would be retiring from politics before the end of the year.

Nettleton had another appointment with Bedingfield next week. The president assured him that no one else would be privy to their discussions about the matter—not even Jerry Goldman. Yet the chief of staff knew. Whether Bedingfield told Goldman, Nettleton couldn't be sure. Perhaps he could glean an answer at the photo op tomorrow in the Roosevelt Room. If nothing else, he would demonstrate in some manner how willing he was to succeed Goldman as presidential chief of staff

But there was one fact spoiling this otherwise rosy scenario. Marshall Grayson had overheard what the cabinet member told Nettleton about the president's off-the-cuff remarks in the China Room and Nettleton's reply that the president needed to make sure that he would benefit from the change in the ticket. All Nettleton knew for sure was that when he and the cabinet secretary stepped around the corner of Nettleton's office in the EEOB, Grayson was standing inside the office door, wearing a Cheshire Cat smile.

Yes, Grayson was now dead, and Nettleton had taken other steps to keep what Grayson had surely overheard from reaching anyone's ears. But what had Grayson told Kendall Livingstone? And what might Grayson have said to his good friend Tom Roper? Nettleton always believed that Grayson was simply biding his time before he'd attempt to expose his rival's political machinations. There was no one in Washington he had feared more than Ed Malloch's chief political advisor. He was constantly rankled and embittered by the thought that Grayson could still destroy him from beyond the grave.

•　•　•　•　•

Robyn was disappointed that no one was waiting for her under the statue of Joan of Arc. She checked her watch. She was on time. The caller assured her he'd be there right at 10:00 a.m. She walked to the statue and stood in front of the pedestal of the bronze statue, reading the French inscription *"Aux Femmes D'Amérique – Les Femmes De France."* For several minutes she looked in vain for an approaching Agent Surrency. She debated how long she'd wait for him. "Damn it, man, come on."

She heard the metallic clang but didn't see the bullet strike the bronze horse's hoof above where she was standing. Instinctively, she turned to determine what had happened. She thought first that someone had thrown a rock or some other object either at her or at the statue of Joan. Then something hit lower down—on the very top edge of the platform on which the statue rested. Now she knew. Someone was shooting at her.

She dropped to the ground and debated which way she should crawl to make herself a more difficult target. But no third shot followed the second. After another thirty seconds, she rose cautiously and looked around the park. Given what she knew about those who'd used the area for drug buys, she wondered if there had been an altercation, with several persons taking pot shots at each other—two of which had hit statue of Joan. She began to move away in a crouch but soon rose and headed rapidly to her car.

Robyn called in the incident and asked to be informed if anyone else reported a shooting in the park. Then she remembered that he hadn't heard the shots herself, only the sound of the bullets hitting the statue. The shooter must have used a silencer. Robyn lowered her head onto the steering wheel. She had to conclude that she was the target. But why would anyone shoot at her—especially in broad daylight, a little past ten in the morning in a public place? She thought first of the serial killer but quickly dismissed the idea. There could be no connection. Detectives and crime lab specialists were not the targets of serial killers. Was it relating, then, to any of the other homicides she was working on? Again, it made no sense. Were she to die, her colleagues would go on without missing a beat. Everything was shared. No one could assume that she possessed knowledge no one else knew or could discover. Approaching DuPont Circle, she resolved to postpone her contemplations until she placed a call to the Hoover Building.

"I'd like to speak to Agent Surrency. This is Robyn Meadows of Metro....All right, thank you, I'll hold." After a long three-minute wait, he came on the line.

"Hello? This is Surrency."

His voice sounded exactly as she expected it would. Not a bit like the voice who had called her earlier in the morning.

•　•　•　•　•

Moving quickly down the hall of the Dirksen Senate Office Building, Carol McCrimmon greeted a score of colleagues, staff persons, and visiting citizens. Robert Gleeson was speaking to her in a half whisper as he struggled to match her pace.

"Senator, I did what you asked me to do regarding Senator Roper, but I'm not sure I understand why you want to get involved in--."

McCrimmon stopped him with a snap of her head in his direction. "Robert." He understood. He was not to ask anything further. She had her reasons. The less he knew the better. He recalled the cliché-filled lesson he'd received by someone far more experienced than he in the way the game was played in Washington. Gleeson turned and headed back to McCrimmon's office as she continued on to her meeting with the minority leader.

•   •   •   •   •

Roper made a second call to the Livingstone farmhouse. He wanted to let the *Post* political reporter know there were a couple of other impressions of the Bedingfield White House he hadn't shared but now wanted to. Again getting the answering machine, he hung up rather than leave a message. He planned to drive back down the farmhouse sometime between 5:00 and 5:30, since Livingstone had assured him that he was always out at the gazebo office at 6:30, right after dinner. Roper would bring a bottle of wine as a token thank you for the hospitality he'd received at the Livingstone's Tuesday night. He hoped to get there a few minutes before 5:00, before the sun had completely set. He wanted to take a look at the area near the road for any indication of where that shot might have come from.

•   •   •   •   •

Exactly at noon, the man entered the gift shop of the Hirshhorn Museum on Jefferson, between the Smithsonian Castle and the Air and Space Museum. He didn't need to eat during his lunch hour, since he'd already had a full breakfast at 7:00 a.m., although he had a candy bar in his coat pocket just in case. He'd come to the gift shop to thumb through a few books and flip through some postcards relating to modern art—an area that had never before elicited his curiosity. In recent weeks he'd begun lamenting the many gaps of knowledge in his life.

But these blank areas were the price he paid for knowing so thoroughly what he did know, a price he more than gladly paid owing to the humiliation and degradation he'd experienced at the hands of his parents so many years ago. He found it the grand accomplishment of his life—that he had so perfectly fooled dear old Mom and Dad. In the weeks following his sixteenth birthday, they'd beamed at how quickly he took to the new field of learning—language and literature. His mother truly believed then that her son would forever leave his numbers alone. That he would forget the role numbers played in the horrifically sinful act, which he would leave alone and buried, for her sake as well as for his. But by this Friday evening his mother would discover soon enough how wrong she had been in such an assumption.

His parents had both celebrated their anniversary. Yes, in less than thirty-six hours, they'd awaken from their blithe slumber—in the very bed in and around which it had all happened. Their remaining years would forever torment them—brutalize them—as they dealt with the fact that all had been of their own doing.

"Can I help you find something?"

The man smiled at the attractive woman, as if he knew her. "Hi. Yes, I think you can."

She waited for him to go on, but he merely looked at her and continued smiling.

"A book? Poster?"

She was dressed conservatively—in a stylish high-collar pink blouse and black pants—but he knew that in other settings she loved showing off her full breasts and sensational legs, as she had done on that early September evening when he first saw her at the softball fields.

"Sir?"

"I'm sorry. I'm just a little embarrassed, that's all."

The woman stepped closer to him and lowered her voice. "But why?"

"I don't know the first thing about modern art, I'm afraid, and my lady friend is up on it enough to make me feel ignorant whenever she sees something in a magazine or in one of her art books and then asks me if I know who painted this or sculpted that."

The woman laughed sympathetically. "Oh, I understand. You'd like to get a crash course so that you don't have to feel so—"

"Right, right. You understand. What I really want is to bone up on as much as I can and then ask her to come here to the museum and surprise the living heck out of her by knowing a little something about what we're looking at. See?"

"I do. Absolutely." She found the man completely charming in his exuberance and ineptitude. Had she seen him before? She believed that she had. "Well, I think this volume over here will serve the purpose. But I have to warn you—it's not cheap."

"That's okay. It'll be worth whatever it costs." She showed him the price. "Wow. Let's just say that it *better* be worth whatever it costs."

She laughed again. "I know it will be. So, shall I ring this up, or do you want look around some more?"

"Oh, boy. I hate to ask you this, but I wonder if it would be possible to purchase it and leave it here so that I can pick it up later today—or at the very latest tomorrow around noon. I have some errands and a lot of walking to do before I go back to work, and my arms would fall off if I had to lug that tome around with me."

"Do you work far from here?"

"No, not at all."

"Then you can take it to your office before you go on your long walk. See?"

The man looked at her without changing expression. He

only responded when she dropped her eyes. "Can't. Have to do the walking first—pick up some stuff. In fact, I'm about two minutes behind my time as it is."

"Oh, all right. I'll keep it here and you can pay for it then."

"Will you be here this afternoon?"

"I'm afraid so. No rest for the weary. I'll be right here until closing—5:30. And I work tomorrow, in case you can't get back today."

"At this time?"

"Yes, I go to lunch at 12:45 every day I work." She looked at her watch. "Ten minutes from now." She was surprised that he nodded as if he knew her schedule.

"Great. Thanks so very much. You've really helped me out."

"You're most welcome. Oh, and remember when you do bring your lady friend for the tour, be sure to visit all three floors and the Sculpture Garden."

"I will. She'll completely flattened by seeing the museum for the first time and then hearing me carry on so intelligently about modern art. Thanks again. Goodbye."

"Goodbye." After the man left the gift shop, she placed the large volume in a bag and realized he'd forgotten to leave his name. But that was fine. She'd remember him easily enough. Yet something else now struck her as most strange. His lady friend was such a devotee of modern art, and she'd never been to the Hirshhorn? The woman shrugged. Perhaps the woman was from out of town.

• • • • •

As he walked west toward the Washington Monument, the man smiled at how perfectly things had gone in the gift shop. She really was a lovely woman—twenty-eight years old, her brand

151

new hair style just perfect for the shape of her face. Earlier he'd looked directly into the faces of the other three women he had killed, knowing that eventually they'd help pay for his past pain and disgrace. Two he had spoken with at the softball fields, the other at a formal reception at the Kennedy Center. And now he had exchanged pleasantries with the fourth.

He reached 14th Street still thinking of perfection. And of the numbers "20-18-11-19-07." Into his mind sprang the words of Descartes—a philosopher his father had encouraged him to read before entering the university: "Perfect numbers like perfect men are very rare." He reached for the candy bar in his coat pocket. Surprisingly, he felt hungry.

Chapter 13

Alyona Novikova lay on her stomach, her face wedged between two pillows. The covers had slipped below her buttocks. Her hair was still up; the nightshirt she wore was bunched above her shoulder blades.

She lifted her head and shot out her right arm toward the clock radio. She slapped her fingers down three times before finally cutting the sound. It was 10:00 a.m. L.A. time. Her visitor would be here in an hour. He had stood her up the night before, and she was still angry.

She had prepared herself impeccably. The new dress and shoes, the nails and hair. Ready at 11:00 p.m., perfectly primed to be charming, witty, and alluring enough to make her very best impression. And now she'd be looked over and otherwise evaluated before eleven in the morning. It wasn't fair, she thought. A bad sign. A very bad sign.

Agent Hendrix apologized profusely when he called last night at 11:10. She could tell he was upset that his colleague from the California Bureau of Investigation had failed to let him know earlier that he couldn't make the scheduled time. As a result, the agent wouldn't be bringing a representative from the film project, as originally planned, but Hendrix assured her he'd arrange another opportunity for her to meet with this person—this time one-on-one, without the CBI agent, which Alyona much preferred.

Again, she had volunteered to speak of her relationship with Senator Roper on the phone, and again her offer was rejected. Hendrix reiterated that he had let his colleague know that the man's last-second cancellation demonstrated a lack of professionalism and respect for Alyona and her valuable time.

•　　•　　•　　•　　•

The knock came at 11:03. She took one last look in the mirror and adjusted the hair draped across the edge of her right eye. She took a deep breath and opened the door.

"Ms. Novikova?"

"Yes, hello. You must be Agent--."

"Arnold. Barry Arnold."

She extended her hand and asked him to come in. "Coffee?"

"No, thank you. I'm fine. But please have some yourself."

"All right." She took his hint and poured herself half a cup. When she returned from the kitchen, she was smiling broadly. She was tickled by the fact that he looked much more like a casting director than a CBI agent. His hair was longer than she expected of someone in his field—the sandy-blond locks resting low on his forehead, touching his eyebrows.

"What's so amusing, Ms. Novikova, if I may ask?"

"Oh, nothing. And please call me Alyona." She couldn't help thinking that in a sense she was auditioning, even if he wasn't the person who could open any casting doors for her. She sat across from him in her favorite plush chair, while he sat on the sofa. He took a quick glance at her legs as she crossed them, but

154

she thought nothing of it, for he was a man who interviewed scores of beautiful women in the L.A. area.

"All right, Alyona, I won't take up too much of your time. Let's talk about your relationship with Senator Thomas Roper.

"All right." She hoped he'd be satisfied with what she could tell him. It wouldn't be all that much, really.

"Do you mind?" He pulled a small recorder out of the pocket of his suit coat.

"Oh. Do I have to be recorded?"

"It's standard, Alyona. If we use anything you say, this protects you, see? This way you'll be quoted accurately."

"I'm sorry to be such a...I don't know...a bother, but if I say something and I realize I misspoke, can we erase what I said and start the answer over?"

"Oh yes, I promise. I'll rewind and you'll hear what you said just before the part you want erased and then we'll record over what you don't want anyone to hear."

"Thank you. It's just that I've never done this kind of interview before." She hated that she sounded so inexperienced. Surely, they wouldn't hold that against her.

"Don't even mention it. Have you ever heard your own voice in a film? Or are you one of those actors who never watch or listen to anything they do on screen?"

"A little, but...." Alyona blanched at the memory of how her voice sounded in those fourteen adult films—not only the jaded dialogue and expressions she was forced to utter but also the many wordless but audible demands of the "script." She found the look he gave her inscrutable. Was it possible that Agent Arnold knew of her previous film career?

"All right, here we go." He pressed the record button. "Alyona, when did you first meet Thomas Roper?"

She answered his several questions truthfully and as fully as she could. Still unable to accept that Arnold wasn't the one who would evaluate her poise, voice, and personality, she found herself attempting to modulate her volume and inject various emotions into her replies. It reminded her of the horrible acting classes she took when she first arrived in Los Angeles. The wearisome and banal scenarios—trapped on an elevator with eight panicky persons and other such nonsense.

"So, you believed that you and Senator Roper had a future?"

She merely nodded. It was too painful to offer an answer. She lifted her coffee cup but her hand shook too much so she put it back down without taking a sip. Had Arnold seen her hand tremble?

"Did the problem between you two have anything to do with the way he treated you?"

"No, nothing like that."

Arnold reached down and stopped the recorder. He rewound it to the spot right before she gave her terse answer.

"Alyona, I think that you'll want to answer that a little differently."

"But why? I don't think that I--."

"Excuse me for interrupting, but such an answer hardly makes this interview worthwhile." He paused for a moment. "You understand that, don't you?"

She was troubled by his characterization. "I suppose, but I can't say something that really isn't true."

"Look, Alyona." She was taken aback by his tone. He sounded strict, like a schoolmaster from another era. "He must have treated you in some way to make the relationship come to a premature end, right?"

"Well, yes. But...."

"No. I'm afraid that's not an answer we can appreciate. I think if you go back you'll agree that you weren't happy with the way he had treated you when you broke up."

She was growing anxious at his stern demeanor, but she knew he was right. She hated that Roper had treated her like some immoral slut when he found out about the films she had made. "All right."

"Wait." He turned on the recorder. "Go ahead."

"I wasn't at all happy with the way he treated me when we broke up." She didn't even realize that she had used Arnold's exact words.

He asked three other questions, eliciting the same admission of unhappiness from her. "All right, Alyona. One more question. We're almost done. "Did he treat you badly over something relating to sex?"

Her eyes welled with tears. She couldn't get the memory of what Roper had said to her that night. Without considering context or consequence, she replied, "Yes."

"I see."

"Wait, wait. Please turn that off. Go back, go back. That sounded wrong." She had completely lost her composure. Her eye liner was starting to bleed from the tears spilling onto her cheeks. "Let me explain what I meant by that."

"All right, please do." He didn't touch the recorder.

She froze. She couldn't tell him. She couldn't let him know exactly why Tom Roper had called it off between them. Or exactly what she meant when she said that sex was a reason for the break up. She knew she'd never get a role in a legitimate movie or TV career if she admitted to having been in pornographic films.

"Alyona, it was his fault, right? What he demanded of you sexually? What you refused to do for or to him?"

She felt her heart breaking. Her head sunk as her hands came up to cover her eyes. She had to answer with a lie. It was the only way she could escape her horrid past and have a chance. Just a chance. That's all she wanted.

"Yes, it's true."

Arnold shut off the recorder and put it into his coat pocket. "Thank you so much, Ms. Novikova." His eyes now stared at the exposed part of her legs, above her knees. She knew he was making his mind up about something. And she knew what it was. She tried to pull her short sundress further down her thighs.

"I wonder if you'd mind my using your bathroom."

She barely pushed out the words. "No. It's back there." She managed to lift her hand and point to the area directly behind her.

As Arnold closed the bathroom door behind him, she wiped her cheeks with the back of her hand. She brought the bottom of her legs up on the seat's cushion and curled herself in a fetal position.

She knew now she'd been set up. Neither Hendrix nor Arnold was a law enforcement agent of any kind. Neither of course was the man's real name. And they surely knew of the filthy movies she had made—many still available on VHS or transferred since to DVD. There would be no audition. She would never have a respectable film career.

She wanted to crawl back in bed under the covers and hide from the realization that she had betrayed Tom Roper—the man she once and still loved. To call him would be impossible. How could she tell him what she'd done? Years earlier, her honesty had left her emotionally devastated. She wouldn't allow herself to repeat the same mistake. Soon he'd know what she'd done to betray him. She didn't want to hear what he'd call her and how he'd express his regret that he had ever known her. No, she couldn't let herself hear any of that. She thought of a fellow performer in adult films who had ended her life when she couldn't live with herself any longer. Alyona put her hands to her ears as if to block the sound of the self-accusations growing louder in her head. She barely felt the gloved hand pull her wrist away before the shot entered her temple. She would never feel the small pistol being placed in her hand or the sound of Barry Arnold quickly opening and closing the apartment door behind him.

•　•　•　•　•

"Tom, you just need to sit on these feeling for a while. I'd say nothing about this to anyone. Look, I understand why you feel the way you do, but we need men like you in the Senate. Hell, we need *you* in the Senate. Okay, end of sermon. I'm paying for lunch."

"Usually the clergyman *asks* for money after his sermon, Tripp."

"Yeah, I know. That's why I didn't follow my father's footsteps and enter the ministry."

Roper appreciated Tripp Wilcox's support, perspective, and especially his sense of humor. "Your counsel is welcome, Tripp. It's just that I feel uncomfortable being here for the next five years when my heart isn't likely to be in it."

"Tom, don't think of it as five more years." Wilcox paused, an impish smile beginning to form on his lips. "Think of it as 1,825 days. No, wait, you're already into your second year now — so 1,811 days, give or take a day or two."

Roper smiled at his friend's facility with numbers. Wilcox often took impish glee in dazzling friends, reporters, and witnesses with rapid-fire addition, division, and multiplication, all done in his head.

"What's on your mind, Tom? You seem far away."

"Nothing. Just thinking about Grayson's murder—and Ian Arrington's."

"I got you, brother."

In truth Roper was thinking about the number Wilcox had just quoted to him. 1,811. 18 and 11. The second and third numbers in the killer's string of five. But again, were these reliable clues by the killer or some kind of sadistic numbers game meant only to frustrate and confuse?

"Excuse me, Tripp. I need to get this." Roper reached for his cell. "Hello? Really? Okay, I'll come right back."

"What is it, Tom?"

"Seems I've been getting a bunch of emails the last hour asking me to take back what I said to Browning and at least apologize to the Bureau for the implications of my remarks."

"Do tell."

•   •   •   •   •

Two hours later, Roper called Robyn.

"Tom? I was just thinking of you."

"Just seeing how you are, Robyn." There was little life in his voice.

"Tom, are you all right?"

"Yes. Yes, I'm fine. I'm....

She waited for him to continue. "Tom?"

"Forgive me, Robyn. It's just been a bit chaotic around here this afternoon. Look, I need to go. Just wanted to say hello and see how your day's been."

Given his low spirits, she decided to share the events at Meridian Hill Park at another time. She also thought it best to wait until later to inform him that Metro had called to ask her to help arrange a time for Senator Roper to talk. And a colleague informed her that the Secret Service was also anxious to sit down with him, and would she be able to assist them as well? It seemed that Metro and the Secret Service were at least respectful of Roper's office—none wishing to embarrass the senator by coming to Capitol Hill or to the Hart Senate Office Building. Then it struck him that Browning might arrange for the Bureau to speak with him as well.

"Tom, I'll be finished here at 4:45. So how about cocktails, dinner, and Netflix?

"Robyn, that sounds perfect, but it will have to be later, I'm afraid. I need to go out to Kendall Livingstone's as a short follow-up to my visit Tuesday night."

"Can't you just call him?"

"I've been trying but I've had no luck reaching him at the house. And I don't have his cell number. He's always out in his office from 6:30 until 10:30, so I'm going to catch him before they eat and he begins work on the book." Roper didn't mention he also wanted to check out the area for clues regarding the shot fired at his car the other night. "I should be back by 6:15 to 6:30. Have the cocktails ready then, okay?"

After hanging up, Roper thought more about the unusual email traffic coming through his office. Roper's entire staff was surprised at the pace of these emails, some coming individually, others in batches of five or six. Back in his office, Roper read some twenty of them. Several messages implored him to apologize or refine his comments as a gesture of good will— with a few noting that he'd made his point and that the Bureau would make sure to be more careful the next time. Others flatly criticized him for political grandstanding. Still others praised him for what he'd done but suggested he end the "war with Browning" owing to the need for cooperation between the

Bureau and Congress. A couple of them remarked that the FBI's over-aggressiveness was necessary "to protect this country in these dangerous times."

Interestingly, the emails were all roughly the same length—three lines or less. All were signed—most purporting to be from his home state. The addresses were all different, but Roper knew damn well that this was some orchestrated effort on the part of Sheridan Browning. But after a few moments of further reflection, Roper wondered why Browning would use such a transparent tactic. In addition, it didn't at all seem like Browning to hand over his sword like this, because these appeals all suggested surrender, a desire for a cessation of hostilities. Roper was perplexed. What the hell was Browning up to? Nathan Roper had taught his son active distrust and skepticism, but Roper wondered if he'd learned his father's lesson too well.

"Senator?"

"Yes, Melanie."

"You better read this."

Roper read the email on staffer Melanie Sheffield's screen. It wasn't like the others. Not at all. There was but a single sentence.

"Senator, the past is prologue. YOUR past is prologue."

There was no signature. "Melanie, see what you can find out about the sender."

"But look." She was obviously shaken, as she scrolled down and opened another email—the same message verbatim but from a different sender. "Senator, what's going on?"

"I don't know, Melanie. I really don't know."

• • • • •

"Marta, the president wants you to visit every member of the committee personally."

"Of course."

"Except Senator Roper."

White House congressional liaison Marta Taubman lifted the pen from her notepad. "I don't understand, Mr. Goldman."

"There's nothing for you to understand, Marta. The president thinks—and I agree—that Roper doesn't need a personal visit."

"But, and forgive me for asking, isn't it going to look rather odd if I see every member of the committee but one. What would be the explanation for the snub? What if I'm asked by Senator Roper, or by Senator McCrimmon, or by someone in the Capitol Hill press core?"

Marta watched Goldman take his feet off his desk. He quickly got out of his chair and walked to where she was sitting. She knew he liked to intimidate her by pressing the distance between them, standing so close as to make their difference in height all the more pronounced. And Goldman was a tall man. But this time he stopped within three feet of where she was sitting. He thrust his hands into his pockets and smiled.

"Good point, Marta. A very good point. Tell you what you do. Don't visit the minority's junior committee member either."

"Senator Yeomans?"

"She's the one. Now, remember that tomorrow afternoon the president wants you to be in the Roosevelt Room for photos with the document from Archives." Goldman took a step back and half turned his body in a clear signal that she should leave now.

Marta stood and smiled genuinely. "Please tell President Bedingfield how much I'm looking forward to being part of the photo shoot. My father will be--."

"The president understands, Marta. Oh, and he wants you to talk to the first lady the entire time we're there. Good bye, Marta."

The phone rang as she left his office. "This is Goldman. Go ahead, tell me.... Wait—wait. Just hold it. God damn it, hold it. For now do nothing more than what I asked you to do." Goldman hung up without the slightest nod toward cordiality.

•　•　•　•　•

At 4:55 p.m., Roper made the turn onto the Livingstones' long dirt driveway. He glanced to his right and took in the tree line flanking the property. How far in or down toward the farmhouse had the shot come from? Perhaps he'd ask Livingstone to walk the area with him. Livingstone might even point out a few trails that could lead to some kind of clue. Roper was finding it almost impossible to fight against the view that it was simply a stray shot from a nocturnal hunter, especially with all that had happened in the past several days: the murders of Grayson and Arrington, the man standing in the shadow of the street light, Lena's menacing visitor, and now emails with the identical message: "Senator, the past is prologue. YOUR past is prologue."

Roper was relieved to see both the Livingstone cars and the lights on inside the living room. After several unsuccessful knocks on the front door, he headed around back. As he began to make the turn from the side to the rear of the house, he thought he heard something moving among the trees to his right. He halted and looked for a place to conceal himself. He was quickly disappointed by his cowardice. "What the hell am I doing?" he muttered. The noise was likely an animal of some kind. Nothing more than an audible manifestation of the environment.

Moving slowly so he wouldn't startle anyone, Roper approached the kitchen window and listened for the sound of voices. He heard nothing. The lights of the kitchen were on but no one was there. What if they were in the bedroom? With Livingstone's insistence on four hours of uninterrupted writing and editing in his gazebo office every night, perhaps he and Sandra wished to catch up on some lovemaking.

As Roper tried to make up his mind about what to do next—he certainly didn't wish to rap on the bedroom window—he glanced behind him to the gazebo. The soft light from its window suggested Livingstone might be working already. Perhaps he and Sandra were eating dinner out there. But something seemed odd: Roper didn't see any smoke rising from the woodstove chimney—and it was cold out.

Roper walked to the door on the right side of the gazebo. He knocked. After ten seconds, he knocked again. Once more he heard rustling in the trees behind him. He paid no attention to that now, because his hand was on the doorknob. If the door was locked, he'd wander about the property and perhaps call out to them. But the doorknob turned easily.

He took in the dreadful scene in front of him. More out of respect for the deceased than from the chill of the air entering the office, Roper closed the door behind him. His mind flooded back to the photographs he viewed of the thirty-one civilian casualties who had perished because he hadn't done enough to prevent their deaths in 1998. The unrecognizable facial features, the displacement of limbs, the twisted positions of the bodies. The macabre mingling of wet and dried blood.

Roper made a feeble attempt to ascertain if there was life in either body, but he had only to breathe to know that they both were dead and had been for some time. He saw Livingstone's cell phone, but didn't touch it, in the unlikely possibility that the killer had left prints. Roper's cell was in his car. He needed to retrieve his phone immediately and call the police.

But he hesitated, absorbing the gruesome scene before him, knowing that Kendall and Sandra were victims of the same man who murdered Grayson, Arrington, and their female companions. But Roper didn't see a note in Livingstone's frozen hand—a note containing the five numbers, with the third one crossed out. He looked on the floor near the body but saw nothing. At a slight distance he examined Sandra's body, keeping his eyes off the brutal damage that had been done to her head. She was in a state of undress, a winter coat draped across her almost sideways and covering the area from her lower back to her upper thigh. But he didn't see any initials in blood on her exposed parts, and he couldn't bring himself to remove the coat to find the bloody signature that was surely there.

He looked around the office for the note. It had to be there. Then he heard the hum of Livingstone's computer. Turning, he saw that the screen was black. But he detected lines on the dark screen. Marks made in blood—an X. Roper took the knuckle of his right index finger and tapped the mouse. The screen came alive. There they were—printed on an otherwise blank page of Livingston's manuscript—the five numbers. The X was placed on the screen exactly over the third number—the "11."

Roper knew he had to leave the scene and call the police. But he'd only taken a single step toward the door when he noticed the knob beginning to turn. He heard the soft thud of something metallic pressing into the wood as the door began to open. In a moment Roper saw the barrel of a weapon appear between the edge of the door and the jamb. The door opened further. When enough of the barrel was visible, Roper launched himself forward, placing both hands around the barrel. With his left foot, he scooped the door fully open. In one continuous movement, he shoved the barrel of the gun forward as hard as he could.

In a second he was outside the gazebo office, on top of the person holding the rifle. Roper quickly moved his left hand down toward the stock and began pressing the weapon on the chest of the person under him.

"What are you doing? What are you doing?" The words came out in a high-toned squeal. Roper moved his head so the light from the office behind him could illuminate the speaker's face. It was a teenage boy.

"Get off me, Mister. Get off me!" The boy winced, expecting to be struck by the rifle now completely in Roper's grip.

Heavily breathing, Roper got off the boy. "Stand up. What are you doing out here?"

"Let me have my hunting rifle back." The boy was already regaining some of his petulance. He was obviously the neighbor's middle son the Livingstones had told him about.

"Not until you tell me what you're doing out here." Roper looked at the weapon. "What kind of rifle is this?"

"It's a Winchester 70. I got it for Christmas. Let me have it back. I'm...I'm not supposed to have it when it's dark out. Let me have it back." He sounded desperate.

"First tell me what you're doing over here."

The boy was looking toward the open door of the gazebo office. "I just came over to say hello to the Livingstones."

Roper could easily tell he was lying. "With a Winchester?"

"What was going on in there? Why are you here, Mister?"

Roper didn't want to get into a "You tell me first" exchange with the boy. "What's your name, son?"

"Brian Felton. What's yours?"

"Tom Roper. Look, Brian, something horrible has happened to the Livingstones."

"What, what?" The Felton boy started toward the door.

"No, no." Roper blocked him from the door, which he now shut. "I'm going to call the police now—so you better go home and tell your parents that the police may want to talk to you."

"Are the Livingstones dead?" The boy's eyes were wide open.

"Yes."

"Oh, man." Brian stared at Roper, who was still holding the Winchester. He spoke in a deliberate yet excitable voice. "You're not going to kill me, are you, Mister?"

"Don't be ridiculous. Here." Roper gave him back the rifle. "Now go home and tell your parents you'll need to talk to the police."

"I'm not going to get in trouble, am I?"

"Have you done anything you could get in trouble for, Brian?" The boy didn't answer. "Brian, tell me one thing. Did you take a shot at my car the other night as I was driving away?"

The boy's face dropped. "No, sir." Now his face regained its animation. "But I saw who did. I didn't see his face, but I saw him, sir. I was out there when I shouldn't have been and heard the shot."

"Do you know where it came from?"

"Oh yes, sir." Roper was struck by the boy's sudden and respectful manner.

"Show me. We'll walk to my car. I have to get my cell phone and call the police first. Then you'll show me."

"You don't have to walk to your car, sir. Here." The boy pulled out his own cell. "Tell the police that I'm cooperating with the investigation. Okay?"

Chapter 14

Roper called Robyn at 6:00 p.m. to say he was talking to the Prince George's County police out at the Livingstones. She didn't have to be told why—she could tell from the somber tone of Roper's voice. He filled her in on the crime scene as best he could, including the third number crossed out in blood on the computer screen and the initials "I" and "S" found on Sandra Livingstone's bare breasts.

"Robyn, I'm thinking it might be a good idea for you to go home to New Hampshire."

"What are you talking about, Tom?"

"Damn it, Robyn, I'm worried for your safety. Don't you see? All three of these victims have known me—all were friends in various degrees and we all played on the same softball team." He hesitated for a moment. "And I didn't want to tell you this, but someone took a shot at my car when I left here Tuesday night."

"What? Tuesday night? And you didn't tell me?" She heard his sigh. "Tom, then why did you go back there—and all alone?"

"I'll explain when I see you. Can you have a colleague from

Metro come over and sit with you until I get there? I still have more with the police here in Maryland. It may take a while before I can make it your place." She said nothing. "Robyn? Robyn, what is it?"

"Nothing. I'm just scared for *you*, Tom." She refused to tell him about the shots fired at Joan of Arc statue—likely fired at *her*. If she told him now, he'd personally drive her home to Concord, she was sure. And there was still the possibility that she was just in the wrong place at the wrong time. "Tom, Metro wants to talk to you formally about the murders."

"I'm surprised they waited this long."

"And the Secret Service."

"Jesus Christ. And now I'll have a third serial killing to discuss with them. And of course something about how all three murders seem to be pointing at me as one of thr two remaining victims."

After he hung up, Roper felt the gentle tap on his shoulder.
"Senator?"
"Yes?"
"Rod Pryor. I'm with the homicide unit."

"Right. I think I answered a couple of your questions earlier, didn't I?"

"Yes, sir. But I'd like you to go over a few other things again if you don't mind."

"Okay."

"You said you knew Mr. Grayson and Mr. Arrington fairly well?"

"Mr. Grayson more personally. But yes, I knew them fairly well."

"Now, you say you were out here Tuesday night."

"Yes."

"And you said that you and Mr. Livingstone talked about his

book manuscript."

"Yes."

"And you left that night and haven't been back out here since."

"Right."

"And how would you characterize your relationship with Mr. Livingstone? And Mrs. Livingstone."

"Excuse me, Detective Pryor, but what are you suggesting?"

"In all honesty, Senator, I'm simply trying to satisfy not only myself but others above me that there really is no reason to arrest you."

"Others above you?"

"Yes, sir."

· · · · ·

"Mr. President?"

"Yes, Jerry."

"Some news from Maryland."

"And?"

"I just received a call...."

"Go ahead, Jerry."

"Kendall Livingstone and his wife were murdered at their farmhouse in Maryland."

Bedingfield stood up from his Oval Office desk and turned his back on his chief of staff. "When?"

"Probably last night."

"I see. And..."

"Looks just like the murders of Marshall Grayson and the other one—Arrington. Shall I give you details?"

"No."

Goldman noted that Bedingfield's right hand was extended somewhat, his forearm moving slightly back and forth. He's seen the president do this before when his boss was thinking through a problem. Bedingfield was rubbing the top edge of his ceremonial letter opener. He raised his head. "What about Livingstone's manuscript?"

"Working on that now."

"I see." The president finally turned around. "Thank you, Jerry."

"One more thing, Mr. President."

"Yes?"

"Tom Roper was the one who discovered the bodies. The police have...they've been talking to him at the scene."

•　•　•　•　•

"Thanks for coming back, Bobby. I'm sorry to call while you were on the way home."

"Is anything wrong, Senator?"

"I suppose I owe you an explanation, for why I had you...."

"No. You don't. Really, you don't."

"Please sit down, Bobby."

Gleeson took a seat in Carol McCrimmon's Senate office. The majority leader began her characteristic pacing in front of her desk. Gleeson noted something rather unusual—she had her shoes off.

She easily detected his discomfort. "Bobby, I understand why you feel upset. I want you to know that I--."

He stood back up. "No, I'm fine. Just tell me what you need me to do?"

"Can you at least sit back down?" He immediately complied, folding his hands in front of his lap like a schoolboy in a Rockwell painting.

"I've been beating myself up the last several hours about those emails."

Gleeson expected as much. What she'd asked him to do earlier was very much out of character for her. "I understand, Senator."

She snapped at him for his matter-of-fact response. "No, I don't think you do. What...what do you have to do to...to...?"

"To stop the emails from being sent to Senator Roper?" She stood directly in front of him. Her eyes were fully open, her lips bent in a sneer. He looked to his left. "Senator, it's easy. If you want them stopped, I'll do it right now." She remained silent. He could tell she was conflicted. "Want me to have them stopped now?"

McCrimmon turned and walked back to her desk, pausing for a moment before sitting. Finally realizing that her shoes weren't on her feet, she bent down to retrieve them.

Gleeson softened his voice. "Senator? Do you want me to stop the emails from being sent?"

Having put on both shoes, she sat squarely back in her plush desk chair. "No, Bobby, not now. Perhaps tomorrow. I'll let you know. Go home. I'm sorry that I.... never mind."

"Then I'll see you tomorrow, Senator."

"Bobby. You understand what I asked you to do is not that uncommon. Believe me when I say it's not meant to hurt Senator Roper, but only to...and that you can never say anything to anyone that you were asked...that I asked you to...."

"Senator, I do understand—I really do. I will never say anything about this. Not to Senator Roper, not to anyone."

"Thank you, Bobby."

Gleeson showed himself out.

Carol McCrimmon dropped her head. She'd resolved to act according to her conscience but had buckled. She knew that if she didn't do as Devin Cassell had specifically advised, her earlier extramarital sexual indiscretion with one of the oil companies' biggest lobbyists would be made public in a way that would certainly disgrace her—ending any chance that in three years' time she'd become the first woman vice president in U.S. history. She believed she had had no choice but to pull her young staffer Robert Gleeson into it, because she was certain the more senior members of her staff would refuse to do what she requested.

She couldn't help feeling that in spite of the affection she felt for Gleeson and her sense that he'd remain loyal to a fault, she had now placed him in a position of ascendancy over her. How might he use these actions against her, perhaps not now but during the 2016 campaign? What might he ask for? Perhaps she could retain his loyalty by promising an important position in the vice president's office. She let out a long sigh thinking that she'd have brought him with her regardless. Now he'd see that it would be at least partly in exchange for his continued discretion. Sure. It was simple. She'd provide him with a job and status *he* would be loath to sacrifice for the sake of conscience or any other motive.

·　·　·　·　·

The man dropped several quarters into a vending machine. For some reason he thought a cold soft drink would be perfect as an end-of-a-very-long-day beverage. When he first came to town, his colleagues thought it odd that he chose not to have that seventh or eighth cup of coffee right before calling it day, as they did. He paused two seconds after hearing each coin drop to make sure that the machine would credit the next one correctly. He refused whenever possible to use a debit or credit card to make beverage or snack purchases.

As in everything he did, he had to follow procedure—a

chronology—without deviation. Even if the goal could be reached by ignoring all preceding steps, doing so would violate his commitment to balance and order. He believed that no great event had ever been accomplished capriciously, no matter what some might argue. Sequence was vital. The numbers had to follow an unalterable pattern. Each number was sacrosanct, holding vital meaning and purpose.

After he had his numbers taken away and all the words put before him by his mother and father, he had circled one of the Latin mottos he found in a volume of Poe short stories that his father suggested he read: *"Nemo me impune lacessit"*—"No one attacks me with impunity." He found both solace and inspiration in several characters of Poe, shrewd and patient men who took their time in exacting their revenge.

Leaning against the vending machine as he enjoyed his soft drink, the man checked the time. 6:35 p.m. Only a few hours until he'd breathe life into the fourth number of the five—19. Breathe life. He wasn't even cognizant of the irony, as he half-whispered the words of W.E.B. Du Bois: "When you have mastered numbers, you will in fact no longer be reading numbers, any more than you read words when reading books. You will be reading meanings."

•   •   •   •   •

On his way to Robyn's, Roper decided to stop at his place for a change of clothing. It was now 7:45 p.m. He was still shaken by the fact that someone of high rank in Maryland law enforcement or more likely in the FBI was actually contemplating his arrest.

After Roper had answered another dozen questions and offered several assurances that his whereabouts on Wednesday night could be accounted for, Detective Pryor had excused himself to take a call, part of which Roper heard.

"So now I should apologize for intimating that he might be held? I'm confused. Yes, yes, I know. But I thought you were contemplating...Sorry. But can I ask who prompted the change of heart? Someone from Washington, I assume?" After getting his reply, Pryor's shoulders dropped as he emitted a frustrated sigh. "Yes, sir, I'm well aware of that fact. I'm just curious to know. He'll ask me why I hinted that he might be arrested, and...." Pryor had turned around and saw Roper standing a mere six feet away from him.

On the road back to Washington, Roper again thought of Robyn. If he couldn't convince her to return to New Hampshire, he was going to spend every night with her. He felt he had to protect her, regardless of her protestations. Someone had threatened Lena Roseboro. It was only a matter of time before Robyn would be approached or, worse, harmed in some way. Suddenly he realized that his being with Robyn might put her in more danger, not less.

Nearing his place, he was careful to check the sidewalk and each street light for anyone looking out of place. He'd spent most of the drive from Maryland adding Kendall and Sandra Livingstone's deaths to the patchwork of evidence relating to the killings he'd so far awkwardly sewn together. Again, the male victim was someone he had known—someone with whom he had played softball.

The murders of the males were uniform. A fairly large knife thrust in the back or swiped across the neck. The three women suffered different fates. One garroted, one stabbed with a smaller weapon in the neck, the last apparently bludgeoned with what Roper wasn't sure. The five-numbered notes—the first placed in the male victim's hand, the second down his sweater and shirt, and the third on a computer screen. Each one with a bloody cross-out of the matching number. "20-18-11." The "19" and 07" remained on the list. Two more planned victims. That the first three had been killed in only a matter of a few days suggested that the killer would strike again very soon.

He considered the murdered women. Not the principle victim in each killing, he still believed, but seemingly important to the serial killer for some twisted ancillary purpose. It seemed inconceivable that they'd be killed merely to provide a surface to accommodate the letters, while the numbers were left in a more traditional manner. The three women had initials daubed in blood on the buttocks, lower legs, and breasts. "M.T."— "L.R"—and now "I.S." Or were they not initials but simply letters?

Again, Roper tried to arrange the letters in his mind. Did they spell out a name or location? Or some kind of justification for these killings? He varied the order. "SIMLRT"? "MRLIST"? "RISTLM"? He saw possibilities, especially in MRLIST—could this be part of a name a "Mr. List-something, but he'd need more letters—another vowel at least before he could shape a useful name or anagram of any kind. Roper squeezed his fingers into the steering wheel and cursed his wish. For him to have what he wanted—that additional vowel—would mean the brutal slayings of two more persons.

Parking his car, Roper had yet another disturbing thought. What if these letters—ten obviously planned in all—stood for one person to be affected, frightened, or assaulted in some way—if not killed? For example, Lena Roseboro's initials were accounted for in the six left at the murder scenes. Robyn Meadows were also included among the six. As were his own. The three of them accounted for only four of the six letters, however. Who then was represented by the "I" and the "S"?

Roper walked to his door still ruminating on the initials of those whom he felt closest to. What of Tripp Wilcox? The "T" was there. Would the "W" be left on the next female victim? He thought of Marta Taubman—the president's congressional liaison to whom he'd taken an immediate liking when he first came to the Senate. Her initials—like his, Robyn's, and Lena's—were accounted for in the six. So many with "M's" as first or last names. Carol McCrimmon. Max Nettleton. Edward Malloch, for Christ's sake. He began to think of "L's." The first name that came to mind was Laurie Eldridge, his mentor's daughter whom he had saved from being kidnapped.

He slammed his hand on the metal railing flanking his doorstep. He had to stop this line of thinking. Highly agitated, Roper pushed his front door open and turned on the lights. His place had been ransacked.

• • • • •

"I think he was too much of an iconoclast to rank among the best contemporary political reporters, Max, but my God, what had he done to deserve such an end as this?"

Max Nettleton thought the vice president was once more giving evidence of his incomprehensible political if not general naïveté. Surely he knew about Livingstone's book and what it was likely to say about Evan Bedingfield. Rumors were rife about the identities of the many unnamed sources who provided so much grist for the manuscript. Nettleton understood that the White House was chewing its nails over the forthcoming publication. He furthermore realized that the dust wouldn't settle on the book until late spring at the earliest. The book's publisher seemed unsympathetic, at least publicly, to the administration's concerns. There was no evidence that anyone had seen any of the unpublished manuscript, but no one had any doubts as to the potentially incendiary nature of Livingstone's work. Why should this book be any different from the kinds of articles the young reporter had been writing since first coming to the *Post*?

As Ed Malloch lamented the deterioration of modern journalistic standards, Nettleton thought only of what was going to happen to the manuscript and how it might reveal or suggest something that would be damaging to him personally. Had it been sent to the publisher piecemeal—chapter by chapter? Or had Livingstone been keeping all of it until he was finished with his own editing? Had he printed off any of it—perhaps placing a hard copy under lock and key? Or was it still in his computer's documents file or on a flash drive, precariously existing in an environment that would obliterate every word with the manipulation of single finger? Or was the flash drive locked away somewhere? Nettleton knew his counterpart in the White House was thinking the same thing.

Nettleton was well aware of Jerry Goldman's connections. Hell, they both had an assortment of eyes and ears reporting to them from every corner of the city and throughout Virginia and Maryland. It would be interesting to see how and if that manuscript surfaced. If it went missing, the *Post* would explode with accusations and forward a host of sinister scenarios—and they'd be right to do so. Nettleton expected the book would be published, but perhaps with some heavy edits the author would never have allowed had he lived. Would the publisher even know edits were made post-mortem?

"Max, damn it. I've kept you way too late. Look at the time. Now past eight. Go on home. My best to your wife and daughter."

"Thank you, sir. As I said, we do have company coming to the house tonight."

"Max, before you go. I seem to have misplaced the correspondence from the attorney general. It's about the ongoing investigation of Patrick Sims over at Justice. Did you see it?"

"No, sir, but I'll look. Want me to...now?"

"No, no. Go home, go home. Look first thing in the morning, though—okay?"

"I will."

Nettleton didn't have to look. He knew exactly where it was—still in the same place he put it after talking it off Malloch's desk.

Chapter 15

Roper found nothing missing from his apartment. The drawers of his desk and bureau had been pulled open and the contents within rifled through. Books and CDs had been yanked from their shelves to the floor below. The closet rummaged through—the pockets of all his pants and jackets apparently checked. Roper felt a twinge of satisfaction in the fact that he didn't have a safe to blow open. At least that item was in his Senate office.

The bedroom window provided the source of entry. After rigging a heavy blanket to block the cold air, Roper went outside to ascertain how the intruder had climbed up the six feet to the window. On the ground was his neighbor's step ladder, which he'd been using to clip some of his own and Roper's branches in the small backyard areas. Roper recalled that his neighbor was visiting his daughter in South Carolina.

Five minutes later, Roper opened the door to the police. The window was quickly repaired, and Roper willingly agreed on the installation of a security system. Metro assured him that his residence would be watched for the time being, and after answering additional questions about the break-in, he grabbed some clothing and headed to his car. When he got to the street he saw three men standing on the sidewalk waiting for him. Two from the Secret Service and one from Metro homicide. He grabbed his cell and told Robyn there'd be yet a further delay—probably a fairly long one.

·   ·   ·   ·   ·

"Jean, no need for you to go out. I'll stop at a convenience store and get some. I'm headed home now. Hang in there. Put a cold cloth to your head and your devoted spouse will have the Tylenol in your hands in less than twenty minutes."

Tripp Wilcox found the drive out to Bethesda as aggravating as usual, made even more so by the idiot following him a little too closely. He could make out that the driver wore a baseball cap but that was it. At least the son-of-a-bitch didn't have his high beams on. Pulling into the convenience store parking lot, Wilcox saw the car behind him slow down as it passed the store.

In line to purchase the Tylenol and a six-pack of beer, Wilcox glanced out the window and saw the same blue car pull into the parking lot from the opposite direction. Rather than park next to Wilcox's car, the driver parked at the very end of the lot—some ten to twelve feet beyond the convenience store.

Coming out of the store, Wilcox looked to his right and saw that the driver was not behind the wheel of the car. What the hell was going on? Without getting into his car, Wilcox placed the beer and the Tylenol on the front seat and locked the doors. Growing up in some of the most rugged terrain of South Dakota, he paid little attention to danger when his curiosity was aroused. He began walking toward the empty vehicle. He caught sight of the clock in the store. 9:40 p.m.

·   ·   ·   ·   ·

Max Nettleton settled down with his second extra dry martini. His wife and daughter hadn't yet returned from shopping. No company was coming tonight. That was only one of the many white lies Nettleton served up to Ed Malloch over the past several years—always garnished with the proper intonations and facial expressions to make them seem true. But deception and indirection were nothing foreign to Max Nettleton, whether in his personal or in his political life.

Until some six months ago, he had only one very brief and to his mind harmless affair in the fourth year of his marriage, one full of romantic interplay and intimacy but which stopped short of sexual intercourse—and his wife never found out. For the next fourteen years he never progressed past "innocent" lunch, drinks, or dinner with other women, which at times he embellished with a kiss or caress. The opportunity for sex presented itself in several instances, but Nettleton feared losing control of his political as well as personal life if he let it get that far. And control was what he had to have. He utterly hated that those in the White House had kept so much from him. He deeply resented the insult of being denied a place in the loop. Jerry Goldman never let him forget that he'd hitched his wagon to the wrong star when he stopped working for Governor Evan Bedingfield and took a senior position with the less impressive Ed Malloch.

And then this past July he met Maureen Blakely. He first laid eyes on her when she sauntered up to him at an outdoor 4th of July party hosted by the staff at Interior. Even though his wife and daughter were away in New York at a summer music camp, Nettleton was quite at home at the party, for he knew many of the guests. Every member of his history club was there, for example, along with representatives of almost every governmental department and every building flanking the

National Mall or situated on the east side of the Capitol. The guest list also included faculty at the American and George Washington Universities, Howard, and Georgetown. Five men and women from the Eisenhower Building were also in attendance—including his rival Marshall Grayson.

Although she'd apparently downed several frozen daiquiris before introducing herself, Maureen obviously wasn't a woman who'd lose control of her balance or her allure. Clearly she was a woman who knew what she wanted and how to get it. Thinking back now, Nettleton realized how foolish he'd been to ignore this trait as a warning. Instead, he'd judged it as an irresistible invitation to which he couldn't help responding. Had he been more perceptive that day, he would have noted that she had approached several other men in the same aggressive manner. What made him think he could ever give a woman like Maureen Blakely all she wanted from a man?

After spending less than thirty minutes in each other's company, they agreed to "bump into" each other at the JW Marriott on Pennsylvania Avenue for one or two drinks. Before July was out, they had seen each other seven times for lunch, drinks and, on one occasion, dinner. On the first weekend in August, when Nettleton's wife and daughter were on holiday in France with his in-laws, he and Maureen had sex for the first time—in another Washington hotel. Maureen had rented the room; Nettleton had been the "surprise visitor."

But Nettleton was completely put off by Maureen's exuberant sexuality and hardly functioned as a lover. The disappointment on her face said as much. Capitulating to masculine vanity, he was determined to perform successfully the next time they had sex. He required no pharmaceutical assistance. He just needed to clear his mind of guilt and take her as both he and she wanted.

Without enthusiasm, Maureen agreed to give him another opportunity to satisfy her. They met in a modest travel lodge across the Potomac the following Wednesday night, after he completed his work at the Eisenhower Building. The minute she pulled the covers back from the bed, Nettleton sensed that again he'd be unable to perform sexually. Burning with humiliation, he simply stood in the room as she lay nude on the bed, spreading her legs and touching herself. He deemed the whole scene appalling.

"Maureen, please don't."

She removed her hand from between her legs and slammed it back against the headboard. "Can't get over your Sunday school training, is that it?" Her face registered the disdain she felt for the pathetic man standing before her and the insult he had paid her. Yet she was not at all embarrassed by the fact that she was lying nude before him while he stood before the bed completely clothed, his hands now thrust deeply into his pockets. She hadn't even brought her legs together. "Good bye, Mr. Nettleton." The formality of her words slashed at his sensibilities.

He didn't see Maureen again after that night. Not even accidentally. For the rest of August and all of September he worried incessantly about her coming forward and telling others what they had done together—and how he had failed the second time. But he heard nothing. No one looked at him with a knowing expression. No one stopped chatting when he walked into a room. His wife didn't give any indication that she had suspicions.

But two months later he overheard Marshall Grayson speaking rhapsodically about his latest love interest—Maureen Blakely. The concerns about a revelation rushed back, and now Nettleton faced the added humiliation of Grayson's likely awareness of his sexual debility. Maureen surely must have told Grayson, knowing full well that both men were political rivals. But less than a month later, all concern and humiliation evaporated. Grayson and Maureen Blakely were both dead.

Nettleton finished his martini and dropped the second of the two olives into his mouth. Entering his den, he opened the safe and pulled out the sheets on which Marshall Grayson had explained why Patrick Sims might wish him dead. The information intended for Tom Roper's eyes only.

The memory was still vivid: Nettleton stepped into Grayson's office to inform him of a change of lunch plans with Ed Malloch and saw Grayson writing on a sealed white envelope. Grayson reacted peculiarly, as if he'd been caught watching porn on his office computer. He shoved the letter into a larger manila envelope and hurriedly wrote an address on it.

Grayson had given the manila envelope to one of the staff interns for delivery to Roper's office in the Hart Senate Building. After Grayson left the Eisenhower Building, Nettleton told the young intern that if he had any mail going to the Capital he'd be happy to take it over since he had a scheduled meeting with the majority leader, thereby saving the busy intern a trip. When the manila envelope was handed over, Nettleton took it straight to his office and opened it.

He drew out the white envelope, carefully unsealed it, and read the letter inside. He was stunned by the damning information Grayson had on Patrick Sims. But more devastating was what Grayson said he'd observed about Nettleton's own comings and goings and the actions Nettleton was taking to get Ed Malloch off the ticket in 2016.

Nettleton knew he couldn't simply burn or shred the letter and the envelopes. Grayson had probably told Roper to expect the material. Neither could Nettleton destroy only the section that spoke of his activities, for he was discussed on three of the pages. Besides, none of the pages ended with a complete paragraph so Roper would know something was missing and would of course contact Grayson. So after Nettleton secured the lengthy letter in his own safe, he took several sheets of blank paper, folded them, and placed them in another white envelope, which he sealed with plenty of scotch tape. He then placed the envelope in another manila folder and wrote Roper's address on it. And just as he promised the intern, Nettleton took it to the Hart Senate Office Building and dropped it on one of the staff person's desks without anyone seeing him do so.

In the aftermath of this reminiscence, Nettleton wondered if the senator had by now opened the sealed envelope and saw the blank pages. Surely he had.

•　•　•　•　•

Given the peculiar and to his mind insulting questioning by Detective Pryor, Roper was grateful that Metro and the Secret Service agreed to a joint and, more important, brief interview. Returning to the kitchen of his apartment, the four men sat around his table while others from Metro wrapped up their investigation of the premises. During the questioning, Roper noted that Metro detective Scott Garrison, whom he had met through Robyn, said very little. The detective jotted down an occasional note, but mainly listened and kept his eyes glued on Roper's. Roper couldn't be sure, but it seemed as though Garrison knew something he didn't. Roper wanted to signal him to stay so he could satisfy his hunch. But it was unnecessary, for when the two Secret Service agents left—content that the senator would be available in the next few days whenever they chose to speak with him—Garrison hung back. Clearly he wanted to speak with Roper about something important.

"Senator, she definitely doesn't want me to tell you this, but I think I should. Someone may have shot at Robyn earlier today."

It took Roper a moment to respond. "What do you mean *may* have shot?"

"She was supposed to meet someone claiming to be FBI this morning about another case she's working on. He told her to meet him in Meridian Hill Park. When she got there, he hadn't yet shown. Two shots were fired and both hit the statue she was standing under."

"But, again, you said *may* have shot at her. What did you mean?"

"There is a chance that they were stray shots fired at someone else—or just fired—perhaps at the statue of Joan of Arc. Or perhaps not."

Roper couldn't believe he hadn't yet asked. "Did she get hit?" Since he'd spoken to her several times, he knew it couldn't have been serious if she had, but he needed to know. "Did she?"

"No. That's one reason why we're thinking they were stray shots."

"Anyone apprehended?"

"Not yet. Look, Senator, she told me but insisted I not tell you. I just think you need to know. In fact, I'm betting she wants you to know in spite of what she said."

Roper thought about the shot fired at him and how he'd dismissed the notion that it was accidental. Unfortunately, he hadn't yet talked to young Brian Felton about the man the boy said he'd seen near the Livingstone house. Roper had called, but the boy's parents were too shaken up about the murder of their neighbors to allow anyone to speak with their son. They told the police that Brian had a propensity for making fictitious claims about whom he was with or whom he had seen do whatever he claimed was done and that Brian confessed in his bedroom that he really hadn't seen anyone. Roper was frustrated that the police let it go "at least for now," but there was nothing he could do. Roper was torn. The parents' depiction of their son as a child often living in a self-created fantasy world seemed more than plausible. Perhaps all three shots—the one fired at him and the two fired at Robyn—had less sinister explanations.

Garrison gave Roper his cell number and encouraged him to get in touch if he thought of anything else or if anything else happened that seemed related—even tangentially—to the serial killings. Roper decided not to mention Lena's frightening experience or the shot taken at him.

•   •   •   •   •

Tripp Wilcox pressed his large, powerful frame against the edge of the convenience store's outer wall. He was about to look around the corner to find out just what the hell the driver of the now vacant car was up to. But as he began to slide his head to the right, he stopped.

He recalled spending the day with members of the Sioux Falls police department when he first ran for the Senate. One of the more experienced officers told him that whenever he had to look around the edge of a building, he'd drop to his knee and look from a lower vantage point. If the suspect was armed and waiting to take a shot, he'd be focusing on a spot roughly at the officer's eye or chest level. So the officer could get a quick peek and cut down the odds that a suspect's bullet would find its mark.

Wilcox dropped to one knee and inched his head around the corner. He was surprised to find a pant leg only inches away from his face. He reached for the calf and for a moment had the one leg tightly in his large grip. He let go the second he heard the pistol shot.

The shot went somewhere above him, followed by a high-pitched grunt from the person now running toward the wooded area behind the store. Wilcox was on his stomach; in a second he was up and in pursuit of the person running toward the woods.

Wilcox never stopped to think of the foolhardiness of chasing someone with a loaded gun, who might at any time turn and fire a shot that would kill him. Since boyhood, Wilcox had always acted quickly on instinct. He sensed that the shooter was scared and wasn't likely to fire again. The original shot was probably an accident, a reaction to the surprise of the large hand grabbing his leg.

Fifty-one but still in impressive physical condition, Wilcox called out for the shooter to stop, but the man kept going, his baseball cap flying off as he ran into the woods. Wilcox's better sense finally kicked in, and he stopped his pursuit. He looked over his shoulder and saw the convenience store clerk staring at him, a flashlight in his hand, muttering "What? What happened?" He was about to signal to the man to stay back when a shot rang out from the woods, followed by a brief series of low moans.

In the woods, they saw the prone body immediately. Wilcox noticed the pistol lying only a foot away. He shined the light on the shooter's face. A man probably in his late twenties, perhaps early thirties.

For the next several seconds the man moaned softly, seeming to shape the words "I wasn't going to...I was told not to...."

Wilcox saw the blood seeping out from the waist area of the man's jeans. He'd obviously fallen and shot himself in the stomach. Wilcox gently shook the wounded man's shoulder. "What weren't you going to do? What were you told not to do?"

"Jesus. I tripped and...I...." He fell silent, reserving his rapidly ebbing strength for the last deep breaths he would ever take.

While the clerk ran back to the convenience store to phone an ambulance and the police, Wilcox searched the man's pants for any identification. There was no wallet, but he found four items in the front left pocket. Wilcox clicked on his pocket-sized flashlight and saw an airport printout suggesting that the man had earlier in the evening flown from L.A. to Washington. The second item was a local phone number following the initials "P.S." The third was an address, with apartment number, for an "Alyona N." Wilcox examined the remaining item—on a folded yellow post-it. Another address. His own.

•　　•　　•　　•　　•

She kissed him hello before he had the chance to drop his smile.

"Robyn, why didn't you tell me someone took a shot at you?"

"Damn that Scotty Garrison." She kissed Roper again and grinned nervously. "I was actually hoping he'd tell you. Anyway, how about a drink? You look like you could use one."

"What's that supposed to be? The understatement of the year?" Roper followed her into the kitchen.

"Here." She handed him some of the Kentucky bourbon Marshall Grayson had given her at Christmas.

"Scott didn't tell me who you went out to Meridian Hill Park to meet."

She took a swallow of Roper's bourbon. "FBI. Or so the caller said on the phone. I knew the name. Agent Myron Surrency. I had worked with him, although I'd never seen him. I was stupid. I admit it. But I figured a public park—broad daylight—

and the reason for his being there seemed plausible enough."

"So he didn't show?"

"Not only didn't show, but never went. I called the Bureau and spoke to him—that is, to the *real* Agent Surrency."

"Robyn, why the hell didn't you...?" Roper couldn't chastise her for keeping from him the same kind of information he'd kept from her. It was time to tell her more about the shot taken at him out at the Livingstones' two nights earlier. But Robyn spoke first.

"I know. I just felt you didn't need to hear that. And remember, it might have been a couple of stray shots from a drug deal gone bad or some asinine prank by some kid. Someone may even have had it in for Joan of Arc. Who the hell knows?" Robyn's flippant remark was belied by the concern on her face. The phone rang.

"It might be Matt Shanahan about the bullets that hit the statue. Excuse me. Hello, Matty?"

"No, Robyn, this is Tripp Wilcox. Is Tom there?"

"Oh hi, Tripp. Yes, he's here. Hang on."

Roper swallowed the rest of the bourbon and took the phone. "Tripp, what's up? I haven't passed the two-billion mark in YouTube views, have I?"

"Sorry, good buddy. I'm not calling about that."

Roper knew something had happened. He thought first of Jean Wilcox, who had been having some medical problems. "Is it Jean?"

"No, no. She's fine. No, I just need to talk to my good friend." Roper could hear voices in the background.

"Tripp, are you outside somewhere? Car trouble? Do you need for us to come get you?"

"I only wish. I'm at a convenience store not far from home. Someone was tailing me."

Roper softly cursed. Of course it was inevitable that someone would get to Tripp Wilcox as they'd gotten to the three murdered men he knew, as well as to Lena Roseboro. And likely to Robyn in Meridian Hill Park. Roper sensed Wilcox had another significant detail to add.

"And it seems this person wanted to take a shot at me as well. Hell, a shot was taken actually. He seemed to be stalking me. It's complicated, but I promise to fill you in later. I have to talk to the police now. I'll call you back in a bit."

"Wait, Tripp. One more thing. Was the shot from a rifle?"

"No, a pistol."

"Pistol?"

"Right."

"Did he say anything?"

"Nada. He's dead. Stumbled as I was chasing him and accidentally shot himself in the gut. Young guy—good-looking—sandy-blond hair. Gotta go. Bye." Roper placed the phone down and looked at Robyn.

"Tom, what is it? Did something happen?"

"We need to talk. Can I have another bourbon?"

Roper shared what Tripp revealed to him and what had happened at the Livingstone farmhouse. He could see Robyn was struggling to maintain her professional detachment as she asked him specific questions about what he saw and did at the Livingstones earlier this evening and on Tuesday night. She couldn't bring herself to assure Roper that the shot taken at him and the two taken at her were both accidental. Yet neither she nor Roper could satisfactorily tie the incident involving Tripp Wilcox to what happened to them.

"Robyn, I don't know if the guy who stalked Tripp was the same one who took shots at you and me. But maybe—just maybe—this will be the end of it."

"I wish I could fully turn optimist, Tom, but that's going to take a while. But perhaps you're right. But..."

"But...?"

"But he couldn't have been the serial killer."

The phone once more interrupted their contemplations.

"I'll get it, Robyn. It's probably Tripp. Hello?"

"Senator? I was hoping you'd be there. It's Tony Braithwait."

"Oh hello, Tony. How did you guess I'd be here?"

"Oh, come on, Senator. Your relationship with Ms. Meadows isn't exactly classified. Actually, I was hoping to get your whereabouts from her and perhaps your cell number."

Roper sighed. He was in no mood to speak of his behavior at the Senate hearing and the number of YouTube views he'd so far chalked up. "Tony, can we postpone this until tomorrow. I promise to give you something about the Browning business then. Okay?"

"Senator, I'm afraid I'm not calling about that." Now it was Braithwait's turn to sigh. "I'm calling as a friend to warn you about what might break tomorrow or on the weekend—although I think it's more likely to be Monday morning."

Roper assumed it was the fact that he was twice out at the Livingstones and discovered the bodies. "And that would be...?"

"Your relationship with a woman named Alyona Novikova."

"Hang on, Tony." He muffled the phone with his hand. "Robyn, can I take this in the bedroom?" She nodded. "Will you hang up here when I get on the line?"

"Of course. Government business for your ears only?"

Roper offered an anemic smile as he stepped into the bedroom and closed the door behind him. "Okay, Robyn, I got it." He heard the click as she hung up the other phone. "Tony, I had a short relationship with Ms. Novikova back home in Wisconsin. She wasn't an agent for the Russians, if that's what's being floated. I would have had nothing to give her anyway." Braithwait didn't respond. "We were very close for a short time, Tony. It wasn't going to work out, so we ended it. Besides, there was never anything serious between us in a romantic way, if that's what this is all about."

"That's not what she said, Senator."

Roper grimaced. "So after all this time she's making a claim that she and I had sex? I assure you that nothing could be further from the truth."

"Not that simple, I'm afraid. She's not only claimed—and this is only what I have been told, I want you to understand— that you made some, well, degrading sexual demands on her that she couldn't perform, but also that 'because of you' she ended up in porn films. *And* that the experience so scarred her that she'd been deeply depressed and often suicidal because of it. Do you deny all or any of this, Senator?"

Roper hesitated. He knew how deeply affected she was by her short career as a porn actress, but he didn't want to confirm the truth of that experience if this story had come from an enemy of Alyona's—her former 'agent,' for example.

"Senator? You chose not to deny what I've just told you?"

"Tony, what you have told me is either utterly false or totally misleading."

"Then at least some of it is true, is that right, Senator?"

Roper couldn't shake his chivalric instinct to protect Alyona. "You heard what I said, Tony."

"Senator, there's one more thing. She agreed to an interview and made these charges against you on a recording device. From what I understand, when they release the story, at least some sources will have it accompanied sound bites of her voice."

Roper thought of the email warning about his past being

prologue. "Tony, who told you all this? Who interviewed Alyona? Who has this recording you mentioned?"

"I can't reveal where I got this information, Senator. You know that. But I will say that regarding who interviewed her or who has the recording, I haven't got the slightest clue."

"Tony, I'm going to get in touch with her. I don't have her number in L.A. but her father does. I'll call him and get it. If necessary, I'll have a god-damned camera crew film my meeting with her, and I'll challenge her to say openly in public whether she wishes to state that we had a relationship we never really had—not even came close to—and that I asked her to do anything that could even remotely be considered degrading."

"Senator..."

"If it takes going to court, that's what I'll have to do." Roper was unaware that he'd been yelling. Robyn opened the bedroom door.

"Tom?"

"Senator?"

"What, Tony?"

"I'm afraid that's not going to happen. It's just been confirmed by L.A.P.D. She killed herself. Single shot to her temple. I'm sorry, Senator."

Chapter 16

"I'm glad we're not going to the movies now, Rich. It's about damn time you guys cooked for us instead of the other way around."

Prem and Anjum Sensharma were sitting comfortably in the apartment of their close friends Richard and Hannah Lloyd. Rich and Prem had worked together at the Library of Congress for three years, until the previous November when Rich took a position working for the Deputy Secretary of the Treasury. His oft-stated ambition was to end up working at the White House—even if he had to "wash dishes." And now, as he said in the familiar punning manner, he was located only a "stoneware's throw away" at Treasury. Still, he missed the convivial gatherings of those his own age working at the LOC, the National Archives, and the Smithsonian. Since moving to Treasury, Rich relied more and more on Prem Sensharma to keep him up to date on what the old "history gang" was up to.

"Angie, want to help with the cocktails?"

Anjum Sensharma had permitted Hannah and all her friends to call her Angie. "Drink them or fetch them, Hannah?"

"Ha, ha. Very funny. Come on."

Prem watched the women leave the room. As much as he loved his wife, he had to concede that his friend Hannah Lloyd was one devastatingly sexy woman. He was still tweaked by guilt for having gone to the Hirshhorn Museum gift shop where she worked, ostensibly to buy a print but really only to see her in another context, one excluding her possessive husband, who just happened to be his best friend.

"Can you believe that this is the first Thursday night movie the four of us have missed in over six months, Prem?"

"Now, now. Don't beat yourself up over it, Rich."

Rich Lloyd lowered his voice. "Actually, it was Hannah's fault. She didn't see that the film only opened in 'select locations' last weekend and won't be opening here in good old Manassas until next week. But at least she insisted on making up for her mistake by cooking a top-notch meal for all of us tonight. You and Angie are lucky. Veal Saltimbocca is her specialty."

"Just as ending our last game by hitting a double play with bases loaded is yours, eh, Rich?"

"You'll never let me forget that, will you, you sub-continental son-of-a-bitch? It's been over three months ago now."

"Hey, I just don't want you ever to forget that you blew my one chance to knock home a United States senator in a softball game. By the way, did you see the utter disgust on the faces of Thomas Roper and everyone else watching you hit into a double play that day, Rich? If looks could kill...."

"As we like to say back in Boston, fuck you, Prem."

•　•　•　•　•

Outside, the man was surprised to find that the house wasn't empty. The two couples were supposed to be at the Mall taking in a movie. But the lights were on and he saw movement in the bathroom window. The garage door was closed, but there was a car parked along the curb in front of the house. The man didn't recognize the vehicle, but he knew who drove it. He surveyed the house and determined his best course for later in the evening. But how much later? He had intended to be waiting in the garage and acting just as soon as they pulled in and shut the garage door behind them. He was rapidly squeezing his fingers into fists. Would the Lloyds' guests stay late—or even through the night? What then?

The man walked back to his car feeling a level of anxiety he hadn't expected. It wasn't there when he first entered the apartment of Maureen Blakely or the vestibule of St. Clare's Catholic Church. He had to act tonight. There was no time for a postponement as there was out at the farmhouse in Maryland. The "day of grace" had already been used. The presence of others could not be permitted. It would violate the process that had to be followed to the letter. There could be no deviations, no resourceful adjustments or adaptations. Anything of that kind would add confusion to what was so very simple. So simple that sophisticated minds would never come close to figuring it out. Not until it was all over. Then everyone would have a complete understanding.

Besides, it had always been in twos, even since he was a small boy. Counting sheep as they leaped over the fence. Two sheep at a time, his mother said, to help him fall asleep faster. Never just one. Never three or more. A boy and girl sheep together. Counting by twos. The sweet comfort of numbers and the feel of her hand on his brow. But then on his sixteenth birthday the twos took on a horrific meaning for him as she showed him what he had only barely seen by accident. And other twos. How that night she wanted him to show her what she said she had never seen since he became her "little man."

•   •   •   •   •

Patrick Sims approached Tom Roper's residence. He'd parked his car several blocks away and walked toward the apartment as casually as any pedestrian on a mid-afternoon stroll. He noticed lights on in Roper's living room. From what he could gather, all other lights were off. A rear entry might be possible. Failing that, he could make a slight noise—something to lure Roper to open the rear door. Sims thought that would be all he'd need. His task then completed, he could begin a new life.

Without altering his pace, Sims saw the police car slow down in front of Roper's and then continue on its way. Sims walked past the house and looked over his right shoulder for any other lights along the side of the building. There were none. Roper was probably in his living room.

Even from a practical sense, it was fitting that he'd kill Roper. Of course he knew Marshall Grayson's promise to send a letter to one of his close friends in government—and it had to be Roper. As he walked another block, Sims reminded himself that he had to accomplish his mission before the morning, when "Barry" told him he'd be leaving for Michigan and then going to Toronto until he flew either to Switzerland or France.

Sims couldn't let go of the fact that a finding of guilt for having obstructed justice would condemn him in the eyes of his country. Even if they convicted him only for improperly handling or stealing a few classified documents—that would be enough to disgrace him in the short term. But he had done more. For one, those periodic chats with Max Nettleton about classified matters kept even from the White House. Yes, Nettleton. Sims wondered if his timing this night would allow him to murder Marshall Grayson's rival as well. He could convince those who hired him to kill Roper that Nettleton's death was also necessary.

But he desperately wanted that envelope Roper got from Grayson—the envelope Sims was certain Roper kept either in his Senate office safe or here at his residence. The good senator had expressed his disdain for the Machiavellian necessity of politics, so perhaps he was right at this moment debating whether to give the envelope to the Justice Department. Then again, Roper might intend soon to reveal publicly what he had already read. Sims felt the pressure in his temples intensify as he stopped briefly in front of Roper's place.

Sims noted that the area around Roper's apartment was devoid of pedestrians. He turned and walked along the side until he reached the rear door. He listened for any movement. He heard nothing, not even the sound of the TV. He debated whether to walk up the rear steps and knock softly in an attempt to lure Roper to the back or just enter on his own and surprise the senator. It was very possible that no would ever tag this murder on him. He had no beef with Roper. Hell, he actually liked the personable senator. And since he was being suspected of other crimes—no one would think he would add murder to the list.

Sims decided to enter through the rear door. Snap memories of similar activities done years before came to mind—the clandestine career he rejected for one more open, though in its own way no less savage. He reached in his pocket for the device he'd need to break in.

Quietly entering through the kitchen, he moved slowly toward the softly illuminated living room. When he peered into the room, he was stunned. The room was a mess, with papers and books strewn about, the cushions of the sofa ripped up, and the desk's drawers pulled out and overturned—contents lying about the rug. What the hell had happened? He stepped into the living room and saw the indented soft chair next to an open plastic water bottle on a side table.

He heard the toilet flush.

Sims pulled a Smith and Wesson M&P from the inside of his coat—one of several weapons he had in the trunk of his car. This piece had been an unauthorized gift from a friend on the Metro force, now deceased. Sims had never fired it. He gave no thought to the fact that its maiden effort would be to take out a United States senator.

He knelt down at the end of the darkened hallway. As soon as Roper came out from bathroom, he'd fire. There would be no point in asking at gunpoint where the Grayson envelope was. Sims knew he would feel for it on Roper's person, but now he knew it was locked in Roper's Senate office safe. He had no choice but to trust that the safe might well never be opened. Or if it was, that the envelope from Grayson would remain sealed, merely bundled up with the rest of Roper's private papers.

Sims heard the water running in the bathroom sink. After a few seconds it stopped. The door cracked open and the bathroom light was snapped off. Sims brought his finger to the trigger. He saw the outline in the darkened hallway. When the figure began to approach, Sims squeezed off two rounds, which slammed into the man's chest. The body hurled backward against a closet door at the end of the hallway.

Sims stepped quickly into the hallway and began groping on the wall for the hallway light switch. He found it and flipped it up.

"Oh, fuck." Sims looked down at the prone figure of a Metro cop, an opened package of snack crackers wedged in his hand.

•　•　•　•　•

"Okay, but this is the last one, Rich. I've got to drive us home in one piece."

"You're not driving us anywhere, Prem." Angie Sensharma had donned her glasses, which meant she was adamant and in no mood for contradiction.

Her husband laughed. "There she is—my lovely bespectacled Indian cobra. Always fearful that I've had too much to drink." He leaned over to kiss her on the neck, but she was having none of it.

Prem was animated and pressed his wife's arm. "Angie, do you know what the saddest two numbers in the world are for Rich here?" His wife shook her head and sighed. "Then I'll tell you. They're 78 and 86."

She felt she had no choice but to play. "Why those two numbers, Rich?" Angie looked at Hannah, who grinned and dramatically buried her head in her hands before responding.

"Bucky Dent and Bill Buckner."

"I don't understand. Who are they, and what's the connection to those two numbers?"

Hannah explained to Angie the misery every Boston Red Sox fan equated with the Dent homer in the 1978 playoff game with the Yankees and Buckner's unfortunate confrontation with a ground ball in the 1986 World Series. Angie shook her head with good-natured disdain. Prem's eyes began to sag.

"All right, it's time for us to go."

As Angie yanked Prem to his feet, his eyes shot open. "I have one more thing to say before we leave, Angie."

"'Good night' would be enough, Prem."

"No, it wouldn't." Prem flashed a wide smile. "Rich,

Hannah. This whole evening was *wicked good*."

Rich broke out laughing. "That's perfect. I'll make a Bostonian out of you yet."

Ten minutes after the Sensharmas drove off, Hannah had the house in relatively good order. She left Rich in the living room and loaded the remaining dishes, glasses, and silverware into the dishwasher. As soon as she pushed the button, she took a step back to make one more check of the area. It was then that she felt the fingers sliding around her neck.

•　•　•　•　•

Roper was both surprised and gratified that Robyn had listened calmly as he described his relationship with Alyona Novikova and what Tony Braithwait had told him about Alyona's supposed confession and accusations. Robyn hadn't interrupted; nor had she reacted with any anger, disappointment, suspicion, or jealousy. She talked instead of Roper's options should the story break nationally. After placing a call to a colleague at Metro who had a contact at L.A.P.D., Robyn was able to assure Roper that someone would soon get back to her to verify Alyona Novikova's suicide.

Robyn had also encouraged him to speak with someone at the *Post* about how to trace back a salacious story offered to the media. Roper knew he'd be facing a public firestorm, but in a perverse sense he was looking forward to meeting all accusations and assumptions head on. "Facing up" was another of the lessons his father taught him very early in life. Tomorrow, however, he would have to call Alyona's father Tolik Novikova and express his condolences and warn him of what was about to be made public.

"Tom, come to bed."

"Robyn, I'm several hours away from being able to sleep, I'm afraid."

"Tom, I'm not asking you to sleep."

Through their mutually shared passion, Roper knew he'd be able to extinguish, if only for a brief time, all thoughts of what had happened to his friends—those who were killed and those who'd been frightened and shot at. Making love to Robyn offered him respite from those five numbers sadistically dangled by the serial killer and from the belief that he was either the killer's fourth or fifth intended victim.

Robyn waited for him under the covers. Roper pulled his sweater off and clicked off the lamp next to the bed, darkening the room to the point that he could barely make out the outline of her body. But as he began to undo his trousers, a circle of light appeared on the curtain of the bedroom window. Roper went to the window and pulled back the curtain of the second floor room. There was someone standing below with a high-beam flashlight shining it in the window. Roper couldn't make out the figure holding the flashlight.

"Tom, where's that light coming from?" Robyn began to get up from the bed.

"No, no. Stay down. Stay down!" Roper no sooner got the last word out when a single bullet sliced through the bedroom window and embedded itself on the far wall just under the crown molding near the ceiling.

•   •   •   •   •

"You know I love this necklace, Hannah. It really gets to me." She smiled as her husband ran his index finger completely around her throat, touching the necklace the entire time.

Often she had been frustrated by an announcement that he

was going to spend a good part of an afternoon or evening playing sports with Prem Sensharma and other friends. She could smile now as she remembered how in early September she refused to believe that Rich had actually hit a double play—or whatever it was--with a United States senator. She was especially dubious when both Rich and Prem went on and on about how "down to earth" Senator Thomas Roper was. The following week she sat in the bleachers and saw that indeed her husband hadn't been exaggerating about Roper, for he was exactly how they portrayed him—friendly and without pretense. She also found him particularly handsome and charming. That night it was she who cooed about the senator—much to her jealous husband's chagrin.

Now, she felt her husband's lips pressing against the necklace. It seemed humorous to her. Rich was playing the role of patient and creative lover while they stood silently in the kitchen—with the dishwasher rumbling and blocking out all other sound. Concerned always that her husband feel good about his lovemaking, she feared he'd get them both in an awkward position if he tried to run his lips all the way around the necklace the way he had with his finger. Accordingly, he decided to turn around in order to avoid any clumsiness. She would kiss him passionately as a form of lover's compensation.

"Rich." She turned to kiss him. "Oh, God."

Her voice was anemic. She was too frightened to push any volume into it. She saw a man standing behind her husband's left shoulder. Her face reflected utter puzzlement as her husband leaned forward to decipher her lovely features. Her face momentarily relaxed. She recognized the face. She had earlier talked to the man standing behind Rich. Yet she was still mute when she saw the large knife rise and then plunge downward into her husband's back.

As Richard Lloyd spun toward the dishwasher with his arms flailing helplessly on the counter, Hannah began to formulate the scream that had been for several seconds inexplicably delayed. But her vocal chords were suddenly caught in the man's right hand. She thought she detected the sound of the knife clattering on the kitchen floor immediately before she felt the fingers squeezing violently into her throat.

The man drove her into the cupboard door. She felt the pain of the handle digging into her lower back. The very last thing she heard was the sound of her husband's groan as she slid down to the floor. She was unaware that both her hands were gripping the wrists of the man who was strangling her. In another moment she saw blackness. Then she felt nothing.

The man released the powerful grip on her throat. He turned and picked up the knife. Less than two feet away, Richard Lloyd was still moving, though barely. The man kneeled over him for several seconds and watched the blood trickling from the wound to the kitchen floor. Lloyd pressed his hands on the floor, in a vain attempt to stand, but his hands gave way and he fell forward on his stomach. The man carefully moved forward on his knees and plunged the knife once more into the area of the back behind where he imagined the heart to be.

Mindful of the seeping blood, the man carefully stood back up. His breathing was finally beginning to slow down. He felt disappointment with himself for being too angry this time—too resentful of the several hours he'd been kept needlessly waiting by the Lloyds and their two friends. The man had expected to be in bed by now. To sleep well on the last night of his life. He cursed himself for his emotions.

Taking out the prepared note, the man placed it on the counter. He dipped the very tip of his knife into one of the two wounds it had created moments before. He brought the knife to the paper and over the fourth number—the "19"—he made an "X." He adjusted his gloves, took the note, folded it, and placed it in the area between Lloyd's instep and his right shoe

Locating a dishrag near the sink, the man twirled it tight and daubed the tip with Lloyd's blood. He straddled Hannah Lloyd's body and carefully wrote the initials "J" and "B" on her porcelain cheeks, right under her now horribly altered azure eyes. He remembered how taken he had been with those eyes when he walked into the museum gift shop earlier in the day.

Chapter 17

At 11:45 p.m., Patrick Sims opened the trunk of his car and placed his Smith and Wesson M&P in its custom made box. The rifle was also in its travel case. He would have no trouble retrieving either weapon to finish the task he had committed to. But if an opportunity presented itself too quickly for him to stop the car and open the trunk, he'd have his .22 Mag. Black Widow on his person. Conveniently, he also had a concealed carry permit—another gift from his late friend on the Metro force.

Roper wasn't at his place, and Sims could see that he was no longer at Robyn's apartment. What had Roper learned from the police the past few hours? What had he concluded? What had he anticipated? Sims long ago embraced the lesson that proper anticipation was the key to success in stalking prey. He hadn't always anticipated correctly—especially of late—but he could soon make up for the errors he had made. Refusing to chide himself for having killed a poor cop by mistake, Sims concentrated only on killing Roper.

Sims went over the plan for the next several hours. He'd be picked up at 2:30 a.m. and would cross the Maryland-Pennsylvania border before dawn. "Shit." He remembered Max

Nettleton and their scheduled meeting. Another mental lapse he couldn't explain. Sims tensed with anger, but he knew he had to maintain control. "You stupid son-of-a-bitch—think." His first priority was to find out where Roper was for the rest of the night. Sims unscrewed a large thermos. Another cup of coffee would help him think more rationally and anticipate Roper's next move. He hadn't finished his first sip when it came to him. "Wilcox."

•   •   •   •   •

"Tripp, I appreciate your asking us to stay with you and Jean. But I'm afraid it might put the both of you in danger. I think it's best if we just warm up and then hit the road."

"Tom, from all you've told me—and from what I've been through myself this evening—I think the road is the least safe place for either of you. It's now midnight. You're staying here."

Robyn interjected. "But Jean? And I hope we haven't awakened her."

"Little lady, she isn't here. I thought it best if she left the premises, at least for tonight. Her sister and brother-in-law picked her up right before you both got here."

"Your brother-in-law the local Fire Marshall, you mean?"

"That's the one, Tom. One of the perks of marrying a Marylander. Jean left in their car with a fire truck escort. We armed everyone, even the god-damned Dalmatian."

"You're one of a kind, Tripp."

"You and me both. Well, you're safe here. My boys will let us know if strangers are in the area." Wilcox's "boys" were two Rottweilers and an aloof but occasionally cantankerous American Staffordshire terrier named Marty. "Let's make ourselves at home and try to put our heads together and figure out just what the hell is going on."

Roper was pleased Wilcox made no effort to convince him to put himself and Robyn under police protection. There was an officer back at his place already, and he wanted to wait until morning before reporting the shot fired through Robyn's window. Perhaps a neighbor already made the call. It didn't matter. Roper wasn't ready to explain all that had transpired and all that he feared. Besides, Wilcox's frontier spirit was contagious. Hunkering down at his place would give them all time to think. There were plenty of weapons at the house, and as Wilcox noted, the dogs would provide additional security. Finally, Roper knew his father wouldn't have approved of his running like a scalded canine into the arms of the police.

Wilcox was just about to pour each of them some expensive brandy when Robyn received a call on her cell.

"Yes? What is it, Sarah? Oh, dear God. Yes, yes, I'm ready. Go ahead." Roper and Wilcox could see her writing furiously on the back of a magazine. "All right. Who? Okay, wait. Spell the last name. Okay. In Virginia. Manassas. The male stabbed in the same fashion as the others. The female apparently strangled—they think by hand. The fourth number was 19, and it was crossed out with blood. The initials left on the woman's face—on her cheeks, under each eye. 'J' and a 'B.'" Okay, thanks so much, Sarah. Bye."

Wilcox had already brought his friend a brandy. Roper twirled the snifter and stared at the liquid circling around the glass. "Robyn, did you get a name of the victims?"

"Yes. Richard and Hannah--."

Roper spoke before she had a chance to finish. "Lloyd. Rich and Hannah Lloyd."

•   •   •   •   •

Jerry Goldman was disoriented for a moment. He checked the luminous dial on his watch. 12:12 a.m. He'd fallen asleep on his small sofa in his White House office. Earlier, the president had bent his ear with another of his diatribes about disloyalty in his party. Tonight, Bedingfield was particularly concerned about the Kendall Livingstone manuscript. Goldman assured him that he had expressed to the publisher the wishes of the White House regarding a careful editing of the book, even though Goldman kept to himself the fact that several of Livingstone's colleagues at the *Post* were pressing hard to have one of their number made ad-hoc co-editor, so that nothing of significance would be excised. Goldman also knew—but the president did not—that there was a major battle being fought with Prince George's County over the release of the laptop and existing pages of the draft. There were also the notes to be examined and the interview material Livingstone had taped. Goldman had received three phone calls since 6:00 p.m. informing him of these matters.

Goldman wondered what Bedingfield would say if he knew just who was making the most concerted push to get his hands on the manuscript material. Unlike Evan Bedingfield, Goldman had his sources in almost every government building in Washington. Hell, he reasoned, he and Max Nettleton were probably sharing many of these sources, who picked and chose what to tell each of them. Earlier Goldman assumed he'd get the preferential treatment, given that he worked for the president, but that bastard Nettleton must have convinced them that Bedingfield would tap him to be Goldman's replacement in a second term. Moreover, he was sure that his old pal Max would use tomorrow's photo op in the Roosevelt Room to remind the president just what he could bring to the table after Jerry Goldman called it quits. Goldman knew Bedingfield was just about convinced that Ed Malloch should be dropped from the ticket in favor of Carol McCrimmon—with Max Nettleton doing most of the prodding.

And then there was the matter of Tom Roper. Tonight the president went off on the senator again, using the kind of language that just might get him impeached if it were made public. Goldman smiled thinking of a sensational trial in the Senate—with Tom Roper breaking party ranks to vote for conviction.

Bedingfield twice asked Goldman if he had taken some "steps" to "pay back that disloyal bastard." And twice Goldman let him know he had. What was so amusing about this assurance was that he hadn't done a damn thing along those lines—although he guessed that much was being done to more than satisfy Bedingfield's demand for "pay back." Goldman's main FBI source had discovered some interesting details and wanted to speak directly to Sheridan Browning or Devin Cassell to find out more, but Goldman had ordered him to tread water. The only action Goldman took regarding Roper was to make it clear to the Prince George's County police that the senator was not under any circumstances to be arrested. But Goldman still didn't know who was responsible for suggesting such a thing in the first place.

•　•　•　•　•

The man had no thought of sleep. It was past 12:30 a.m., and it would be another hour before he'd be tired enough to close his eyes. The tip of his knife had dug into the oak veneer top of the dining room table in his apartment, defacing it beyond any hope of repair. It was to be expected. The day after he turned sixteen, he had gone outside with his pocket knife and dug the blade into his favorite baseball bat until he rendered it useless for play. His father had once played baseball. That was reason enough.

And the man was still upset over having to wait so long before he could cross out the fourth number. What if the two couples had driven off for a three-day weekend? What would have happened then? But the fourth number had indeed been crossed out. And it had been done with time to spare. Time and precedent were his masters, and time had given him some flexibility at least. As for the fifth number, he wouldn't have precedent to worry about. He'd be setting it.

He watched TV for forty minutes before he felt a slight heaviness in his eyes. Perhaps now he could climb into bed and fall asleep. He stepped into his bathroom to continue the habit he'd begun when he moved out of the family house—the day he went off to college. He checked the waste basket—as he did every night. It was empty. He knew it was, for he had emptied it hours earlier. But he had to be sure.

He checked the bedroom door which was, as he expected, closed but not latched. He slowly pushed it open a few inches. Then a few inches more. He bent his head and listened. There was only silence, although his memory often brought up frightening sounds from his past. It always took him a few moments standing rigidly in the darkened room before he felt comfortable enough to turn on the lamp next to the bed.

Lights turned on and then off—the hesitation in doing either. How his mother wished to alter what after that night couldn't possibly be amended. Her feeble attempt to make peace with him and with herself by placing in his lap a paperback book of crossword puzzles and taking from him the notebook which included all of his additions, subtraction, divisions, multiplications, and percentages. And the batting averages of his favorite ballplayers. She was desperately adamant that they begin their relationship anew—encouraging her oblivious husband to purchase for their son a book of famous quotations they wished their son to commit to memory. How he loathed the very first quotation his father insisted he memorize—from Plato: "A good decision is based on knowledge and not on numbers." But there were other quotations he memorized then that comforted him and would later inspire him to this act of retribution against the parents he despised.

Exhausted by memory, the man was finally able to sleep.

•　•　•　•　•

"All right. We now have these initials: 'M, T, L, R, I, S, J, and B.' I can't get anything by way of an anagram. There still aren't enough vowels."

Robyn understood what Roper was imagining about victim number five; therefore, she gently added, "There may likely be two vowels intended for the final victim's wife or love interest, which would then perhaps spell something specific."

Tripp Wilcox had been listening intently. "You think these letters spell out the killer's name, Tom?"

"It's possible, but they could also spell out a location or a single or a double word statement of some kind."

"Or maybe it doesn't spell out a god-damned thing."

Wilcox wasn't trying to ridicule his friend's efforts, but Roper pressed his fingers into a fist to suppress his sudden flash of anger. In a moment he relaxed and opened his hands. "Maybe you're right, Tripp. So let's look at the location of each murder."

"Robyn?"

"Yes, Tripp?"

"Don't you have a squadron of Metro cops dealing with all

this? I imagine the FBI and Secret Service are on it as well."

"Excuse me." Roper headed for the bathroom. Wilcox had many attractive traits that drew Roper to him. Tact wasn't one of them.

Wilcox watched him walk away. "I said something wrong, I take it."

Robyn took him by the hand. "Tripp, Tom believes he may be the intended fifth victim."

"Hell no. There's no way."

"I agree, but even if he didn't think that, he just has the kind of mind that can't let anything like this go. He's got great instincts for this kind of thing. He's actually helped me several times in my own investigations."

"So you're saying he's missed his calling."

"Something like that. Please don't try to play devil's advocate with him, okay?"

"Honey, there was a time in my life when I would have gladly been head of Satan's legal team, but those days are long gone."

Wilcox laughed and gave Robyn a hug—which he broke only when he heard his American Staffordshire terrier barking at the side door. He stepped out of the room, as Roper returned. In a few seconds he walked back in, with Marty at his heels. Robyn reacted with trepidation. Marty cocked his head and gave her a puzzled look.

"Don't be afraid of old Marty here, Robyn. He's as cool as they come. Has a good sense for who the good guys are." Wilcox bent down and roughly caressed the dog, bringing his hand up under Marty's throat and almost lifting him off the ground. "But if you're one of the bad guys, I don't give you much a chance with this tenacious hound. Now that's not the way it is with Heckle and Jekyll out there—the two Rotties.

They think everybody but Jean and I are the bad guys. Hey, Tom, forgive my advocating for the devil a couple of minutes ago. You know how I am on committees and such."

"Yes I do know. I just prefer to be your colleague rather than your adversary."

"Hell, there's no way in Hades you'd ever be that. Here, let me go out and give Marty a snack and I'll be back to see if I can add anything to what you two have been talking about."

As soon as Wilcox left, Roper smiled at Robyn. "So you begged him not to contradict my impeccable instincts?"

"Hope you don't mind."

"Not at all." Roper poured himself another brandy. "I'm making history, Robyn. I've never before been drinking brandy and analyzing a crime at 12:40 in the morning."

She could offer only a smile at his levity. "Tom, do you think there's something in the locations of the killings?"

"Well, one was in the city proper, one in Georgetown, one in Maryland, and one in Virginia. I suppose we'd have to get a ruler and a good map to see if it's possible that there's a pattern. So we now have a victim who worked at Treasury to go along with those who worked at the Eisenhower Building, State, and the *Post*. I can't detect a clear pattern there either." Roper wondered if adding the Capitol would complete some kind of geometric design intended by the killer.

"The murders took place at three residences and a Catholic Church, Tom. Again nothing there—at least on first blush."

"I know, Robyn. Jesus Christ, I know."

"Tom, I'm trusting you when you say that Richard Lloyd wasn't a close friend. Because if he was, I wouldn't want to talk clinically about his murder. Are you sure you were only casual acquaintances?"

"I'm sure. We played on that softball team—that was it. I

never socialized with him. I met his wife once. We just played on the same softball team." Robyn was discomforted by the repetition of that fact. "Wait, Robyn. Jesus. Oh, Jesus."

"What is it, Tom?"

"Get a piece of paper or something to write on."

She found a sheet of blank U.S. Senate stationary on one of Wilcox's side tables. "Okay, got it."

"Take down these names." Roper rattled off three names quickly and then brought his finger to his lips, trying to recall more. "I gave Metro the names of some of the others on the team, but I couldn't remember these three at the time."

"Wait, Tom. How do you spell this Prem person's last name? Did you say 'Sensura' or something like that?"

"I think it's 'Sensharma.' Spelled as it sounds. Remind me to think of others. We need to get as many of these names to the police as possible. It's a link, Robyn, don't you see?"

She wanted to say—to believe—that it was probably only coincidence, but she wouldn't contradict him now. "I understand. Do you think, then, that another one of your teammates could be the next intended victim?"

"It could be that I'm the linchpin in this." He thought of all that had happened to those closest to him. "Perhaps someone was punishing me for something I did."

"Who would be punishing you, Tom?"

"I don't know." The first face that formed in his mind was Iraqi. The face of a man whose child was killed on the bus along with thirty others in early 1998. "Or..."

Robyn knew what he was going to say. She desperately didn't want him to. "Please, Tom. Don't."

"Or I'm the next one on the list. The four killings may not have spun *from* me but rather have been directed *at* me all the time. It's just that I can't understand why two shots would have been taken at me before the fourth victim was found—or the ones at you—or the one at Tripp. And the break-in. And Lena and the emails. God damn it, Robyn, it's becoming more and more likely that I'm the target of more than one killer."

No, damn it, Tom, you are *not*." She immediately realized her anger was a transparent mask for a fear that he might be right. "I'm sorry, Tom."

"Don't worry about it." Roper debated whether to have another brandy. "Robyn, where the hell is Tripp?"

Chapter 18

"No problem, sir....Yes, I'm sure. I was up reading anyway. Right, right. I understand. Goodnight." He hung up the phone and stared at the clock. 12:55 a.m. "Browning, you big league bastard."

Devin Cassell hadn't been up reading; he'd just gotten off to sleep. Nor did he appreciate the latest idea his boss had conjured up to get back at Thomas Roper. It was so damned brilliant that Browning couldn't wait until morning to tell his associate.

For the first time since he'd been publicly embraced by Browning as "my kind of guy," Cassell felt trapped—as though his life had entirely slipped out of his control. He of course understood that, after the Senate hearing and the public relations spanking Browning had received at the hands of Tom Roper, his boss would expend much energy and, if necessary, capital in order to make the senator pay for his serious lapse of judgment. But matters had now gone too far. Browning was committed to destroying Roper however he could. That Cassell advised a postponement of such strategy until it counted—in the summer and fall of 2018—only raised Browning's ire. He would hear nothing of such rational counsel. "Revenge is a fucking impatient beast," he told Cassell.

Other members of the Bureau understood their colleague's characteristic intemperance. At times they ridiculed or contradicted Browning's arguments and tactics. At other times they stood back while he did all the political dirty work for them. They needed Browning in the fraternity but had no love for him.

Browning's late night phone call seemed totally unnecessary. What he'd suggested—another form of private harassment of Roper—was hardly worthy of such immediate sharing. No, it seemed to Cassell that Browning was fishing for something—a reaction of some kind from his associate. Cassell was now certain that he wasn't privy to all that had been and was now going on.

•　•　•　•　•

"My God, was that a shot, Tom?"

"Stay here, Robyn. Get away from the window." Roper ran toward the side door.

"Tom, don't go out there!" Robyn rushed to the hallway knowing full well that Roper wouldn't heed her command.

Roper pushed the side door open carefully, although he didn't hesitate to step through it and kneel behind the wood stack next to the Wilcox house. He heard the dogs barking, which was more intense than when he and Robyn drove up to the house. He grabbed a round piece of oak to use as a weapon, refusing to accept that this piece of wood, some twenty inches long, would do him absolutely no good against a handgun or rifle.

Roper heard the dogs continue to bark but nothing else. He

decided not to call out for Wilcox, but rather to move in a low, quick sprint to the 1955 Chevy his colleague had been working on in his spare time and then to the tractor parked twenty-five feet further away. His movements reminded him of the first time his father had taken him to a military obstacle course and had him play soldier. "Plot your course, make your decision, and then go," his father advised. Roper's course was taking him to where he believed the dogs were barking. He was sure Wilcox had been hit.

As he peered from behind the tractor wheel while keeping his head down, he realized the dogs had stopped barking. In a moment he heard the sound of heavy footsteps, accompanied by a lighter patter across the field that led down to the fence line. Roper gripped the piece of oak, deciding he'd jump from his place of concealment and surprise the shooter. If he got lucky, he'd at least make sure Robyn would be safe. Then he would try to find Wilcox. Perhaps his friend was only wounded.

He now detected both a man's sigh and dog's whine. It made no sense. The dogs would have torn into an intruder. Roper moved his head slightly beyond the tractor tire for a better look. Quickly, he stood up.

"Jesus Christ, Tripp, what the hell happened?" His friend was holding one of the Rotties in his arms, its head flopped lifelessly to the side. The second Rottweiler and Marty the American Staffordshire circled him.

"I went down to give Heckle and Jekyll something to eat and when I bent down to put the food in the trough, Jekyll started licking my face, knocking the flashlight upward into my eyes. A split second later someone took a shot. He was probably trying to kill me and ended up shooting Jekyll. Look at him, Tom." A substantial section of the dog's head had been blown away.

Roper could hear the emotion in his friend's voice, a

haunting blend of sadness, fear, and billowing anger.

They walked to the rear of the house, where Wilcox laid the dog down on a large tarp while Heckle stood guard over his fallen comrade. Marty had gone back to the side door, apparently to protect Robyn, who was still inside the house. As Wilcox began folding the tarp over the dead animal, Roper ran past the terrier, unafraid that it would react to the sudden movement and attack him. He entered the house and informed Robyn what had happened.

Within a few minutes, they were sitting in front of the fireplace. Wilcox had a shotgun across his lap. Robyn had called the Maryland police in spite of Roper's protest. Roper was pondering the nature of the shots taken at him, at Robyn, and now twice at Tripp. As Wilcox had informed him, the man near the convenience store had fired his pistol only when Wilcox had grabbed his leg. The two shots fired at Robyn—and Roper firmly believed that they were directed at her—had been close but had still missed by several feet. True, the one fired at Roper's car missed as well by a foot or so, but he was a moving target, making a turn in his vehicle. Neither Robyn at Meridian Hill Park nor Tripp Wilcox were such difficult targets. Tripp said he'd been very close to the Rottweiler when the shot hit. Roper couldn't shake the fact that if the same person did all the firing—at Roper, at Robyn, and at Tripp Wilcox—he was a pretty lousy shot, unless....

"What are you thinking, Tommy boy?"

"I'm just wondering if the shooter really wanted to kill you, Tripp."

•　　•　　•　　•　　•

"Senator, are you sure this time?"

"Yes, I'm sure, Robert. Don't ask me to explain. Just do what I ask."

Gleeson yawned out his reply. "I will, Senator McCrimmon. You know I will."

McCrimmon held out the hope that the emails already sent to Roper would satisfy her promise to Devin Cassell and prevent the revelation about her sexual indiscretion with the oil lobbyist when she first came to the Senate.

"Robert, are you still there?" She thought he might have fallen back to sleep.

"Sorry, Senator. I'm listening. So you want me to put a stop to the emails."

"Yes, and I want you to forget we ever had them sent. Is that understood?"

"Completely."

"Is that clear?"

"Perfectly."

"All right, Bobby. I'm going to call Senator Roper and tell him."

She could hear him sitting up in bed. "Senator, you can't expect him to understand why you'd have done such a thing."

"Do you really think I'm that stupid, Robert? I'm only going to say that we've discovered that some college student computer geniuses set up a program that sent these emails and that they didn't come from any legitimate constituents. That's all I'm telling him."

"I'm sorry, Senator. I'm just trying to consider whatever could be misconstrued, in order to protect you—you know that."

"I do know that, Bobby. That's why I'm so happy you're with me. Look, I'm sorry to call you at this hour, but I couldn't sleep until I resolved this matter."

"I understand, Senator. I'll make a call first thing in the morning."

"Make the call now, Robert."

"As I was about to say—why wait until the morning? I'll call the head computer geek now, who will then make calls to the other computer geeks and have the emails stopped."

"Good, Bobby. Thank you."

"Senator, I heard from Melanie Sheffield in Senator Roper's office that they've also been receiving emails warning him about his past being his prologue. Do you know who's sending those?"

"I assume they're being sent by the same computer geniuses you contacted."

"I don't think so. Anyway, good night, Senator McCrimmon."

"Good night...oh, Bobby, your mention of that other email reminds me I want you to do me yet another favor tomorrow. Some chaperoning if you will."

"Chaperoning? Oh, what we talked about at the end of last week?"

"Yes. I'll explain more in the morning. Now get some sleep."

•　•　•　•　•

Max Nettleton checked his watch for the third time. He'd kept his car running because of the cold. Where the hell was Sims? Nettleton imagined having to roll down his window to a cop who wanted to know why he was sitting alone in his car near the George Mason Memorial in East Potomac Park at 1:30 in the morning.

He was to wait until he saw Sims walking across East Basin

drive and then he would hit the high beams. Sims would get in the car, and they'd drive across the Potomac and travel along the George Washington Memorial Parkway until their business was concluded. Nettleton would then circle back and drop Sims back off near the Mason Memorial.

Nettleton wasn't happy about the 1:15 a.m. scheduled meeting time. He would have preferred anytime between nine and ten, but Sims insisted it be at a "safer" hour—whatever the hell he meant by that. But Nettleton was in no position to argue because he has mistakenly relied on this man to do a job for him that he couldn't have done on his own. And then of course there was Sims's deteriorating mental state. For the first time, Nettleton feared he'd be powerless to command one of his many foot soldiers.

Since mid-December, Nettleton had wisely dangled the possibility of assisting Sims should he need to leave Washington in the wake of an indictment. But he'd be expected to do Nettleton one last favor. He had asked Sims to find out from the Bureau if there was any information on Marshall Grayson and his philandering ways. He had thought it possible that he could ruin his rival with such information, even if it were nothing more than the tried-and-true method of raising questions and spreading doubt. Perhaps Grayson had shared something sensitive with Maureen Blakely that she'd mentioned to someone else. In any event, Sims had agreed to see what he could dig up.

Nettleton had done about all he could to keep matters bottled up as they related to Patrick Sims. He'd even purloined the correspondence from the attorney general to the vice president about the probe. But now Nettleton couldn't be sure what Sims would do—or, for that matter, what he'd already done. Concerned about his own safety, Nettleton tried to keep him at bay as long as he could, but he believed he had no choice but to agree to this clandestine meeting—at Sims's suggested time and place. And Sims was now late by over fifteen minutes.

When first learning that Grayson and Maureen had been killed, Nettleton initially thought Sims was the murderer. After all, that was Grayson's own assumption before the fact, wasn't it? The idea was frightening in itself, but soon another possibility became even more dreadful to contemplate. What if Sims learned about Nettleton's affair with Maureen and therefore believed that he had Grayson murdered—or that Nettleton had done it himself?

And Nettleton recalled Sims's chiding him for cultivating his "garden of petty little spies" who fed Nettleton all kinds of specific information about Grayson's comings and goings. Nettleton protested that it couldn't really be helped, for Grayson was often indiscreet to a fault and spoke freely of his sexual triumphs to anyone listening—especially to those he wished to impress. After all, the Office of the Vice President had to be protected.

If push came to shove, would Sims speak to prosecutors about Ed Malloch's chief of staff and Nettleton's asking Sims to look into FBI files for any damning evidence or innuendo? What kind of embarrassment would all this lead to? Could Nettleton's career survive a nefarious link between himself and Sims? Or between him and the woman who had been brutally murdered?

There were still other possibilities to consider. What kind of request would Sims make of Nettleton in exchange for his silence regarding half a dozen matters? In addition, there was the Kendall Livingstone manuscript. What had the *Post's* reporter said about Malloch's chief of staff? Nettleton reasoned that perhaps it was nothing serious on its own—but when combined with whatever Sims might say, such revelations could destroy him.

Nettleton decided to wait another ten minutes—he really had no choice but to listen to what the man said. Again, he could only imagine what Sims might ask of him. Nettleton certainly had other political chips he could cash in, but there was no way he could derail a Justice Department investigation of one of its own—one this far along in the process, on the very eve of an indictment.

"Come on, you mother fucker." Nettleton turned up the heat in his car and opened his glove compartment. The pistol was there, fully loaded. He checked to see if the safety was off. It was.

Chapter 19

Devin Cassell sipped some Irish whiskey as he spoke to one of Sheridan Browning's "field employees," who assured Cassell he'd done what was asked of him—from firing two shots in Meridian Hill Park in broad daylight, as well as one through Robyn Meadows's bedroom window, to entering both Thomas Roper's apartment—indiscriminately ransacking it without looking for or taking anything—and the residence of Lena Roseboro, successfully frightening the woman so she had to leave town. The caller added that the other man working with him was the one who stood outside Roper's apartment near a street light, turned the doorknob at Robyn Meadows's apartment, and sent the ominous "past/prologue" email to Roper. Cassell merely nodded as he listened to the caller and recalled Browning's order that Roper and everyone close to him were not to feel safe.

"Anything else?" Cassell reached for his glass. The caller didn't respond. "I said, is there anything else?"

"Barry Arnold's dead."

"What are you talking about?"

"As you instructed, he left the airport as soon as he got back from L.A. and eventually tailed Wilcox to a convenience store. But Wilcox went after him. Arnold ran into the woods, tripped, and the gun discharged into his stomach, killing him."

"Oh, Christ." Cassell looked at his whiskey. "All right. Anything else?"

"Yes. The Russian girl in California."

"Don't tell me that Arnold…"

"He had his orders, Mr. Cassell."

"I gave no such orders. I made it clear she wasn't to be harmed."

"We know that. But Arnold made it look like she shot herself. It would make sense, right?"

Cassell hung up without responding. Finishing his whiskey, he lifted the phone and called the woman who was with him the first time he called Alyona Novikova from Virginia. "Hello, Kate? Sorry to wake you. But I need you to set up breakfast tomorrow with Sheridan, okay? Call him as soon as he gets up. Hmm? He'll be up at 6:00 a.m. Where? The Willard Room."

Cassell poured himself another drink. He checked for a number in his files. Finding it, he picked up the phone and dialed.

•　•　•　•　•

"All right. But I want the area scoured clean. The god-damned son-of-a-bitch shot my dog." After hanging up, Wilcox turned to Roper. "They're going to be delayed. Big crack and meth bust just wrapping up—dozens of suspects, some they have yet to yank out of an apartment complex. Can't believe what they just told me. 'Don't be too concerned, Senator. It was probably some sick kid who had it in for your Rottweiler.' Maybe I should call the god-damned Secret Service." Seeing that Robyn had returned to the room, Wilcox apologized for his profanity.

Wilcox's mention of "some sick kid" reminded Roper of young Brian Felton and the possibility that he might actually have seen the man who shot at his car as he was pulling out of the Livingston's long dirt driveway. Roper couldn't be sure whether the Prince George's County police had by now interviewed the boy. He also wondered if either Metro or the FBI was making any headway in deciphering the serial killer's numbers and initials codes.

"20-18-11-19-07." Roper wanted to start his analysis over. What had the number "20" to do with Marshall Grayson? Roper couldn't remember Grayson's birthday, but perhaps that was it—that he was born on the twentieth of the month. If so, he'd find out the birthdays of Ian Arrington, Kendall Livingstone, and Richard Lloyd. Then what? There would have to be an immediate notification to every single government agency and local media that anyone with a birthday on the seventh of any month might well be the potential fifth victim of a serial killer? Roper felt some relief in that fact that his birthday didn't fall on the seventh of the month.

Roper took yet another sip of brandy Robyn handed him—only this time diluted with half a cup of coffee. A "small Irish," as she termed it. He was impressed. Robyn showed no visible fatigue or fear, in spite of the late hour and all that had happened to her and to the man she loved. A tough but wonderfully tender lady.

Another thought hit him. What if each of the five numbers was really the day of the month in which each *female* victim was born? Roper had no idea what Maureen Blakely's birthday was—or those of Arrington's girlfriend, Sandra Livingstone, or Richard Lloyd's wife. But Robyn Meadows had celebrated her thirty-third birthday on November 7th.

"Tom, you look like the day is finally beginning to crash in on you."

"No. It's nothing, Robyn. Really."

Wilcox came over with the brandy. "You've got too much damned coffee in that cup, partner. Here. Let me rectify that."

"Whoa, whoa. That's good, Tripp."

"Now if you'll excuse me for a minute, Tom."

"Where are you going?"

"Out to put Jekyll in the barn."

Robyn pulled him by the arm. "Can't it wait until the police get here?"

"Little lady, you've got a mighty powerful grip. Don't let your bosses know about it, or else they'll yank you out of that lab and give you street duty."

"Please, Tripp."

Roper tried to laugh but the events of the day made it impossible. "Tripp, perhaps you'd better listen to her."

"I thought you said no one's been trying to kill us with these rifle and pistol shots, Tom. They're only trying to frighten us, remember? So what the hell do I have to fear?"

"I know what I said, Tripp. I also know I occasionally get things wrong."

"I'll be fine. Here." Wilcox patted the sidearm on his belt and smiled broadly. "Robyn, you take the shotgun, because I know Senator Roper has a very, and I mean a *very* low rating among us Second Amendment boys. Hell, don't worry. I'll be fine. I just can't leave Jekyll outside wrapped up in that tarp. I'm putting him in the barn." He headed out the side door.

Robyn whispered to Roper. "Tom, maybe you'd better go out there with him."

"Maybe I better. I'll just give him a minute so he's not offended. I'll just tell him I want to see the inside of the barn.

Besides, I've never actually seen the inside of a barn—although I could always hit one with a baseball." Roper could tell from her expression that the joke and the sports cliché were completely lost on the woman he loved.

•   •   •   •   •

Certain that the deliberate near miss of Tripp Wilcox would convince Roper to stay in the house, Sims re-assured himself that he still had time to kill the senator before the police showed up. And he'd be much closer to Roper than he had been when he took a shot at his car out at Kendall Livingstone's place.

Sims was surprised the other dog hadn't started barking by now. Earlier, he'd expected to shoot it when it ran toward him at the fence line, where he now stood. If Wilcox came out again alone, he'd shoot him and then move toward the house. But if Wilcox and Roper remained in the house, Sims knew he'd have to find a way to draw them out or make his way close enough to the house to shoot through a window. Failing that, he'd have to enter.

•   •   •   •   •

Wilcox opened the barn door with his foot and carried the tarp inside, a greatly subdued Heckle following at his heels. Marty remained at the door to the house as his owner had instructed him.

•   •   •   •   •

Sims moved carefully through the snapped barb wire opening. As he did so, his rifle became snagged near the trigger housing.

Sliding his hand down to free it, a piece of barbed wire dug into his thumb. The trickle of blood and pain only served to infuriate him. His eyes were dry. He felt the heat in them. He saw Wilcox enter the barn.

Sims paused every ten feet in anticipation of the remaining Rottweiler's springing at him from the darkness. He carried the rifle in military fashion—his right index finger on the trigger housing, the other hand under the barrel. The way he'd been trained when he was in his early twenties, before he had a change of heart about his career and chose political warfare rather than the real kind.

Sims had to be ready to kill the dog before it reached him. If he couldn't use the rifle, he'd stab the Rottweiler with the hunting knife strapped to his lower leg. He knew that even if he were bitten, his adrenaline would carry him through to the fulfillment of his mission.

Hearing nothing, Sims moved as lightly and quickly for another fifteen feet, this time altering his course toward the house. It was then that he caught sight of the barn door slightly ajar. A narrow beam of light cast a sharp diagonal on the ground in front of the barn. Sims dropped into the classic crouching position and raised the rifle. He would fire at least two rounds into Wilcox as soon as he stepped outside the barn door. He assumed he'd then have very little time to turn the weapon on the other Rottweiler. After killing the dog, he'd move to the house and find Roper.

"Come on, Heckle boy. Come on!" Wilcox's booming basso voice cut through the night's silence. When he spoke again, however, his voice was more subdued. "All right, stay as long as you like. You boys sure went through a lot together."

Sims saw the barn door open wider and Wilcox's shadow encroach on the beam of light. He placed his finger on the trigger. Wilcox now stood in the door's opening, his head turned to his left, looking downward inside the barn at his dogs.

"Tripp?"

"God damn it, Tom, get in the barn."

Sims watched Wilcox jerk Roper by the shirtsleeves into the barn. He had no opportunity to refocus his aim on his intended victim. The other dog—the American Staffordshire—was still guarding the entrance to the side door of the house.

•   •   •   •   •

Max Nettleton made yet another pass near the Mason Memorial in the vain hope that he'd find Patrick Sims waiting for him. He now assumed Sims was in flight, probably with the help of one of his own contacts who'd make it possible for Sims to remain in hiding for the rest of his pathetic life. Or better yet, he'd die fleeing the authorities—in a car wreck or shoot out, it didn't much matter. The disturbed bastard would then take to the grave any incriminating evidence against the vice president's chief of staff.

As for what Kendall Livingston might have put in his book, Nettleton was deeply troubled by the call he'd received earlier from Russell Donaldson, an old friend now working at Justice. Much to Nettleton's dismay, Donaldson told him that Livingstone's home computer, all his flash drives, and all his hard copy materials were made off limits by the Prince George's County police. Worse, they hadn't backed down when Donaldson made the case that Justice and the FBI needed to examine the document immediately. When he was politely refused, he became indignant and played the trump card Nettleton had given him—the threat that they would hear from the Secret Service and the V.P.'s office if they failed to appreciate that the manuscript contained material that might very well "compromise national security." But the boys from southeastern Maryland refused to budge, and Donaldson was forced to leave empty handed.

But they had said one thing that especially disturbed Nettleton. According to Donaldson, one of the detectives replied to the threat that they'd be risking the wrath of the Secret Service and the V.P.'s office by noting that they'd already been assured such would not be the case. When Donaldson asked who so informed them, they replied, "Mr. Goldman, the president's chief of staff." Donaldson added that Goldman had subverted what seemed to be a request to take Roper into custody. But Donaldson had no idea who might have pushed that matter.

Nettleton was as perplexed as he was angry. First, he couldn't imagine who might have wanted to have Roper arrested. It couldn't have been the president since Goldman took the action he did. Some notable in Prince George's County looking to make some kind of political hay? An enemy of Roper's in the Senate?

But more significant was Livingstone's book. If anyone wanted the manuscript suppressed or selectively edited, it was Evan Bedingfield. So why was his chief of staff assuring the Prince George's County police that they could keep it until their investigation was completed? What the hell was Goldman up to? Did the president even know what Goldman had done? Nettleton concluded that attorneys for the publisher and perhaps even the *Post* would soon make it impossible to get a look at the manuscript and expunge any damning information about the vice president's chief of staff.

And what if Livingston had interviewed Patrick Sims, for Christ's sake? Furthermore, if Sims was arrested and went to trial, why wouldn't he open up about what he knew? Given his medical history, his new lawyer would insist that he plead not guilty and actively seek any favor from the court. Sims might offer information about anyone in government—including Max Nettleton.

Nettleton again parked his car and waited for Sims. This time he pulled the gun from the glove compartment and rested it close by on the passenger seat.

• • • • •

Inside the barn, Roper held the shotgun, while Wilcox dealt with the remaining Rottweiler. "Heckle, cut, boy, cut." The animal was banging against the closed barn door, letting Wilcox know that the shooter was nearby. The dog obeyed and came back to Wilcox. "Jesus, Tom, you should have stayed in the house."

Roper understood that shots were likely to be exchanged. Wilcox tried to push him down. "Wait, Tripp. Robyn's alone inside."

"Get down, get down!" Wilcox almost jumped on Roper's back to make him comply. "Give me that." Wilcox took the shotgun and racked it. The Rottweiler again began barking viciously at the closed door of the barn. "Cut, Heckle. God damn it, cut." Once more, the dog obeyed.

"Tripp, I can't leave Robyn alone. Let me get out through the back of the barn and go to her."

"Damn it, Tom. There are two pistols lying on the table next to the sofa. She's a cop. She'll grab a weapon and be ready for anyone who comes through the door."

"Here you go, buddy." Wilcox handed Roper the small Kel-Tec .32 he had on his hip. "Tom, listen." Both men leaned their heads forward near the closed barn door. They could hear footsteps approaching them.

Roper couldn't help thinking of John Wilkes Booth trapped in the tobacco barn at the Garrett farm in Virginia during the wee hours of April 26, 1865, twelve days after shooting Lincoln at Ford's Theatre. Perhaps it was the large cracks between the planks of wood on the side of the barn that brought the historical moment to mind. For an instant, Roper feared the assailant, whoever he was, would set the barn on fire, as had the Union soldiers that April.

Roper saw Wilcox looking around the barn. Wilcox stepped further to his right—toward the split in the planks. "Gotta get this light off, Tom." A single bulb hung from a suspended wire.

Roper continued to think about Booth and how he'd been shot through a similar opening at Garrett's barn. "Tripp, get the hell away from the..." The bullet struck Wilcox and sent him reeling toward Roper, who grabbed the larger man around the waist as he was sinking to the ground. "Tripp, Jesus Christ." The remaining Rottweiler growled and bared its teeth, his eyes menacingly trained on Roper.

At that moment the barn door was kicked open and a man entered with a rifle leveled and ready to fire. The dog's attention now shifted. It spun to its right and headed toward the intruder. It never had a chance. The bullet caught him flush in the head.

Roper could see the man's face clearly under the dark wool cap. A face he knew. "Patrick. What the hell are you doing?"

Sims stepped into the barn but continued to aim the rifle at Roper. "Sorry, Senator. I just can't let you share what I'm sure you know." Roper shook his head in confusion, which instantly infuriated Sims. "About what I've done, god-damn it! The fucking stuff Marshall wrote you about." Sims seemed on the verge of panic. In spite of the near freezing temperature, Roper could see the perspiration on Sims's face.

Roper realized he'd have only one chance to talk Sims out of pulling the trigger. "Patrick, if you mean that envelope that Marshall sent to my office, I did open it."

Roper saw Sims's finger begin to curl around the trigger. "Wait. Wait! There was nothing but several blank pieces of paper in the envelope. That was it."

"Sorry, Senator. I'm not buying."

"I swear that's what was in the envelope, Patrick. There was nothing else. I don't know anything. Come on. Don't do this. It's not worth it." Roper winced at using such a hackneyed line, but he had simply run out of things to say to save his life.

"It doesn't matter anyway, Senator. I have my orders."

"What do you mean?" Roper knew he wouldn't get an answer before Sims fired. At that moment another trick taught by his father jumped into his mind. Roper moved his head to the left and looked past Sims's shoulder. "Robyn, get away from that door!"

As Sims spun around, Roper grabbed the .32 he had dropped near his feet when Wilcox sagged to the floor of the barn. It was a miracle he located the pistol on his first attempt. He rolled further to his right—completely over the prone body of his friend. He thought he heard Wilcox groan as he fired two rounds from the .32. One shot clipped the stock of the rifle as Sims turned back toward him. The other one caught Sims right under the chin. For a moment Sims seemed to be in suspended animation—his head bent back, the rifle lifted grotesquely as if he were suspended from it. In a second both the rifle and man who held it fell backwards onto the dirt floor.

Roper rushed to Sims. He watched the man's jaw and mouth move in contorted fashion. "Patrick, Patrick. Did you kill Marshall and the others? Did someone order you to kill them—

and to shoot at me?" Sims's mouth was frozen open. There was no point in feeling the carotid artery on his neck. The man was dead.

Rushing past Roper and the body of Sims, the American Staffordshire terrier entered the barn and located his master. It licked Wilcox's face but ceased when it smelled the blood coming from the bullet wound near the top of Wilcox's shoulder.

Wilcox's head quivered. "What the hell happened? Marty? Tom? I blacked out, I think." Wilcox attempted to rise but immediately grabbed his shoulder. "Jesus mother, that hurts like a bitch. I got shot, right?"

Roper could only shake his head incredulously at his friend's reaction to nearly being killed.

"Yes, Tripp. You took a bullet."

Wilcox finally stood. He looked down at Sims and then back at Roper. After wincing from the pain in his shoulder, he smiled. "Hey. Nice shootin', cowboy."

Chapter 20

The dream left him sweating in its aftermath—as it always did.

He first had it soon after he discovered evidence of his mother's fertility in the bathroom garbage pail. He was simply unaware at that age that a woman in her mid-forties still bled like teenage girls and young women. How could he have been so unaware? His discovery offered him a partial yet painful understanding of why, on the following night, his mother did what she did to him.

He remembered on the eve of his sixteenth birthday feeling the intense pressure in his temples. He just couldn't comprehend how his mother could receive his father in that sordid state. They'd gone to bed early, and the boy was old enough to understand that since his father had been away for over a week he'd want to have sex with his mother. But when she was like that?

The boy moved toward their bedroom door and listened for the same muffled sounds he'd heard several times before. Instead of then going to his room, he slowly pushed open his parents' bedroom door to see if his mother was truly allowing his father entrance to her body. However, by the time he placed his head into the room, they had stopped. But his relief was short-lived. He would never forget his mother's smile as she looked at his father. Later he'd learn the adjective to describe it—conspiratorial.

Early the next evening, on the night he turned sixteen, he had come into the kitchen and watched his slightly inebriated father rubbing his wife's buttocks and fondling her breasts through her blouse. The boy had already been disturbed at the sight of his parents sitting on the sofa while he opened his juvenile assortment of gifts from them. How proud his father was as his son opened the final present—the collection of sterling silver ingots his father foolishly believed would inspire his son to become something important. The boy feigned enthusiasm as he always did, and owing to his skill in artifice, he easily tricked his parents into believing that he had received the best gift of his young life. He watched his father rubbing his wife's ankles and feet and finally gently kissing the tears of joy and satisfaction that had fallen on both her cheeks.

Even years later, the man couldn't believe he'd actually returned to his parents' bedroom later that night—after his discovery in the bathroom the night before. His father had just left the house to pick something up at the convenience store at his wife's request. The following morning the boy would see the opened box of tampons on the kitchen table.

But on his birthday night his mother invited him into her room and patted the bed, asking him to sit while she remained under the covers. As soon as he sat, he asked.

"Mom, can I ask you something?"

She smiled. "Of course, my baby, whatever you want to know."

"Why do you have sex with Dad when you're bleeding?"

The man remembered how tightly she closed her eyes and

then started counting slowly backwards from ten. Her "ten, nine, eight" were in her deeply angry voice—the one he'd rarely heard throughout his boyhood, only when he'd done something disrespectful or unsafe. The "seven" and "six" lost all traces of anger but sounded to him contemplative, as when she was in the process of changing her mind about granting a request she had first rejected. The "five, four, three" put a lilt in her tone, the same tone she employed when she was playful and flirtatious with him—either alone or in front of others. Her eyes reopened on the "two" and "one." She was smiling now, as she reached for his hand. He was looking into her eyes when she reversed the last two numbers—"one and two"—as he felt his hand being placed on each of her breasts.

He'd been completely still as she adjusted her body and brushed his face with her tousled hair. There was alcohol on her breath mixed with the heavy application of the perfume she'd daubed on before going to bed. He saw her bare legs and feet slip from the covers as she repeated the "one and two"—this time touching him between his legs over his sweatpants. She kept repeating the two numbers as she reached under the fabric. In a moment she was counting backwards from ten again, almost hypnotizing him with the now ethereal sound of her voice, gently manipulating him as she counted. His stillness and silence were unaltered, even as he felt the touch of her gentle though firm hand.

When she finished saying "one," she whispered to him playfully that all the ten numbers together added up to fifty-five, his current uniform number for his high school's basketball team.

Further sounds caught in her throat as she slowly removed her hand from the inside of his sweatpants. Then, just as deliberately, she turned her head and readjusted her body under the covers. She began to count again—this time from one to ten—her voice sounding to him distant and frightened now, with no deviation from the sound as she forcibly made her way to "ten."

Finally, she was turned completely away from him when she softly inquired what he wanted to ask her. He was struck by the pain in her voice and for a moment suppressed the fresh memory of what had just transpired between them.

The boy didn't hear his father's steps toward the bedroom as he repeated the earlier question about why she had sex with his father when she was bleeding.

He barely had time to lift up his hands in self-defense when his father grabbed him by the hair, and hurled him against the bedroom wall. Nor did he cry when his father began beating him with his belt. The boy was sixteen now. He prided himself on being tough. But he did hear his mother sobbing under the covers under which she was now hiding and his father castigating him for having "humiliated" his mother.

His attorney father normally spoke to him as lawyer to client, in soft and measured terms, always offering advice and challenging the boy's uneducated views. But this night he had more to drink than usual and was highly embarrassed and infuriated by his son's shocking question to his mother. In the bedroom and in front of his wife, he cursed his son profusely for speaking about his wife's period and cruelly reminded the boy of the times he'd caught him masturbating. The end of the tirade came when his father took the kitchen knife he'd brought into the bedroom to cut the seal off another bottle of champagne and held it out toward his son, warning him to leave his penis alone when he went to bed "or else."

Two days later, the boy paid a visit with his father to a professional therapist—a woman in her late twenties. The boy was taken by the woman's appearance; she was of the sort he'd actively fantasized about after he reached puberty. He sat morbidly as his father explained that his son had a "predilection for masturbation" and perhaps a "perverse preoccupation with the female menstrual cycle." The therapist put up her hand to silence him, attempting to re-establish the professional environment the boy's father had so unforgivably violated. She offered the boy a half smile meant only to assure him that everything would be all right. To the boy, however, it was an exact replica of the conspiratorial smile his mother offered his father when he had pushed open their bedroom door. The boy ran from the office and did not return.

The following week, his father let the matter drop and began honoring his wife's desire that their son's shift from numbers to language and literature. Years later, with another female therapist, the man would try to understand what had happened to him. This therapist was interested in what he dreamed and fantasized about; as a result, he told her about his recurring dream—featuring the bloody residue of his mother's body; his father's touching and kissing of his unclean mother; his father's revelation to his mother that he was masturbating; the knife his father pointed at his genitalia; and the birthday gift of the historical ingots. Soon after, the therapist recommended that he see a male psychologist because she felt too uncomfortable listening to her young client speak of another prevalent dream—the one he had of hurting her.

•　　•　　•　　•　　•

The numbers of the digital bedroom clock informed the man of how long he had left to sleep. Once awakened, he had no intention of ever sleeping again. Soon his parents would see that he had used everything they'd given him against them. They had inadvertently shown him the way. It mattered little to him that his mother had now passed the age when she stopped bleeding and that his father's intimate touches of her body had likely also ceased forever.

As he was drifting off to sleep, he muttered to himself the words of Honoré de Balzac, which he had memorized his freshman year of college and repeated often since: "Numbers are intellectual witnesses that belong only to mankind."

• • • • •

As soon as the men returned to the house and Robyn saw that Wilcox had been shot, she put down the pistol she was holding and called for an ambulance. Rejecting Wilcox's plea that it was "only a scratch," she began to tend to his wound and found that the bullet hadn't passed through the shoulder and would have to be taken out surgically. She dismissed his suggestion that she heat up a hunting knife over of the flames and let him remove the slug himself.

"I've done it once before, Robyn. Hunting accident when I was twenty. I can show you the scar."

"No. You're not touching that wound, Tripp."

"Then how about a nice tall shot of brandy to ease the discomfort?"

Robyn smiled. "All right, that I can allow."

After the police and EMTs arrived, Wilcox grabbed Roper by the arm. "Tom, it seems that Sims was trying to kill you all along."

"Seems so, Tripp. But..."

"But...Hey, hey! Take it a little easier, boys. Hurts like a mother...like *my* mother wouldn't have wanted it to hurt."

Wilcox often hated the fact that, as a U.S. senator, he had to watch his mouth. The two young EMTs were grinning as they attempted to examine Wilcox's shoulder wound.

"Excuse me, sir, but you need to get to the emergency room right away for this."

"Yes, son, I know that. Now just leave me be for five minutes. The lady here patched it up so I'm not going to bleed to death."

Soon Roper heard the other young man speaking softly into his cell phone. "Karen, the price—with all the add-ons—is $1,483.00. Did you get that? No?" He laughed. "Right. What should I expect from a girl who couldn't get into Yale? Okay, got a pen? Ready?" As the young man repeated the number more slowly, Robyn pulled Roper toward the front door.

"Tom, we should go to the hospital with Tripp. We can spend the night at my place if you think it's now safe, or we--."

"No, Robyn, it's *not* safe. Not yet."

There was still too much that didn't make sense. In addition to the four serial killings and the promise of a fifth, Roper remained in the dark about who shot at Robyn in Meridian Hill Park, who fired the round through Robyn's bedroom window, and the shot fired over Tripp's head at the convenience store. Who was Sims working with or for? What had Marshall Grayson originally planned to put in the envelope that rested inside Roper's Senate office safe? Could he really have sent blank pages? Perhaps Roper would deduce what Grayson had intended him to read when the details of the Sims investigation were released by Justice. One thing seemed highly certain. Patrick Sims could not have been the serial killer. There was no note found on his person with the five numbers.

Roper's carousel kept spinning. Was Patrick Sims the intruder who frightened Lena Roseboro? Who got the purportedly recorded admission from Alyona Novikova? And what of her death? Was it really a suicide? And did the death of Patrick Sims mean that he and Robyn were now out of physical danger? It was possible but not at all certain, because there was still the haunting thought that the serial killer had him in mind for the last number—the "07." Each of the four men killed had a sports connection to Tom Roper—the Filibuster softball team. Had the signs been pointed toward him all along? Were he and Robyn destined to be the final victims?

"Robyn?"

"Yes, Tom."

"I want you to go with Tripp to the hospital."

"You're not coming?"

"No. I think it best that we...that I stay away from you until all this is over.

"Tom, this isn't necessary."

"Robyn, just humor me. Please." He knew she understood what he was thinking. She only needed to be assured that he would be safe until the morning. "I'm sure the police will want to talk to me for another hour at least. Then I'll go back to the city and crash in my office. Don't worry. I'll be safe enough in the Hart Building."

Roper wanted to be alone behind his desk. He was determined to come up with some understanding of the sequence. There had to be something less complicated in the numbering than Metro assumed. He had at least to satisfy himself as to whether he was or was not the intended last victim of the serial killer.

Before he resumed his interview with the Maryland police, Roper accepted that his career in the United States Senate was over. He'd have to call the governor of his state and resign his seat. Who in his position had ever gone through what he had in the past several days? If nothing more than being shot at and then killing a man in self-defense. Again an example from American history came to mind. Roper considered that his tale might one day come to rival that of the South Carolinian congressman Preston Brooks, who beat Senator Charles Seward senseless with a walking cane on the floor of the Senate in 1856. He could imagine his father chuckling, "Well, Tom, at least you'll make the history books. Just like your mother wanted."

Chapter 21

Devin Cassell sipped his Viennese coffee in the elegant Willard Room, a mere two blocks from the White House.

"So what's the big fucking emergency that's caused me to change my breakfast plans, Devin?" As soon as Sheridan Browning sat down, the server was at his side with a menu. Browning looked at Cassell. "You ordered yet?"

"No."

Browning grunted at his associate's terse reply. "All right, let me see. I'll have the orange juice. And drop a few shards of ice in there while you're at it. Then I'll...let's see. Yes. The Vanilla Dusted Brioche French Toast. Easy on the maple syrup."

"Coffee, sir?"

"No. Just the orange juice. With the ice."

Browning jumped in before the server could ask. "Devin?" He bore his eyes into Cassell's.

Without dropping his gaze to look at the menu, Cassell ordered the three-egg omelet.

"Another coffee, sir?"

"No, thank you. Nothing else."

Browning leaned back in his chair as the server walked

away. "Nice place." Browning waited for Cassell to respond. The younger man remained silent. "Was in here last month with my six-year-old granddaughter for their Nutcracker Brunch. Melissa adored it. You should bring your kids here, Devin." Apparently Browning had forgotten that Cassell's children were both in college. "God damn it. Something on your mind, boy?"

"Did you have anything to do with the death of the Novikova woman, Sheridan?" Cassell neither raised nor lowered his voice when asking.

Browning lowered his. "What the hell are you talking about, Devin?

"I asked you a question, Sheridan."

"Fuck you."

"I'll ask it again. Did you have anything to do with Alyona Novikova's supposed suicide?"

Cassell had been sympathetic to the young woman's situation when he spoke with her on the phone, while posing as a federal agent. He had decided to contact a real agent in L. A. to see about setting up a legitimate audition for the woman.

The server interrupted with the orange juice. Browning began toying with his silverware. Cassell kept his eyes trained on his boss, who held his reply until the server left the table. "Look, Devin, something happened that we didn't foresee. I don't know what the hell went through the mind of that character who went to her apartment in L.A. Maybe she got suspicious and she threatened to call the police. I just know that he killed her and made it look like she took her own life." Browning had begun tapping the fingers of both hands on the table cloth. "Who the fuck knows why."

Cassell decided to shift subjects. "Thanks for verifying that it wasn't really a suicide, Sheridan. Now do you know about the shooting out at the Maryland country house of Senator Tripp

Wilcox?"

Browning stared into Cassell's eyes and took his time with the reply. "I heard there was a shooting but nothing more than that Wilcox was wounded."

"You also know, I'm sure, that Barry Arnold—or whatever his real name is—you know, one of your most ambitious young minions—accidentally shot himself in the stomach while trailing Wilcox."

"I've already seen to it that his wife and young kid will be taken care of financially."

"Well, he was just doing what you wanted, Sheridan. Just supposed to frighten Roper's closest friends, right?"

"Casualties of fucking war, Devin."

"Oh, did I mention that Tom Roper was out at Wilcox's place last night when the shots were fired?"

"Roper?"

"Yes, Sheridan. Tom Roper."

Browning's voice took on a tone of forced bemusement. "Well now, Devin. Are you telling me that Thomas Roper, son of the famous general, shot a fellow U.S. senator?" Browning lost his balance as he stood up and grabbed the chair for support. "I'm going to take a leak."

"Sit back down, Sheridan. You seem uncomfortable talking about the shooting out at Wilcox's. But of course you knew nothing about that, did you?"

Browning's features immediately darkened. "Where the hell do you get off taking to me like that, you son-of-a-bitch."

Cassell understood that Browning was about to pull rank, and he was in no mood to listen to his boss recite his resume and elaborate on his national significance. "Sheridan, the facts are that Roper killed a man in self-defense. But not one of ours, right? Or *not to my knowledge* one of ours. But perhaps you might have a different perspective on that, Sheridan. Seems I've not been privy to everything you've been up to lately."

Cassell's restrained contempt suggested to Browning that the younger man was now a serious threat to everything Browning had and still wanted. Still, he was left with no choice but to mollify him. "Listen, Devin. I like to keep you out of such things. You have that charming quality of integrity that on the one hand makes you so valuable to me but on the other annoys and worries the shit out of me. That fucking Roper should never have made it alive out to Wilcox's in the first place, and Sims should have been on his way to Michigan. Okay, you happy now? You know it all. So do your job and figure out a way we can turn this so that Roper was planning on killing Sims all along."

"Sheridan, you're getting silly again."

Browning again drew his fingers into fists but fought to maintain a more pleasant tone of voice. "All right, all right. But don't you see how perfectly it's all worked out so far? The nature of those emails is beginning to get a little press attention—not to mention the effect on Roper and his staff from the extra little message sent about his past being his prologue. Tell me again, where does that quotation come from?"

"Shakespeare. *The Tempest.* And in case you didn't know, Sheridan, the lines are carved on the National Archives Building."

Browning squeezed his fists tighter at the derisive manner in which Cassell challenged his intellectual curiosity, but he was determined to remain in control until he figured out what Cassell was trying to tell him or threaten him with. "And on top of that, Devin, we've managed to upset Roper's equilibrium and scare the shit out of everyone close to him here in D.C."

"Did the Novikova woman have much time to be frightened

before she 'took her own life,' Sheridan?"

Browning dug his fingers into the tablecloth, bunching up the fabric and jeopardizing the place setting and the glasses of water and orange juice. The plastered smile on Browning's face was now grotesque. Cassell knew he wouldn't be able to keep his volatile personality in check much longer. For a moment, he wondered whether the deputy director of the FBI would have a stroke at his table in the Willard Room.

Browning tried to sip his orange juice, but his hand was trembling too much to lift the glass to his mouth. "Devin, listen to me now. What we got from that Russian girl was more than we could ever have hoped for. The story's all set to break on Monday. Some will leak out today and on the weekend—just to get everyone salivating."

"You were going to have Roper killed and still have this stuff published?"

"God damned right. So the way it is now the whole pile of shit dumps on Roper Monday morning. God damn it. There isn't a fucking way in hell he can survive this. Who gives a fuck if the Russian girl's dead? All she could have done was retract what she said and make a god-damn martyr out of Roper— turning this whole thing around and having it spit back right into our faces. I wasn't going to let that happen. Can't you see that? Good Jesus Christ, I've still got that fucking prick Roper right where I want him. Better that Sims didn't kill him. He'll be a walking dead man in the space of four days from now anyway. A fucking disgrace to his country. Nobody—and I mean *nobody* fucks with me without paying a steep price. And let me tell you something, you smug piece of shit, if you think you can hold my ass over a barrel, you better start thinking about what I have done and what I still can do. Don't fucking smile at me, you cock sucker. *Do you hear me?*"

"Sir."

Browning turned sharply to find two members of the Willard staff standing a foot away from him. One of them touched Browning's arm.

"What the hell are you doing?" Browning didn't remember standing up. Nor did he realize how loud his voice had gotten since he began his tirade. He also didn't recall seeing the person at the table behind where he was now standing. There was a lone man sitting there—a cup of coffee and a folded newspaper in front of him. He recognized the face. The man had interviewed him several times in the past.

Browning turned back to Cassell, who had remained seated but who now was nodding in the direction of reporter Tony Braithwait. "Devin, you mother fucking Judas."

•   •   •   •   •

"Jerry."

"Yes, Mr. President?"

"Has everyone been contacted about the change of time?"

"Everyone but Max Nettleton, sir."

"Damn it. I need him here. He's got to be in the photo."

"I understand, sir."

"Just for the sake of impression, not reward for any assistance. Everyone knows he's in charge of that history club, Jerry."

"You've still got the history professors. They'll be here."

"I know, but I need Nettleton."

"I'll try again." Goldman headed out of the Oval Office.

"We've got less than an hour."

"I know, sir." Goldman got to the door this time.

"Jerry, was Archives fine with moving it up?"

"Yes, Mr. President."

"Majority leader?"

"She's fine with it too. And she reiterated her apologies about not being able to come over for the photo op."

"Fine. Any problem with the document?"

"None, sir."

"Marta Taubman's been informed?"

"Of course."

"All right. Jesus Christ, I wish the Japanese would understand that getting here Friday afternoon instead of Saturday morning, as we agreed two weeks ago, makes keeping my schedule a little difficult."

"You could be a hard ass, sir, and tell them to wait until tomorrow morning, as you first agreed."

"Not done to be rude, Jerry. Especially to the Japanese."

"I understand, sir." Goldman hesitated this time before stepping through the door. He fully understood the comic use of the phrase "wait for it."

"Jerry, is the Roosevelt Room ready to go for this morning?"

"Not a problem, Mr. President."

•   •   •   •   •

"Bobby, they're changing the time of the photo shoot to this morning."

"I assume you still want me to ride shotgun on the document."

"Yes. I don't know why, but I'd feel better knowing that you're keeping an eye on it. I've had second thoughts about letting Archives house the document, although I know it's much safer there. It's just been in the family for over two hundred years—never out of our hands." She offered an embarrassed laugh. "I think I'm really afraid one of the historians is going to nab it and whisk it back to his university."

"Doubt that."

McCrimmon decided not to tell Gleeson that it was Max Nettleton she didn't trust, not the historians. "Once more, thank you for your admirable service, Bobby."

"Glad to help."

After he left her office, she felt more confident that Gleeson would keep to himself her involvement with the emails sent to Tom Roper.

•　•　•　•　•

"Max? Glad you called. The president's been looking for you." Goldman heard nothing on the other end of the line. "Been trying to reach you over an hour—since 7:00 this morning. Anyway, it's the photo shoot with the McCrimmon document from Archives. We've had to move it up to 9:15 this morning. That's right, 9:15. The president insists that you make it. Hmm? You're already on your way in to the city? Just get here by 9:00. Okay, good, good. I'll tell the president now. Say, Max, you sound tired. Get enough sleep last night?"

•　•　•　•　•

Tom Roper had only slept for two and half hours on the sofa in his Senate office before Melanie "Early Bird" Sheffield arrived. Fortified with caffeine and sugar from the coffee and pastry she brought him, Roper called Robyn's cell to find out where she'd spent the night. She hadn't slept much either, but was staying at the house of her Metro crime lab partner, Sarah Brownstein. She assured Roper that Metro had two officers watching over them.

257

Tripp Wilcox was resting comfortably in the hospital, she added. The removal of the bullet from his shoulder apparently went easily enough, although Wilcox bucked wildly after being told he couldn't be released immediately after the operation.

Promising to see her later in the day, Roper retrieved the change of clothes he kept in his office as well as his toilet articles and reconstructed himself the best he could. Feeling at least partially refreshed, he sat behind his desk and asked not to be disturbed. He saw that it was ten till nine. For a moment he wondered how Lena Roseboro was faring and decided to call her in the afternoon. But now there was work to do.

He soon had several sheets of blank paper spread before him. He quickly ran back through the possibilities for anagrams. The initials left on the slain women were M.T.L.R.I.S.J.B. Again, there weren't enough vowels to flesh anything out. If an anagram would identify the killer, he assumed there had to be two vowels intended for the final desecration of the female victim. Was that the killer's sadistic scheme all along? Make the police wait until he had completed all of the planned murders before giving them a satisfactory roadmap to his identity? Roper began adding vowels to the other letters to see what he might come up with. He devoted only two or three minutes to this futile exercise, however. He knew he was being led on by the specious assumption that there was a name to be identified. Even if the last two initials were needed to discover the killer's identity, it would of course be too late for victim number five.

He believed there had to be another way to solve this maddening puzzle. He went back to what he had earlier believed about the sequence—that the last number—07—had to be a date. Once more, he tried to recall what had occurred in 2007, 1907, and 1807. The only thing that stuck this time was the legal fate of Aaron Burr in 1807. The name repeated itself in his mind. Burr. Burr. Could that be the name of the intended victim or of the killer? Roper began thinking of anyone he knew with that last name. Burr shot Alexander Hamilton, after all.

"Jesus Christ. Jared." Jared Hamilton was on Charlie Hefferen's staff. Twenty-seven years old. Lost an arm in the invasion of Iraq—in the spring of 2003. In spite of his disability, he'd twice played with the Filibusters. Roper grabbed the phone.

"Frieda, this is Senator Roper. Can I talk to Jared, please?

"I'm sorry, Senator, he's not here."

"Can you tell me where he is? This is very important."

"Of course. He's home in Indiana. His sister's getting married this weekend. To a young professor at the university."

"When did he leave for Indiana, Frieda?"

"Wednesday, Senator."

"Have you heard from him since he left?"

"As a matter of fact he called not even twenty minutes ago. You know how he is. He can't believe we can actually do without him for a few days."

"And you're sure he called from Indiana?"

"Yes, Senator. From his house right outside of Bloomington. Is anything wrong?"

Roper realized how peculiar he must have sounded to Frieda. "No, no. Just something to do with...basketball."

"Oh, of course. He said he was going to an IU basketball game this weekend."

"Right. I just wanted to make a friendly wager. But it's no big deal. I'll make another one when he gets back to Washington. Thanks much, Frieda."

Roper had no time to chastise himself for the awkward call to Hefferen's office. However, he drew a parallel between Hamilton's close ties with the state university and Tripp

Wilcox's love of South Dakota. Their home states. Roper paused, titillated by a thought. Yes, home states. Roper pulled another piece of paper and wrote down the state of Marshall Grayson's birth. Kentucky. He then wrote down Arrington's and Livingstone's—both from Ohio. But what was the birth state of Rich Lloyd? He couldn't remember off the top of his head. He thought back to the times they talked after Filibuster games. Of course, Lloyd kept up a running discourse on the great Celtics teams his father and grandfather knew, going back to their first championship in 1957. The colloquialisms and the tell-tale accent. It was clear. Lloyd was from Massachusetts.

Kentucky, Ohio, Ohio, and Massachusetts. Was there a pattern here? Did the killer draw some overall connection of the murders to some famous events occurring in these states—or to famous persons born in these states? But why then the repeat of Ohio? Two events occurring in Ohio? Two famous persons born in Ohio?

Regarding the fourth victim, Roper realized that Rich Lloyd had the same kind of accent as that young EMT at Wilcox's. Now following where his instincts led, Roper replayed the young man's phone conversation with his wife or girlfriend. What had the EMT said? That he had noted something about the amount with the "add-ons" being $1,400 and something.

Roper pressed his forearms on the desk. And what was it that the EMT said to the woman on the phone as Robyn was pulling him away? Yes. He asked if she had gotten that dollar amount and teased her about not being able to get into Yale. He teased, "Ready? One more time" and repeated the numbers. Roper remembered them now. "$1,483." The EMT playfully told his wife or girlfriend that if she added up each of the individual numbers she'd get "16." That is, she should add 1, 4, 8, and 3 together to come up with 16.

Roper reached for another blank sheet and jotted down the five numbers the killer left as a clue or calling card: "20-18-11-19-07." He thought of the first victim, Marshall Grayson, and where he was born, Kentucky. Who else had been born in Kentucky? If there was any connection it had to be someone very well known. Roper had always loved western lore and easily recalled that Jim Bowie and Kit Carson were from Kentucky. But what did each have to do with the number 20, even if it was the total of the numbers in a date? Bowie was killed at the Alamo in 1836. Roper added the four numbers of that date, as the EMT had added the numbers of the monetary amount. Adding the four numbers in 1836 came to 18. Roper squeezed his fingers into fists. The second number of the killer's sequence. But Grayson was born in Kentucky and the number 20, not 18, was associated with his death.

Roper knew he was in danger of heading into quick sand with this method of inquiry, but he couldn't help thinking of other famous native Kentuckians before trying something else. Henry Clay, Adlai Stevenson, and Muhammad Ali. But he couldn't think of anything about their lives that would allow for an understanding of the killer's sequence. He began tapping his red pen on the paper, deciding whether to cease this mathematical nonsense, when another famous native Kentuckian suddenly came to mind. Perhaps the most famous of them all—even if he was more often associated with another state.

Abraham Lincoln.

Roper wrote the year of Lincoln's birth—1809. The four separate digits added up to 18. 18 again, but still not 20. Next he wrote 1861, the year of Lincoln's first inauguration and the beginning of the Civil War. The four numbers totaled 16—a number not in the sequence. He had one more date to consider—1865. The addition of the four digits equaled 20. Roper suspended his pen over the paper. The year of Lincoln's death. No…the year of his assassination. The first presidential assassination.

He circled the name of Ian Arrington—born in Ohio—and added 1-8-8-1, which came to 18. He quickly did the same for Ohio's Kendall Livingstone—1-9-0-1—and then Massachusetts native Rich Lloyd—1-9-6-3. The numbers came to 11 and 19 respectively, as Roper knew they would. Abraham Lincoln. Born in Kentucky, assassinated in 1865. James Garfield. Born in Ohio, assassinated in 1881. William McKinley. Also born in Ohio, assassinated in 1901. John F. Kennedy. Born in Massachusetts, assassinated in 1963.

Now the meaning of the 07 number on the killer's list was clear. Roper quickly folded the paper and jammed it into his pocket. He left his office and was soon standing outside the Hart Senate Office Building.

Chapter 22

Nettleton passed through White House security and expressed feigned dismay at the news passed to him from one of the guards—an ambitious foot soldier whom Nettleton had months earlier cultivated as a source. Patrick Sims had been out at Tripp Wilcox's place in Maryland and was shot to death. The guard had no other details to share. Nettleton asked if Wilcox had been shot. The guard shrugged his shoulders and apologized for not having more information. As soon as Nettleton entered the White House, he smiled broadly at the good news. His relief was palpable. Still, what the hell had Wilcox to do with Sims? He trusted he'd know soon enough.

Just as suddenly his spirits sagged. He realized how close he'd come to killing Sims himself. He had even concocted a story before he headed to the Mason Memorial hours earlier. It involved threats Sims made against the lives of his wife and daughter, with a plausible blackmail component to the tale. Nettleton would have claimed that he shot Sims to protect himself and by extension his family. He'd only driven out to the Mason Memorial because Sims insisted on it—and that much was indeed true.

But during the night, Nettleton also decided that if and when Sims began speaking of Nettleton's relationship with Maureen Blakely and Nettleton's possibly tampering with private communications between Marshall Grayson and Thomas Roper, Nettleton would simply remind everyone of Sims's history of mental illness—a recent record of appointments with a Baltimore psychiatrist going back a few years—again all true, though known to but a few in Washington. It would then come out that the real reason Patrick Sims wasn't named deputy attorney general was that Leon Johnson either knew or suspected that Sims had psychological problems which disqualified him from the second highest position at Justice. Nettleton learned all this from several sources—at Justice and at the FBI, not to mention what Sims told him directly or at least hinted at. Nettleton felt immense satisfaction at the number of political allies he had in the city—from the White House and the Congress to the Smithsonian and the Library of Congress, not to mention several university faculty members.

But now heading toward him with hand extend was Jerry Goldman, who likely knew whether Kendall Livingstone interviewed Patrick Sims for his book and whether there were a few passages in the manuscript that might bring Nettleton down.

"Max, good to see you. You're right on time—9:00 a.m.—right on the nose. Coffee?"

"No, thanks. So, tell me again. Where will the photos be taken?"

"Roosevelt Room. But we have a little time. Let me get you that coffee and we can sit in my office."

"Then why did you tell me to be here at 9:00?"

"Wanted to be sure you'd be on time. You aren't always the

most punctual beast, Max. Besides, this way you and I can have a little chat."

Nettleton didn't like the pleasant tone or expression on Goldman's face. What was Goldman up to? What did he want to chat about? Nettleton's voice betrayed his nervousness. "Shouldn't we head to the West Wing, Jerry?"

"All right. Then just step inside the Map Room for a second, Max."

Nettleton had no choice but to agree. The men went inside and headed for the two stuffed red armchairs among the Chippendale-style furnishings. Goldman gestured for Nettleton to sit.

"For Christ's sake, what the hell is it, Jerry?"

Goldman smiled. "Max, why the concern? You look like someone about to receive his two-week notice." Nettleton couldn't think of anything witty to say in reply. He was well aware that his face registered considerable apprehension. Goldman continued. "I just want to let you in on the fact that I received a fairly good report regarding the contents of Livingston's manuscript. Parts of it may interest you."

Nettleton's instinct was to grab Goldman by the throat and slam his fist into his face. "Parts may interest you"? What the hell kind of euphemistic bullshit was that? But Nettleton remained silent, although he felt his knuckles pressing firmly into the arm rest of the chair.

"And what parts would they be, Jerry?"

"It's complicated, Max." Goldman looked at his watch. "We'll have to talk later. Let's get to the Roosevelt Room." Goldman rose and walked toward the door, leaving Nettleton frozen in the chair.

Nettleton finally stood to follow. He could only curse Goldman silently. "Son-of-a-bitch. *Son-of-a-bitch.*"

•   •   •   •   •

Roper told the driver where he needed to go. "As fast as the law allows, Andrew. Just don't get us pulled over."

"Do my best, Senator. Uh, you need to buckle up, sir."

"Right." As he secured the seat belt, Roper's mind raced back over the events of the previous week. It was there all along. History. God-damned history. He'd even contemplated the date 1865 when he thought of Booth's fate out at the Garrett farm in April of that year. Why then didn't he think of Booth's victim? The killer had a fascination or at least a strong interest in history—American history. A student or professor at one of the nearby universities? Georgetown? George Washington? Howard? Up at the University of Maryland? "Oh, Jesus Christ."

"What's that, Senator?"

"Nothing, Andrew." Roper had just remembered that Max Nettleton had a history club.

•   •   •   •   •

"Jerry, remind me again."

"Mr. President, the gray-haired man to the right is Professor Trent Ballenger. History. Harvard. The younger man speaking with him is Professor Ryan Davies. History. Georgetown. He's a good friend of Max Nettleton's. And the woman speaking with the two of them is Grace Westcott from the National Archives. She brought the document, so I thought we ought to invite her into the Roosevelt Room. It will only enhance the photograph."

"Yes, yes. Good call, Jerry. And the man talking to Marta?"

"That's Robert Gleeson. From Carol McCrimmon's staff. Serving as chaperone, it seems. Apparently she sent him to represent her—and to keep an eye on the family document."

Bedingfield grabbed the sleeve of Goldman's coat. "Who's that young professor again?"

"Ryan Davies of Georgetown."

"Seems nervous, wouldn't you say?"

"A bit of a scholarly loner, from what I've gathered. But a rising superstar in late eighteenth-century American historical studies, his department head tells me. He's the one who won the history award. He's now working on a new assessment of Washington's second administration."

"All right. The photographer is here. Ah, and there's Max Nettleton. He looks preoccupied, Jerry."

"He does, doesn't he? Wouldn't know why, though."

"Where's the first lady?"

"Saw her a second ago. Likely went to freshen up."

Evan Bedingfield stood in front of the Roosevelt Room. "Good morning everyone." The introductions were made, but still his wife hadn't joined them. Bedingfield suppressed his impatience. "Is everything set up inside, Cam?"

Cameron Whitney, the official White House photographer, answered in the affirmative. "All ready to go, sir. The chairs have been pulled away from the conference table, and the document is situated on it. And I've just told everyone where you'd like each of them to stand."

"Good, good. The first lady will join us in a moment, but since we're here, let's go inside and I'll give you a tour of the Roosevelt Room. I'm sure she'll be here any minute. Marta?" She was talking with Robert Gleeson.

"Yes, Mr. President?"

"No, wait. Never mind, Marta." Bedingfield shot Goldman a look.

"I'll find the first lady, sir." As Goldman walked away, the president noted the far-away expression in Max Nettleton's eyes, as though he were making up his mind about something. Professor Davies of Georgetown came up to Nettleton, who nodded to him and patted him on the shoulder without speaking.

"Jerry, wait." Nettleton caught up with Goldman.

Bedingfield was now annoyed at the prospect that Nettleton's would hold everything up. He turned to his left.

"Oh Mr. President?"

"Yes, Marta?"

"Since we have a minute, I wonder if you'd mind my taking Mr. Gleeson into the Oval Office for just a second. Just so he can say he was once there."

"Never been into the inner sanctum, son?"

"No, sir. Senator McCrimmon described it to me on several occasions—and I've seen the official photographs—but I've not been lucky enough to see it first-hand."

"Sure, go on in. But stay only a second. Who knows? A miracle might occur and we'll get everyone in the Roosevelt Room and get this photo shoot done. Oh, in case I forget, please express my appreciation to the senator for her generosity in permitting the document to travel over here from the Archives.

"I will, Mr. President."

"Now go ahead the both of you and take a quick look at my digs."

Bedingfield's congressional liaison took Gleeson into the Oval Office. The president was delighted and amused by the young man's eagerness, but his smile evaporated when he thought of Nettleton's demeanor as he headed toward Goldman. The expression on the V.P.'s chief of staff seemed borderline malevolent.

•   •   •   •   •

"Okay. Thanks, Andrew."

"Should I wait, Senator?"

"No, I'll walk back to the Capitol when I'm done."

"Are you sure?"

"I'm sure."

On the way to the White House, Roper had gone back over the first four numbers on the killer's list. It could be no coincidence. The simple adding of each year of the four presidential assassinations resulted in the total left behind at each murder. Lincoln in 1865. The four digits of the year adding up to 20, and so on. Each man killed was born in the same state as each president. The final number 07 was even more dreadful in its simplicity. Add 2 to 0, then to the 1 and finally to a 4 and the numbers would equal 07. 2014—the current year. Since the other murders fell almost on consecutive evenings, the fifth killing—the 07 killing—might well happen tonight. This was something Roper couldn't speak about on the phone. It had to be in person. He feared the president wouldn't believe him otherwise. Roper wondered if Bedingfield would even believe him now.

•   •   •   •   •

Nettleton grabbed Goldman's arm. "Are you going to tell me what was in the Livingstone manuscript that I might need to worry about?"

"Max, I never said anything about your needing to worry—did I?"

"Look, you fucking bastard..."

"Max, lower your voice. This is the White House, for God's

sake." One of the White House staff came around the corner. "Katie, where's the first lady?"

"She's on the way to the Roosevelt Room, Mr. Goldman. Sorry. Nature calls for her as well as for us average female peons. You know her. She'll check to be sure every facial line is smoothly caulked before emerging."

After she moved on, Goldman removed Nettleton's fingers from his sleeve. "Max, we need to get you back to the Roosevelt Room pronto. Just be patient. We'll talk about what Livingstone dug up after the photo shoot. Come on."

Nettleton once more hesitated before following. His head was spinning. He wanted to kill that lousy bastard Goldman. Goldman knew. The son-of-a-bitch knew everything.

•　•　•　•　•

Roper looked at only one portrait inside the Entrance Hall before it hit him. While he'd figured out the meaning of the numbers, he'd completely forgotten about the initials left in blood on the female victims. The initials left on Maureen Blakely's body were "M.T." It was again so simple. 1865—the year of Lincoln's assassination. "M.T." Lincoln's wife Mary Todd. Ian Arrington's girlfriend had "L.R." imprinted on her ankles. Garfield's wife was Lucretia Randolph. Sandra Livingstone had "I.S." on her breasts. William McKinley was married to Ida Saxton. It was Robyn Meadows who only recently informed Roper of Garfield's and McKinley's spouses' names when the two of them were playing, of all things, a political trivia board game.

The letters on Hannah Lloyd's cheeks were "J.B." John Kennedy's widow, Jacqueline Bouvier.

Roper realized that if the killer succeeded in murdering his fifth intended victim, the initials he would wish to leave in blood would be "T.P." Teresa Patterson. The wife of Evan Bedingfield. But Roper knew the killer wouldn't expect to have any time to so mark the first lady.

American political history was the framework for these killings, and Roper was certain the killer had to be someone in government—someone with easy access to the President of the United States.

Chapter 23

"Come on, Bobby." Marta Taubman stood at the Oval Office door and started waving the visitor toward her.

"Sorry. I just wanted one more look at the south lawn out of that magnificent window."

Gleeson joined her and they stepped across the hall to the Roosevelt Room. Indulging her flirtatious side, the one the president never saw, Taubman remarked, "Just remember who got you into the Oval Office, Bobby. Okay?"

"Oops, sorry, Marta." Jerry Goldman nearly collided with her as he rushed into the Roosevelt Room.

Gleeson looked over his shoulder and saw an agitated Max Nettleton walking deliberately toward them.

"You okay, Max?"

Nettleton stepped into the Roosevelt Room without even acknowledging Gleeson's question.

Marta whispered to him, "You and Mr. Nettleton know each other?"

Gleeson nodded, but she could see that he was physically uncomfortable. "Yes. I just wonder if he's upset that Senator McCrimmon didn't come."

"Tell me. Is there something up between the two of them? I've been hearing rumors that he's jockeying to get your boss on the ticket in 2016."

"Don't know what you're talking about, Ms. Taubman."

She laughed at his formality. "Like hell you don't."

Gleeson's face was now contorted in pain.

"Bobby, what is it?"

"Nothing. Just...just..." He adjusted his body by lifting his right hip, forcing his left side to fall against the door frame. "Oh geez, I think it's a spasm. Anyway, it's nothing. Come on. We need to go in. They're about ready."

•　•　•　•　•

"Where is he? I need to see him immediately." Roper was standing in the Cross Hall.

"Sorry, Senator, you can't interrupt him now." Katie Holland wished that Jerry Goldman were standing next to her. She saw the urgency in Roper's face, but she had also just heard talk about some Russian woman in his past who might destroy his career. She was therefore concerned that he was going to embarrass himself and the president by making an improper request.

"Is there a problem?" One of the Secret Service agents quickly assessed her concern.

Roper put his hands up to calm any suspicions about him. "Look, I have information I have to share with the president. You know who I am. I'm a United States senator. Take me to him. Please. This is no joke. The president is in serious danger."

"All right. Where is he, ma'am?"

Katie Holland was convinced. "He's in the Roosevelt Room for a few photos. Senator, you can wait outside the door until they're done. They're taking photographs of the president with some important historical document."

Roper stiffened. "Katie, is he alone?"

"No, Senator. He has some historians and archivists with him. And Mr. Nettleton."

"Katie, please. We need to get in there now."

She led Roper and the Secret Service agent toward the West Wing.

•   •   •   •   •

Bedingfield seemed satisfied with the arrangement of the Roosevelt Room, and was impatient to get it all done with. "All right, are we finally set, Cam?"

"Yes, Mr. President, but I wonder if Mr. Goldman can join us in the shot. We need one more person for balance."

Goldman nodded. "No problem. Where do you want me?"

"Let's see. Mr. Goldman, just stand to the right of Mr. Nettleton." Nettleton was positioned on the far right of Bedingfield. On the same side of the president were the two history professors. To Bedingfield's left were the first lady, Grace Westcott from the National Archives, Robert Gleeson from Senator McCrimmon's office, and congressional liaison Marta Taubman.

Goldman stepped down to Nettleton's right.

The photographer looked at the grouping once again. "We'll have to close up a bit. Hip to hip, everyone."

Nettleton felt Goldman's body press firmly against his right side, as if he were pushing him—bullying him. That Goldman was three inches taller made his tight proximity even more discomforting to Nettleton, who had the urge to push back. But what the hell was he going to do? Shove Goldman over the table? Nettleton understood that Goldman was smug with the knowledge that he knew enough to end his career and perhaps send him to prison.

The catalogue of his many sins raced through Nettleton's mind. His betrayal of his wife with Maureen Blakely. His betrayal of Ed Malloch. His manipulation and concealment of documents and personal correspondence. His use of contacts to provide him with inside information about policy and personality. His sitting on information that impeded official investigations. His dealings with men such as Patrick Sims. And his providing information to a handful of eager foot soldiers in the expectation that they would act in nefarious ways—without direct order or overt suggestion—to satisfy both Nettleton's perverse curiosity and his taste for revenge.

As a result, Nettleton found that his normal cool headedness had deserted him. He was terrified that he was about to lose control and say or do something that would finish him politically.

"Could I suggest that Ms. Taubman and I trade places?" Everyone looked at Robert Gleeson. "I just feel a little funny pushing her to the very end of the photo."

"Quite a gentleman, isn't he?" Teresa Bedingfield winked at the younger woman.

The president held up his hand. "I have a better idea. Since you are the representative of Senator McCrimmon, Robert, why don't you stand between me and the first lady? I think that will be better for what we want to show here. Don't you think so, Jerry?"

"I agree, Mr. President."

"Then if you don't mind, Mr. President, may I suggest that Professor Davies switch places with me, since he's the one writing on Washington's second term." Trent Ballenger of

Harvard pulled at Davies's arm. "Please, young man, switch with me."

Jerry Goldman could sense Bedingfield's impatience building at Ballenger's interruption. The president was always put off when someone else "took over" the proceedings. Professor Davies stepped next to Bedingfield, who disguised his pique by patting the historian paternally on the shoulder.

Marta turned toward Gleeson, still concerned that he was in pain from what he said was a spasm. Gleeson nodded and stepped back so he could move behind the others and come down between the president and the first lady, who along with Grace Westcott shifted to their left to make room. As Gleeson passed behind her, Marta caught sight of a damp stain on the side of his left pants leg, visible beneath where his suit coat hit his trousers.

• • • • •

Roper, Holland, and the Secret Service agent reached the door of the Roosevelt Room, which was now closed. The agent was beginning to explain to one of his colleagues standing nearby what was going on.

Katie Holland was clearly nervous that Roper would disturb the photo shoot. "I promise, Senator, that you can speak to the president just as soon as they finish taking the pictures."

Exasperated, Roper leaned against the wall and stared at the closed door. The two Secret Service agents kept their eyes firmly on Roper. In a moment Roper noticed something unusual along the door frame of the Roosevelt Room. He stepped toward the door.

"Senator, don't go in there." Holland literally wedged herself between him and the door, brushing her pale blue suit coat against the frame.

"Look at your jacket, Katie."

She bent her head and noticed the reddish smear on the light fabric. "What is that?"

Roper put his finger on the frame and swiped the still moist splotch on the frame. "Blood."

Roper and the Secret Service agents needed no other prompting. They pushed open the door just as Cameron Whitney was about to take the first photo.

Roper got it out before either agent could even formulate the words. "Mr. President!"

Standing over Bedingfield's left shoulder was a young man with his right arm above the president's right ear, a sharp knife-like object gripped tightly in his hand.

Bedingfield instinctively dropped his head and jerked his body to his left as Roper ran forward and hurled himself over the ornate table, scattering the historical document as he did so. The persons to the left and right of the president fell like dominoes away from Bedingfield. Only Marta Taubman cried out—the others articulated nothing but stifled gasps.

Robert Gleeson was so startled by the entry of Roper and the agents that he held the blade in the same position for several seconds. His hand began to tremble as he raised it slightly higher. Neither Secret Service agent could get off a clean shot because both Roper and the president blocked their line of sight. Taking firing positions, the agents stood in front of the table waiting for the bodies to reposition themselves.

By the time the blade started downward, Roper had grabbed both of Bedingfield's arms—above the elbows. Although almost completely prone on the conference table, he managed to yank the president's body further to the left as the blade reached the level of Bedingfield's back. But the president was now tilting over the body of his wife, who had completely sunk to the floor. The blade continued down until it bit into the middle of Roper's forearm.

The passage was now clear. With Roper's cry of pain as an unintentional prompt, both agents fired once. The bullets caught Gleeson squarely in the upper chest, sending him straight back into a cabinet. His grip was so firm that when he fell back he pulled the blade out of Roper's forearm, which began to bleed profusely. Grace Westcott immediately wrapped her woolen neck warmer around his forearm as he began to pull himself off the table. Everyone else remained sitting or half squatting where they were, except for Marta Taubman who was standing three feet from Gleeson's body, with her open hands in front of her face, her eyes in an attitude of utter horror.

The president helped his wife up and then assisted Roper from off the table. One of the Secret Service agents had come around, his gun now trained on Gleeson, who had not yet expired. Katie Holland ran to sound the general alarm and call for the medical team. Jerry Goldman's eyes were trained on his boss. Max Nettleton had fallen back against one of the walls, staring helplessly at the mad scene before him. He couldn't believe that the would-be assassin was a member of his history club, a fellow Phi Beta Kappa whose Master's thesis on American history he had months earlier read with pleasure—a young man whom he had often advised and with whom he had privately shared his utter contempt for Marshall Grayson along with details about Grayson's personal life and habits.

Gleeson opened his eyes and saw Roper standing before him, pressing the neck warmer tightly against his forearm. "Senator Roper, can you... can you do me a favor and apologize to Senator McCrimmon for me?" The young man's eyes filled with tears. "I'm afraid she's really going to hate herself for telling me about the president's letter opener and for insisting that I come here today and chaperone the document. I had another…another plan to come here and see the president, but this made it easier and I…" Gleeson took a difficult breath. "You figured out the numbers, didn't you?"

"I did." Roper winced from the pain in his arm.

"Look at you. You're just like Major Rathbone. Well, I guess I should end by saying…*Sic semper…parentis.*" Gleeson's eyes remained open. But he was now dead.

Trent Ballenger from Harvard came up next to Roper. "Major Henry Rathbone was the one Booth stabbed in Lincoln's box at Ford's Theatre. But the boy got it wrong. Booth cried out '*Sic semper tyrannis*' —'Thus ever to tyrants'—not *"parentis"*—"Thus ever—or death—to parents." Roper offered the professor a weak smile, made all the more difficult because of the intense pain from his wound.

"Thank God, thank God." Ryan Davies was holding the Archives document in his hand. Roper's heroic effort had not damaged the artifact after all.

The arrival of the medical team and other members of White House security didn't stop Evan Bedingfield from reaching down and removing from Gleeson's hand the ornate "Samurai" letter opener kept on the table behind his desk. Later, they'd determine that the blood on Gleeson's pant leg had come from a gash on his thigh caused after he'd concealed the letter opener down the side of his trousers when he was exiting the Oval Office with an unsuspecting Marta Taubman.

Chapter 24

After everyone had gone and the president had been ushered off by the Secret Service, Jerry Goldman stepped into the Oval Office to see if Robert Gleeson had disturbed anything else in the short time he'd been in the room. It was clear to Goldman that the next several days would be agonizing. Although the American public would not believe the attempt was an act of terrorism or part of a larger plot, it would still suffer the insecurity and general fear from this attempt on the president's life—surely more so than following the one on Reagan in 1981. A serial killer had actually gotten into the White House and almost stabbed to death the President of the United States. This event would also far eclipse the bungled attempt to kill Truman outside the Blair House in 1950.

The serial killer was a staff person for the Majority Leader of the United States Senate. And among the distinguished guests for the photo shoot was a man who'd likely bring disgrace to the administration—the vice presidential chief of staff. Nettleton had given himself away through his voice, demeanor, and gesticulations before he and Goldman entered the Roosevelt Room. In truth, Goldman had no idea what if anything Kendall

Livingston had said about Max Nettleton in his manuscript. Until now there were only suspicions flitting through various Washington corridors about Nettleton's imprudent personal behavior with other women, his improper communications with Devin Cassell of the FBI, and his possible tampering with evidence gathered by the Justice Department. Then there were the strong hints that Nettleton was working hard to get Carol McCrimmon on the ticket and himself appointed Jerry Goldman's successor. Goldman also knew there was a nefarious connection between Nettleton and Patrick Sims, and now wondered if his friend Max had anything to do with the shooting out at Senator Wilcox's place in Maryland.

And Goldman was well aware that Nettleton was perceived as a mentor to the other younger men in the history club—young and earnest types like Robert Gleeson. Goldman was inclined to dismiss the possibility that Nettleton was in any way behind the attempt on the president's life—and on Marshall Grayson's. Nettleton was devastated following the events in the Roosevelt Room. His body language gave validity to his barely audible insistence that he didn't know what Robert Gleeson was capable of. He confessed that he genuinely liked the young man and at times mentored him. It was probable that Gleeson might have been relaying information about the majority leader that Nettleton could use in his efforts to get her on the ticket in 2016. But the most chilling admission Nettleton made was that he'd informed Gleeson of Grayson's ongoing affair with Maureen Blakely.

In short, Goldman could see that Nettleton was genuinely horrified that he might have inadvertently contributed to the double murder. Even so, Goldman made up his mind to contact the attorney general later this afternoon and set up a meeting regarding the legal and political fate of Max Nettleton.

Goldman also would send a note to Tom Roper thanking him for the quick explanation, after the events in the Roosevelt Room, of Gleeson's other murders and what the numbers code and the bloody initials actually meant. Other questions regarding motive would be asked and answered—satisfactorily or not—in the weeks and months to come. Of course, Goldman realized he'd have to get in line to thank Roper properly, for Bedingfield was likely to adopt the senator as his son for having saved his life. Goldman felt quite pleased with his decision to take no hardball political action against Roper when Bedingfield had so wished it.

Goldman stood behind the famous Resolute Desk and looked down at the table from which Gleeson had taken his weapon. There was something foreign resting against the stand that previously held the letter opener. It was a folded sheet of high quality resume paper. Goldman opened it with care.

•　　•　　•　　•　　•

Tom Roper had made it back to his office after his treatment at the hospital and one more round of interviews with the Secret Service and the D.C. police. He was glad he was wearing a colorful sling—one small way he thought might help cheer up his staff. He was about to place a call to Lena Roseboro, when Melanie Sheffield walked in.

"Excuse me, Senator."

"What is it, Melanie?"

"This came for you about an hour ago."

"Something from Senator Hefferen?"

"No, sir. From the White House. It's from Mr. Goldman."

Roper opened the envelope and pulled out two sheets of paper. The top sheet was on White House stationary. The note was brief.

"Senator, I thought you'd like to see this before I turn it over to the police. Gleeson left it in the Oval Office right before the attempt. I've kept it so that you could see it first. Thanks for sharing your formula for how you figured out the numbers sequence and the initials. This note might provide some answers you don't yet have. Best wishes, JG."

On the typed sheet there was no narrative, only a series of phrases and clipped sentences which provided in outline form Robert Gleeson's connection to his victims and his familiarity with their habits, private lives, and loves. Leaning forward to read the ten-point font, Roper stared at one of the remarks, "Why the four other men? Born in same states as the other presidents. No other reason. Just had to die first and in that order. Historical symmetry." Roper could see that Gleeson gained most of his knowledge of the other victims from direct conversations with them and with those who knew them well. Gleeson concluded this section of the note with "So much gotten from Max Nettleton—history club."

All that Roper read fell above the fold line on the thick sheet of resume paper. Below the fold line, however, the message—in smaller eight-point font--was directed more specifically.

This is to my parents, Charles and Melissa Gleeson.

What I did today, I did because of you. I need say no more, but I will—for both of you deserve to hear it.

First, thank you for the presidential ingot set you got me for my 16th birthday. It truly inspired me. It showed me the way. And that's what you both wanted, wasn't it—that I would find the way—another way.

To you, my father, I hope now you feel some of the humiliation you made me feel when I was a boy. And now I will make you feel it even more.

I have waited so long to tell you what you never knew.

To you, my mother, I will say that I came to think of you as four different women. Repulsive mother, unfaithful wife, sinister counselor, and disgusting whore. That's why I killed those four women. It's time you look in my father's eyes and explain why on many of those nights he was away you kept me close to you in your bed. How important you said my being there next to you was. How safe it made you feel. You said it was special that you could still listen to me count the sheep, even though I was really too old to count them. You said you loved to hear me say the numbers, especially when they climbed higher than 100. And then the night you spoke the numbers as you made me touch you and you touched me and moved so that you could make me a man.

You never told me that you bled. You made it clear to me that night—when you had finished—that what happened between us was a sin. Yes, it was a sin. And now, my mother, I have damned the both of us for it.

So let me leave you both with four lines from Longfellow, one of your favorite poets, whom you, my mother, insisted I read soon after that night. I know now that my numbers only reminded you of your sin.

And so I read Longfellow. I carefully read him and never forgot.

Tell me not, in mournful numbers,
Life is but an empty dream!
For the soul is dead that slumbers,
And things are not what they seem.
YOUR son—and always remember that,
Bobby

Chapter 25

"Good morning, Senator. I'm back, and my first order of business is to tell you that I just adore that sling. It goes so well with your personality."

"The sling is red, Lena."

"Just as I said. Fiery red for passion and courage."

"Please. Don't you know that ever since I was a little boy, I've always wanted to defy the federal government and slide on my stomach across the conference table in the Roosevelt Room?"

"Hey—as my granddaddy No-Web Stevenson would say, 'A man does his best sliding when you do it Roosevelt style—as in Jack Roosevelt Robinson.' So where did you get the crimson sling?"

"A gift from Laurie Eldridge. She brought it by the hospital when I was there yesterday. She thought it would go well with the wound." Roper smiled at the thought that the two major scars he'd carry with him for the rest of his life came from his having saved Laurie and a few years later the President of the United States—one person he completely adored, the other he barely tolerated. "Laurie also called me twice, once last night and once ten minutes ago."

"That is a special child, Senator Roper."

"Tell you what. You need to start calling me Tom, Lena."

"Well, maybe in private—during the holidays."

"The holidays are over."

"So they are."

"Tell me. How does it feel to be back at work?"

"Like the weight of the world is off my back. Now, you are *sure* no one else is going to break into my house and scare the ever-living hell out of me?"

"As sure as I can be. As I told you on the phone, Devin Cassell has come clean about what happened to you—and to Robyn—and for the most part to me. Anyway, Cassell is cutting a deal with prosecutors. I'd say that Sheridan Browning's lawyer is the only person standing between his client and his spending the rest of his miserable life in jail."

"What made this Cassell person find religion all of a sudden?"

"Seems he couldn't reconcile what he was doing for his boss with the murder of Alyona Novikova. He called Tony Braithwait and set Browning up in the Willard Room while Tony was there."

"How did you find this out? Did Cassell tell you?"

"No, Tony Braithwait told me. He also said he's got a Pulitzer waiting in the wings after he gets through with his series of stories on Browning and all that happened. He'll want to speak to you as well, I'm sure."

"I can do without that."

Melanie Sheffield bounded into the office. "This is for you, Senator. It's from the majority leader." She placed a box of candy and a card on his desk and then left.

"Candy from Carol. Don't let me start making assumptions,

Senator Tom."

"Hush, Lena." Roper opened the card.

Tom, this is a little token of my concern over all you've had to endure and of my and the country's deep appreciation for all you've done.
Lunch is on me. Sunday, if you're staying in town this weekend.
Carol

Roper wondered how long it would take for her to get over the fact that she was so fond of a young man who had brutally murdered eight people and almost took the life of the president.

"Well, Senator?"

"Don't look at me, Lena. I haven't got the slightest clue why she decided to send candy."

"And speaking of things sweet, how are things going between you and Ms. Meadows?"

"Believe it or not—and in spite of all that she's gone through this week—she still wants to continue our relationship."

"No, really? Marriage in the future?"

"For her or for me?"

"Funny." Lena dropped her effervescent pose. "Senator— Tom—the one thing you told me on the phone that really has me worried is that you're thinking seriously of resigning your office."

"Lena..."

"No, no. Let me say my piece. You're now about to be the biggest hero this town has seen in a long time—if ever before. That business with Browning was chump change compared to the outpouring of love you're about to receive. And I'm talking about some big, *big* love. 'The man who saved the president.' Talk about writing your own ticket. Mr. Thomas Roper, you could walk right down Pennsylvania Avenue—right to the White House—and demand that Evan Bedingfield empty his closet and move on out of there immediately, and the public would have no objection. You could paint that building the color of your sling and they'd have no problem with that either. I just wish you were coming up for re-election this year. How does ninety-nine percent of the vote sound? Now how many millions would that be? 3.2 million votes, or something like that?"

"Please, Lena. No more numbers. Not for a while, okay? Anyway, as some wise man once said, fame is fleeting—or haven't you heard?"

"You mean *Sic transit Gloria mundi*, don't you, Senator? Look, I'm just saying that you saving that young girl from kidnapping got you into the Senate. Imagine what having saved the life of the president of the United States will get you?"

"Aggravation, I'm afraid. Plenty of aggravation."

"Senator Tom, are you really going to quit?"

He smiled. "Lena, I've decided that I'll make that decision in May. I want to see the cherry blossoms in Washington one more time before I submit my resignation."

When Lena got to the door, she began talking to herself, muttering loudly enough for Roper to hear. "Girl, you may be out of a job before summer. Then again, you never know. As Granddaddy used to say, 'Time heals all wounds—except those that a good woman can heal much quicker.'"

Regardless of what he might never know for sure, Tom Roper felt immense satisfaction at having figured out the numbers code in time to save Evan Bedingfield's life. But he also felt deep sadness for not being able to solve the riddle in time to spare the other men and women who died after Marshall Grayson—particularly Kendall and Sandra Livingstone. He'd previously had enough to contend with for the deaths of those innocent Iraqis in 1998. Would he ever get over what had happened to them, let alone to those who lost their lives in the past week? Perhaps leaving Washington was the only way he could put closure on this part of his life. Perhaps, but then...

He looked at the framed photograph of him and Nathan Roper, taken when Tom graduated from high school. He always loved that photo. The look of love on his father's face had so often comforted him and reminded him how to live his life. Roper was sure that right now and wherever he was the old man was awfully proud of his boy.

—The End—